THEO AND THE FORBIDDEN LANGUAGE

MELANIE ANSLEY

Cover Design: Monica Zek

Cover image courtesy of Evgeny Hontor

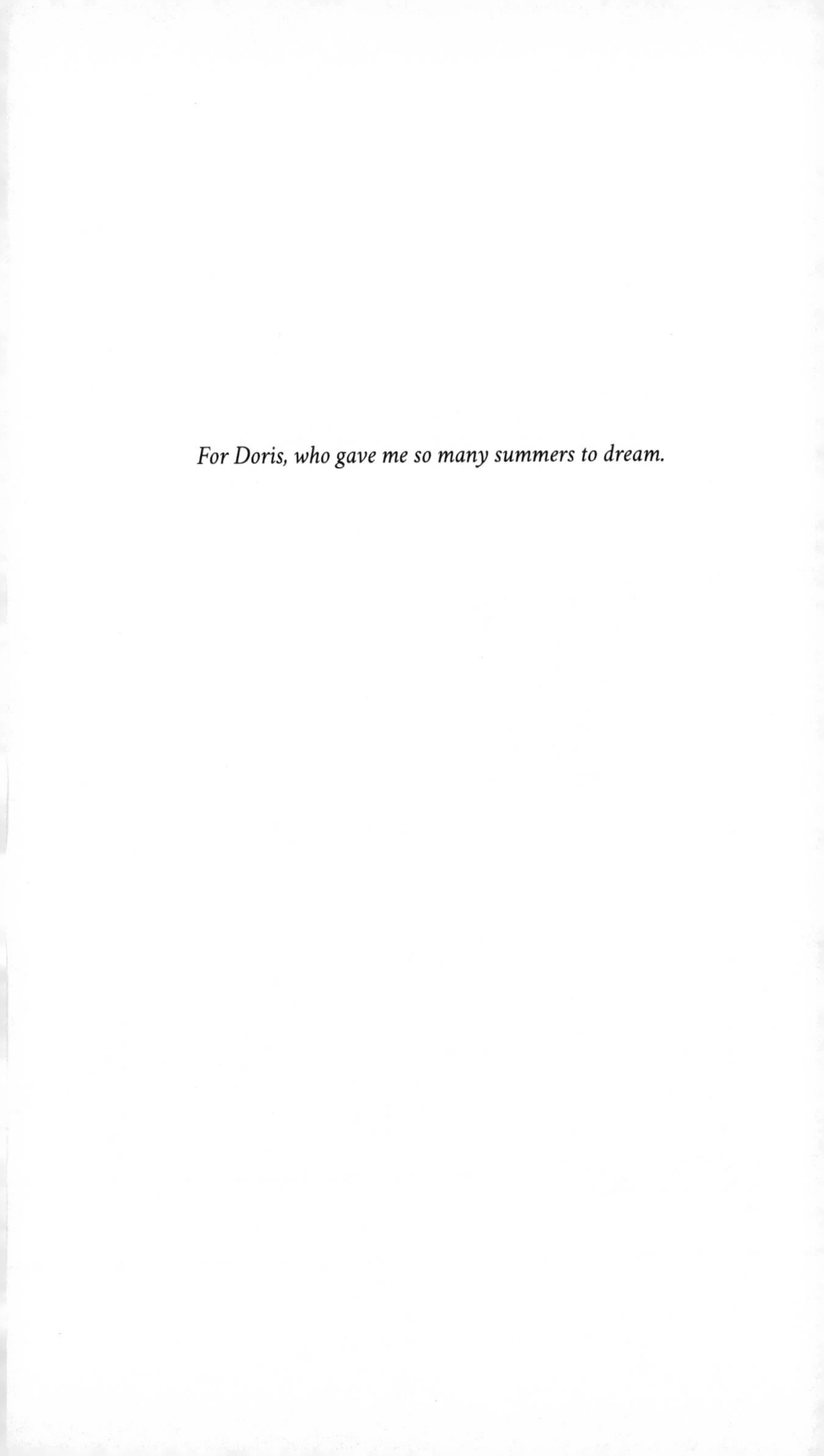

For Doris, who gave me so many summers to dream.

FREE BOOK OFFER

Join the author's reader list and receive the prequel *The Queen and the Dagger* free.

www.melanieansley.com

"A wild ride for adventure lovers of all ages."
- *Goodreads review*

"A beautifully told story of fighting for what you believe in, growing up, and self-understanding."
-*Amazon review*

CHAPTER ONE

The two travelers had been cautious, avoiding any settlements. Bears and rabbits rarely mixed, which was why the sight of the hulking male and his constant companion, a rabbit doe, drew side glances from the odd traveler they encountered.

The bear was young. Though some of his lighter cub fur remained, most of him had darkened to a mature black, the thick hairs like slivers of ebony. He peered into every shadow and bared his teeth menacingly at anyone who stared too long.

His companion wore a rough cowl to conceal her tapered white ears and the intricate blue tattoos that gave away her identity.

As they penetrated the forest's heart, they hadn't encountered another soul.

The bear was the first to sense something amiss. His upright hackles brought his companion to a halt behind him.

"Kuno?"

The bear rose onto his stout hind legs, sniffing the air to sort out the various smells of pine, moss, and damp wood rot.

"Something's not right," Kuno growled. He flicked his small round ears back and forth.

The rabbit could find no sign of danger in the surrounding foliage. Nevertheless, she drew her sword, the blade whispering as it left its scabbard.

For a moment neither moved. They stood, listening to the wind slither through the canopy of leaves above. A crow snapped his wings in flight somewhere close by.

"Let's head back and skirt the creek," the rabbit said.

As she turned, the forest floor rippled and erupted into a wall of armed warriors, leaves and dirt falling from them like sloughed skins. They were tall, two legged, their furless bodies protected by coats of stiff leather armor.

Urzoks. Though they called themselves "man," after the land of Mankahar, they were better known by the ancient word for "disbeliever."

The rabbit turned instinctively towards Kuno and saw that they were surrounded. She counted at least twenty warriors. A vulture settled on the branches above, his eyes alight with blood lust.

The Urzoks loosed a war cry. Weapons drawn, they descended on the pair.

Kuno roared his response, towering over the Urzoks on his hind legs. His paw carved through the first two attackers like a fish carves through water. A third swung his sword at Kuno's arm, but the bear sent him sprawling, pulverizing the attacker's jaw.

The rabbit fended off the assailants with her sword, their assumed superiority allowing her to catch them off guard. A bearded one lunged forward, arm raised and shoulder chink open. The rabbit drove her blade home into the gap. The man howled in surprise as much as pain, blood streaming from the wound, and crumpled to the ground.

She threw off her hood and prepared to dispatch the next two descending on her, when she felt herself swept up in Kuno's paws. With a bellow that reverberated off the surrounding trees, the bear smashed through the enemy line. She heard the snap of wood, the bite of swords into flesh, but could see nothing. His vice-like paw crushed her face to his chest, his fur so thick against her that she could scarcely breathe.

The impact of the ground jolted her bones as Kuno ran the best he could, his thick legs pounding the forest floor, hurtling through branches and dead wood. His breath was a gurgling rasp, as if his mouth was filled with water, and his heartbeat hammered through her body.

Just as suddenly as he had swept her up, he dropped her. Years of training made her roll and regain her hind paws, while the shouts of their pursuers grew louder.

"Run, Princess!"

The jagged ends of four arrows protruded from his shoulder, and his fur stood stiff and dark with blood.

"I cannot leave you here, Kuno!"

"Yes you can," the bear said through gritted teeth. "I will hold them, and throw them off your trail. Go now!"

"No, I won't leave—"

"I said run, Princess!" The bear's roar left no room for disobedience. "For once in your life, do as I say!"

Her breath snagged, tight and hot in her throat. With a final, fearful look at Kuno's pain clouded face, she turned and ran, the yawning black forest swallowing her white form.

CHAPTER TWO

The arrowhead sank into the bright red wood with a solid *thwack,* and a cheer arose from the assembled guests.

Theo watched the rabbits slap Harlan's back in congratulations. He'd lost track of the times Harlan had made someone stand against a tree with a crabapple or pear balanced on their heads. Then came his short arrow, hard and fast, so that the "volunteer" almost wet himself before the arrow hit home. More often than not that volunteer was Theo.

But there might be no more of that, now that his brother was getting married.

Not for the first time, Theo wondered how he and his brother could have shared the same womb. Where Harlan was long limbed, with tall, proud ears, Theo was short and round, his ears too wide to be considered handsome; where Harlan had a coat the color of warmed honey, Theo was a dull grey with charcoal-colored paws and eyes.

At the bridal table in the far pavilion, Keeva, the bride, sat flanked by her sisters. She clapped her paws in time as she watched the well-wishers perform the nuptial binky — the rabbits' traditional celebratory dance.

Theo took another swig of currant ale, trying to ignore his sense of dejection. The shrill blend of flutes and pipes, along with the jumping dancers, were giving him a headache. Or perhaps that was just the ale.

His wooden bench groaned as a portly black and white patched rabbit sat down next to him. The newcomer draped a furry arm over Theo's shoulders.

"Well, Theo me friend, you can't wear that dour face to a buck's wedding, now can you?"

Theo turned and tried on a smile. "Do I look dour, Pozzi?"

Pozzi's eyes twinkled as he erupted in laughter. His whiskers shook until the mirth ended in a ferocious belch.

Theo wrinkled his nose and took another sip of ale, hoping to hide his mood. Likely impossible, seeing as Pozzi was his closest friend.

Pozzi wiped a paw across his mouth and reached for the ale jug. Fermented brew was the dominion of those over seventeen summers, and Pozzi and Theo were just two months shy. But most of the elders who would have protested were too doused in drink themselves to pay them much mind.

Pozzi poured himself a healthy gobletful and filled his friend's cup too.

"Who would have thought it, huh? Her marrying Harlan."

Theo twitched his nose in reply. Keeva was accepting a gift from Jasper the metalworker. Some sort of kitchen utensil. Theo silently hoped that Harlan would fall on its sharp end.

Pozzi swirled his ale, casting a speculative eye on Theo. "You're not still hankering after Keeva, are you?"

Theo flushed to the tips of his ears, though not from the ale. His failed courtship seemed a good summation of his attempts at everything. As a kit he wasn't good enough to play with the others. Later, he never made the yearly games during the harvest festival, for which other young bucks competed for prizes. And when, like so many others, he had felt that first heady bloom of love for Elder Yeth's youngest daughter, he'd been gently but firmly rebuffed.

Pozzi kept time to the music with one paw and continued to watch the bridal table. "Keeva was never the sort to marry below her, Theo."

"Who can blame her? Would you want the healer's apprentice of Willago, when you could have the richest brewer this side of the River Tithe?"

Pozzi snorted. "And now he's eyeing Elder Yeth's seat on the advising circle, if the rumors are true. At least you had the courage to tell her."

Theo regarded his friend over the rim of his cup. "Why didn't you?"

Pozzi shrugged, keeping his tone jovial. "Keeva always did like the thin, muscular sort."

Theo frowned at his belly. "Fat or no, I can't throw a short arrow."

Another cheer arose from the arena, where Harlan had scored the latest round and was lapping up shouts of praise.

"So what?" Pozzi slapped his companion on the back. "Neither can I. You're a fine rabbit, Theo, no matter what anyone might say."

"And what do they say?"

Pozzi averted his eyes, realizing his slip. "Aw, nothing, Theo, don't mind that."

They let the subject idle, neither of them in the mood to discuss it.

Theo felt a persistent tug at his coat sleeve. He turned to see a scruffy-faced rabbit at his elbow. The critter's cheek was patchy with remnants of sticky caramel, and one paw clutched some rapidly melting toffee berries.

"Found your way into the sweets barrel, eh, Walnut?" Pozzi gave one cheek an affectionate pinch.

Bezwal was short, plump, and dull brown all over, which had earned him his nickname. Even his mother called him Walnut, only using his real name when he stole her famed carrot tarts or played too close to the stream.

"A story, Mister Theo?" His eyes brimmed with expectation.

Theo sighed and put down his cup with a dull thud. "Not tonight, Walnut. Go on, play with the others."

Walnut's ears drooped. "They won't let me, Mr. Theo. They say I'm too fat for Eagle Catches the Rabbit."

Pozzi nudged Theo in the ribs, sending a stab of guilt through him. How many times had he been excluded for that same reason? He stood as Walnut gazed up at him.

"Well come on then, I'll fix you a cup of almond milk and some chestnut bread, but then it's off to bed with you, you hear?"

Walnut beamed as he latched onto Theo's paw.

He cast one last look at the bridal table before taking Walnut back to the warren he shared with his grandfather, Father Oaks. No doubt the old rabbit would be asleep. Theo would have to try and keep Walnut as quiet as possible.

As soon as Theo had opened the door, Walnut settled himself in the heather stuffed chair in the corner. He fidgeted as Theo lit a candle.

"What shall it be, Walnut? The tale of Kalmac and the Wolf Pack again?"

"I want to hear a new story, Mister Theo."

Theo glanced towards the back of the warren, where he knew Father Oaks was sleeping. When he was sure his grandfather hadn't stirred, he sighed. "Walnut, I don't have any new stories. It's forbidden."

Theo rubbed at one ear, remembering how Elder Yeth had taken a switch to him when he caught Theo reading a story to Walnut. They'd snuck down behind the woodpile Walnut's father kept, thinking they'd be hidden. But Theo should've known Elder Yeth seemed to have more eyes than he had whiskers. The portly Elder had proven stronger than he looked, and warned Theo that the next time he caught him corrupting the young he'd bring Theo before the other Elders.

Walnut grinned, his eyes knowing. "That's not true, Mister Theo. I saw you with a new one. Yesterday by the tool shed."

Theo crossed his arms. "You spied on me?"

"I'm tired of the same stories. I want a new one, a scary one!" Walnut's voice rose in pleading.

"Sshh!" He checked to see Walnut hadn't woken Father Oaks, then whispered, "We agreed last time that you wouldn't ask anymore, remember?"

"Just one more time! I won't tell anyone. Please, Mister Theo."

Walnut's earnest face eventually won out.

"Alright, but we have to be quiet and not let Father Oaks know, agreed?"

Walnut nodded. Theo opened a pine cabinet above the potbellied stove, careful to not let it creak, and removed a cloth-bound volume, its edges stained and moth eaten.

"Does this story have a monster in it, like the porcupine with poison on his quills?"

Theo put a paw to his mouth to hush him. Sitting down on the hearthstone he whispered, "This is a story about the Griffin, from the land of Nightmares. You sure you won't be scared?"

Walnut grinned in anticipation and sidled closer. "What does the Griffin look like?"

"He has the body of a lion, the wings and head of a giant eagle, and he haunts you in dreams," Theo said, opening the book to the page with the drawing of the Griffin.

"Why?" Walnut asked, peering at the image of the mythical beast.

"Well, if you don't tell him the truth, he'll eat your flesh and gnaw your bones!"

As he watched Walnut shiver in glee, he knew that for all his reluctance, he too relished these secret stories. They were the only things he felt he truly owned, for they spoke to no one but him. As he freed the words one by one for Walnut's waiting ears, he felt the familiar comfort of building a private world. A world that didn't include Harlan, Keeva, or his failures.

Theo leaned against his rake and took a gulp of water from the earthenware flask strapped across his shoulder.

He and Father Oaks had climbed to this mountain ledge before dawn to avoid the heat. Below them the sun now poured its light into the Willago valley like water into a cup. From the northern hills above the rabbit warrens, one could see the entire town and its surrounds, from the craggy mountains of Balsar in the south to the distant forests that bordered the mighty River Tithe in the east.

"Easy on that water, lad!" Father Oaks grumbled from his rock in the shade of a knotted birch, where he sat plucking rowan berries. He lovingly stored each one in a cloth sack. "If ye'd not tucked into that ale so healthily last night, ye wouldn't need so much to slake yer thirst now."

Theo started. How had Father Oaks known?

"Was it the drink that made ye defy your taboo when Walnut asked ye to?"

Theo cringed. Though Father Oaks's grizzled fur had silvered and his whiskers had paled to thin, crooked strands, he had kept his sharp eye and sharper tongue.

"Don't you know what's fer yer own good, m'boy?"

The young rabbit's ears drooped.

"I suppose it's my fault," Father Oaks said, almost to himself. "I should never have agreed to teach ye how to catch words. If Elder Yeth knew what ye were up to, after that last thrashing he gave ye. I should have followed his advice years ago and burned those blighted books."

Theo gripped his rake. "But they're the only things left from Kalmac's journey from the Old World."

Father Oaks snorted. “And all they do is get ye in trouble, lad! Ye need to be more like a rabbit, not keep to yer odd ways and odder ideas.”

Theo hefted his tool and began digging around a stubborn patch of iris roots. “I still don’t see why word-catching is so bad. Who does it harm?”

“’Tis sorcery, lad,” Father Oaks pointed his trowel at his grandson. “Don’t ever let anyone else hear ye say it does no harm.”

“If it’s such a terrible thing, why did you learn to catch words, Father Oaks?”

The old rabbit seemed caught off guard. “I had no choice, m’boy. My father insisted on passing on his black art.”

“Why?”

Father Oaks grunted. “You and yer constant ‘why’. What have I told ye about that curiosity of yers?”

“That rabbits should be less curious and more cautious, I know. But if it’s so bad, why would he insist?”

“He thought it was special, I s’pose. Something that would one day have a purpose.” Father Oaks tossed away a spoiled berry, then fixed Theo with stern eyes. “But he also made sure to teach me about the power in the grasses and roots. As he often said, everyone loves a healer but no one trusts a sorcerer. Best not to deal in things you can’t touch.”

Theo worked at the iris root in silence, his gaze straying occasionally towards the eastern forests.

“Do you think there are word-catchers like us beyond the River Tithe?”

“The Old World is a land of barbarism, no place there for peace-loving folk such as ourselves. Here at least we don’t kill those who can catch words. There’re those over in the Old World who would skin ye if they knew what ye were, lad. Yer lucky to be right where ye are, and if ye knew what were good fer ye ye’d never want to leave.”

Father Oaks lumbered to his feet and hobbled over, clapping a paw on his grandson's shoulder.

"Now enough of this nonsense. If ye don't stop asking questions and start digging a little, we'll be on this mountainside 'til winter."

As Father Oaks and Theo ambled along the path to Willago, the late afternoon sun warmed their backs. Their packs bulged with rowan berries, iris, and the elusive bloodroot, ready to be ground into poultices or dried into teas.

Theo was debating whether the precious bloodroot could be traded for a watertight satchel for some of his more worn-out books, when he noticed Father Oaks shading his eyes with a dirt crusted paw.

Following his gaze, Theo saw a lone, plump figure running up the path, a wake of dust blooming behind him.

"Isn't that Walnut?"

Father Oaks nodded. "Wonder what he's in such a rush for."

As he drew closer, Walnut waved his arms, the words falling from his mouth in half gulps so that Father Oaks had to stop him and get the poor creature to regain his breath.

Bent double, Walnut panted for several shakes of a tail, before blurting out, "At the well ... it's a ... a ...!"

Father Oaks frowned. "What d'you mean? What's at the well?"

Again Walnut gestured with his paws, babbling about collars and gold and birds. Theo and Father Oaks had no choice but to hasten after him, bewildered.

CHAPTER THREE

When they reached the village square, they found a dense crowd gathered, its excited chatter drowning out individual voices.

"What's going on here?" Father Oaks pushed his way through, Theo following. Elder Yeth and the other three Elders stood in a circle around the village's central well, conferring in agitated tones.

Theo could now see the cause of their consternation. A black and ginger owl sat atop the well stones, its orange eyes perched wide apart above a chiseled beak. But what held everyone's attention was the magnificent collar the bird wore. A thick band of gold and silver studded with two rows of multi-colored jewels encircled the owl's neck. Whenever the owl moved, the collar clinked as the stones slid against each other.

"Father Oaks!" Elder Yeth grasped the old rabbit's arm. "Thank Kalmac."

"I thought owls only existed in the Old World, Father Oaks?" Theo whispered, curiosity taking hold.

"Shush!" his grandfather snapped, before turning back to Elder Yeth. "What's happened?"

"We don't know." Elder Yeth tried to keep his voice from the crowd. "It wants our help getting its collar off. Perhaps it's a gift from Kalmac."

"It said that?" Father Oaks asked, suspicious.

Elder Yeth shook his head. "Seems the poor rascal's a mute. But the collar must be worth all of Willago, several times over."

The owl stretched its wings, the sudden movement making the skittish throng fall back. It peered at the gathered rabbits and pointed a razor-sharp claw at one, beckoning. A murmur of fear rippled through the crowd, and a skinny roan shrank into himself.

"Me?" asked the stricken roan.

The owl nodded and curled one claw for him to come forward.

"Don't do it! It'll rip you to shreds sure enough!" came a shrill voice.

The owl frowned at this and stretched out his neck, shaking the collar in invitation.

The chosen rabbit swallowed on his fear, trying to melt back into the crowd. The owl's eyes darkened, before he turned an inquiring gaze on the rest of the rabbits.

"What's in it for us if we free you?" one of the Elders asked, loud enough for the crowd to hear.

The owl flicked his ear tufts, refolded his wings and jangled the collar.

The Elders glanced at each other, eyes filled with the thought of riches.

"Elder Yeth, send the owl on its way," Father Oaks said in a low voice. "Theo's right, the bird's from the Old World. Nothin' good comes from there. It's why Kalmac led our ancestors here and warned us never to return."

The Elders murmured of this amongst themselves, torn. But the lure of the collar overruled their usual caution.

Elder Yeth turned to the gathered villagers, rapping his staff against the well to gain their attention. "Who's to say that the collar is not a gift from Kalmac, a reward for following his rules all these generations? The owl requires our assistance, and will reward us with its magnificent gift once it is freed. Who will try his paw at removing the collar, and win this prize for Willago?"

"I will!"

Theo recognized Harlan's voice even before his brother emerged, sizing up the owl and flexing his arms.

"It's ours then, if I take it off?"

The owl nodded.

Harlan grinned. "Don't worry, I'll remove it. Be sure to remember this at the next Elders election."

The villagers jostled each other to get a better view. They began shouting encouragement and caution equally as Harlan reached forward and grasped the collar with both paws. He pulled, his arms bulging like risen bread.

The owl watched as the rabbit panted, grunted, wrestled and pushed, but still the thing remained locked. At last Harlan was forced to stop.

"Just a little stuck," Harlan reassured the Elders. He turned to the crowd and shouted, "Where's Arlo?"

"Here!" came the reedy voice.

"Get your tools!" Harlan commanded.

Arlo and Mort, Harlan's constant shadows, hurried off.

"I tell ye, it's not meant to be unlocked," Father Oaks protested.

Elder Yeth patted his arm. "We'll soon see, Father Oaks."

Arlo returned with his trade tools of whisker-thin picks, keys, chisels and metal-working supplies, and began examining the collar.

"Pick this collar and I'll share the prize with you," Harlan promised.

Arlo turned the collar, his paws running over the surface to feel for a telltale lock. Theo moved forward for a better look. From this distance he could see that the rows of stones were in fact tiles, decorated in strange patterns, and when they shifted the pattern changed with them, like a fluid mosaic. There was something familiar about the way the yellow garnets were arranged.

"Is this going to take all day?"

Harlan's impatient question scattered Theo's thoughts. The owl was observing him, the locksmith at his neck forgotten.

Arlo absent-mindedly cleaned one ear with the curve of his lock pick. "There ain't no lock, Harlan. I can't get it open. You think it's some kind of sorcery?"

The word fell like a spark amongst the Elders.

"Nonsense!" Elder Yeth admonished, though his voice held uncertainty. "Try again, and stop your scaremongering."

The owl took a step forward. Theo's heart thudded as the bird pointed with one hooked claw, beckoning.

Theo hesitated, then took a step.

"No!" Father Oaks objected, using an arm to hold Theo back. "Ye've had yer try, Elders, now let the bird go on its way and find someone else to open the collar."

"But Father Oaks," Elder Yeth admonished, "there's no harm in letting—"

"That's the end of it," Father Oaks thundered, in a voice Theo had never heard him use with anyone, much less an Elder. He seemed to collect himself, and continued in a more respectable tone. "The thing's not meant to stay in Willago. You think Theo here can break that collar where Harlan can't?"

Guffaws and laughs rolled through the crowd, loudest amongst Harlan's cronies. Theo felt scalded by shame, even more so because he knew his grandfather was right. But why did he have to say it? In front of everyone?

Father Oaks turned and motioned to Theo. "Come now, son. We've wasted enough time here on this foolishness, we have tonics to brew and our winnow baskets need mending."

Theo hesitated, but finally followed his grandfather, trying to avoid the derisive looks Harlan and his friends shot his way.

They left the crowd much as they found it: a jostling tide of chatter as Elder Yeth organized more volunteers to try their paw at the collar.

~

"Why do you always let Harlan treat me like that? Why do you never let me fight back?" Theo said as soon as they had walked out of earshot. "You've never once believed in me, that I might be able to stand up to him. What if I could have pulled that collar apart? You made me feel—" He struggled for words. "You made me feel like a runt."

Father Oaks stopped and turned to his grandson. "He who sows thorns reaps brambles, Theo. Harlan sows his own harvest, and one day ye'll see where it gets him."

The young rabbit kicked at a nearby dandelion, sending its seeds bursting in a cloud. "I don't see Harlan reaping brambles, Father Oaks."

"Live a little longer then." His grandfather continued walking.

When they had put away their collected roots and dragged the winnowing baskets out for mending, Elder Yeth arrived. Father Oaks glanced at him, but said nothing.

"Evenin', Father Oaks." The Elder fiddled with a loose button.

"The answer's no." Father Oaks opened his pack on a kitchen stool and began unloading the morning's harvest.

Elder Yeth bristled. "You don't even know the question."

"I know it's got to do with that bird, and whatever it is, the answer's no."

The Elder sighed. "It's been hurt. That silly dunce, Mort, tried to use fire on the thing and, well ...."

"Is it bad?" Theo asked.

"A little singed on the leg is all."

"He's not staying here," Father Oaks cut in.

"I'm afraid it's already decided." Elder Yeth plucked his button free and pocketed it. "Harlan agreed."

"Well Harlan doesn't own the warren."

"But he does own the supplies shed where you keep your medicines," Elder Yeth pointed out. "It's the only place large enough to accommodate the beast."

Father Oaks muttered an unintelligible oath.

"It's just for one night, Oaks. You can't begrudge an injured creature one night's board?"

The grizzled healer looked up at Elder Yeth, then cast a worried look at his grandson. His bewhiskered face contorted with resignation. "Very well. One night and that's all."

CHAPTER FOUR

The priest wheezed as he reached the meditation hall and burst through its doors. The badger's bulky frame, combined with his age, had made the steep climb arduous.

"It's worse than we feared, my Lord! The princess has not arrived in Jaipri. Most worry she's been killed, like the others."

Lord Noshi took a deep breath, trying to hold onto the vestiges of calm that came through communion with Aktu. He needed to stay unruffled. If he lost his composure, his opponents would blame it on his being a man and vote him unfit for leadership within the Order.

"When was this?" Lord Noshi's voice, solid as the ancient trees that grew in the mountains about them, calmed the priest's own panic enough for him to catch his breath.

"A few days ago, my Lord. Near the Blackwing border. There have been sightings of the empire's forces near there."

"And Kuno?"

The badger shook his head. "We don't know. Should we try to find the princess?"

"A rescue party would not find her in time, I fear." Lord Noshi wrapped his woolen robe about him and stood from his rush mat by the altar, wincing as his joints protested. Having seen eighty winters, a little stiffness in his wiry body was to be expected, but at times like these he felt the years weighed more.

"But, my Lord, we can't leave her alone with those barbaric Urzoks hunting her!" the badger blurted. Realizing his mistake he clasped his paws in apology. "I am sorry, I did not mean to say that all men are ... are ...."

Lord Noshi looked down at the badger, his dark eyes soft in an otherwise hard and weathered face. The badger priest always tried to keep in mind Lord Noshi's bloodline so as not to insult him. Many in the Order were not so kind or thoughtful. Those who opposed or mistrusted him called him monster; many a fellow man called him traitor; his brother, the Red Emperor Dorgun, would be thrilled to see his severed head gracing his castle gates.

"I know what you meant. Let us call a meeting with the Order. Perhaps we can send a message to Jaipri, have them help us find her."

The badger cleared his throat. "My Lord, this makes the third we've lost. How will we defend Ralgayan without their help?"

"We do not know that the princess has been killed." At the badger's doubtful expression Lord Noshi added, "Remember, Aktu will show us the way. Go, notify the Council."

The badger bowed and retreated.

As always, the thought of his brother Dorgun stabbed him with anxiety. The emperor's ruthless assassination of the land's best warriors, especially those he suspected as having been summoned by Noshi to defend Mankahar's last free city, had struck fear not just into the common folk but within the Order as well. Dorgun was ever a master at terror and demoralization, even during those hot summer days when they had played horseball.

Like all children of Dakus nobility, Noshi and Dorgun were expert riders before they could walk. Noshi's boyhood horse, a beautiful bay named Kite, had been one of the finest in the stables. Noshi could still remember the rush of the ground flying beneath her hooves. Nothing Dorgun said could convince his brother to sell the horse to him.

By the closing of the fourth round Noshi's team had been close to winning, and he was about to send the goatskin ball through the last hoop at the end of the field when his older brother had galloped up hard alongside him. Dorgun had leaned down from his sweat-drenched horse, its sides showing the red welts from Dorgun's heels, and raised his club high. Noshi had expected his brother to hit the goatskin, but instead Dorgun had connected the ball end of his club with Kite's foreleg. Noshi would forever remember the sickening sound of bone splintering, the shriek of his beloved horse beneath him before she buckled and dove to ground like a wounded bird. Dorgun had insisted to their father it was an accident, but even now Noshi could remember his brother's satisfied smile.

That day, the stable hand had helped him slit Kite's long, silken throat. That day, watching the life fade from Kite's panicked eyes, the young Noshi had realized where his future lay. From that moment on, he began seeking a life far away from his fellow kind. Far away from his brother.

CHAPTER FIVE

"What's it like beyond the River Tithe, in the Old World?"

The owl blinked at him, silent. Theo sighed. "The only one I've ever met from the Old World, and you're mute."

They were in the supplies shed, the owl nesting comfortably on a side bench that had been cleared of its baskets and jars of old herbs, seeds, and dried poultices. Theo had dressed the owl's inflamed leg with a salve of chickweed and comfrey, then bandaged it with clean linen. He was amazed at how quickly he'd lost his fear of the owl. Throughout his ministrations the bird had been the ideal patient: quiet, cooperative, his eyes observant but not hostile.

As he packed away Father Oaks's medicine kit, Theo stole glances at the collar. Up close he could see that the stones were not set in place at all, but rather slotted into grooves, with an empty space between two of them.

He reached forward with a tentative paw, and pushed at a stone. It slid to the left. The owl watched him, unblinking. He pushed another stone, this time moving it up. The collar was designed so that every piece could be moved one spot over, down, or up, creating new designs.

"It's a game?" Theo asked. The owl blinked his eyes. *Yes*. "If it's a game, what's the goal?"

The owl shook his head, ruffling his feathers and making the stones clink. Theo brushed the feathers aside and looked again. The gems on the right, now that they had been moved a certain way, looked like—

"Theo!"

He jumped. His grandfather stood frowning at him from the warren doorway. "Yes, Father Oaks?"

"Mind the bloodroot's not boiled over. And stop messing about with that creature."

Theo took one last look at the owl, who stared back with round eyes.

"Sleep well, owl."

As he left he thought about the pattern the stones had made. He had to have imagined it, but for a moment he thought that the gems had formed a caught word.

The violent slap of wings and a sharp scream of pain sent Theo bolting from his bed and running into the supplies shed.

He was just in time to see a group of youngsters rush out, laughing and whooping as they escaped into the pre-dawn light.

Theo rushed to the beast's side. Fur and feathers hung in the air, remnants of a scuffle. The owl stood on its good leg, and swiveled towards Theo at the sound of his voice.

There came a whimper. Owls couldn't whimper, could they?

"Did they hurt you?" Theo asked.

The owl stepped aside to reveal a crying Walnut in the corner.

"Walnut, what are you doing here?"

"They were going to feed me to the owl," Walnut's paws

trembled and his belly heaved with hiccuping sobs. "They said if they fed the owl it would give them its collar."

The bird's head pivoted back to the terrified youngster. Theo sighed.

"Well as you can see, Owl's not going to eat you."

Walnut stood on unsteady legs. "You sure?"

Theo thought he saw the owl's eye gleam with amusement.

"I'm sure. Now get home. And Walnut—" Theo hesitated. Like most rabbits, Father Oaks disapproved of fighting back. "Try to avoid those troublemakers."

He watched Walnut nod and hurry home, then turned to the owl. The collar glinted in the morning light that stole, furtive and hesitant, through the roof cracks.

This jeweled band was causing trouble. Though Walnut had always been bullied, no one had ever tried to do him physical harm.

Theo shut the shed door, then turned back to the owl.

"There must be some way of unlocking this," he muttered. As if in agreement, the bird moved toward him, angling his neck to give Theo a clear view of the collar.

It glowed with a secret all its own, the intricate tiles patterned with onyxes, rubies, amethyst and gold. No wonder everyone in Willago desired it. The memory of his public shaming washed over him, along with a sudden desire to prove Father Oaks wrong.

The pattern was still there. He hadn't imagined it. Determined, he began rearranging the tiles, changing the empty space so that it started on the left side but moved steadily to the right.

All the while, the owl watched him, motionless, until Theo forgot about him entirely and became absorbed in clicking the jeweled tiles. A pattern was emerging. He was close. This tile needed to move further left, to complete the mosaic of tiny rubies there, while if that tile could be aligned with the violet colored stone on the right ....

Surer of himself, his paws moved more quickly, until the

stones formed and reformed like chess pieces, the free space moving until he slid the last tile into place.

I'VE FOUND YOU

A sharp click punctured the silence as the jeweled collar fell to the floor, unlocked. Theo grinned. He had been right! The tiles did form words! That would show Harlan. That would show Father Oaks.

Theo looked from the collar to the owl, whose eyes burned with awe and—had he imagined it?—fear.

"I have to tell Father Oaks!" Theo said, excited.

The owl shook his neck feathers, as if to test that the encumbrance was truly gone. He then snatched up the collar with his injured leg, wincing, and made for the door.

"Wait! Where are you going?"

The owl glanced over his shoulder, brows creased. It bowed its head, as if in thanks, then pushed open the shed door and rushed from the warren.

"Wait, you can't go!" Theo bolted after the bird and was just in time to see the owl take to the sky. He called several more times, but was unheeded. Helpless, Theo watched as the owl's ginger flecked wings sliced the sunlight, taking him east past the treetops and towards the River Tithe. Towards the Old World.

~

"Gone? What do you mean gone?"

Theo tried not to flinch under Elder Yeth's glare, while Walnut stood wide eyed in the corner, watching. The Elder's hearth room had the telltale remnants of an interrupted breakfast: a pitcher of milk, a patty of jam, and a bowl of half-eaten barley meal lying ignored on the table. Elder Yeth's wife cleared away what she could and hurried out.

The Elder turned his full frown on Theo.

"The collar came undone, and then he left." Theo tried to

avoid details about unlocking the collar. Above all he wished he'd thought this through more.

Father Oaks cleared his throat. "Well, the thing's gone. Leave it be."

"Where is he?"

They turned to see Harlan surge through the door. "What's this I hear of Theo letting the owl go?"

Elder Yeth glared at Father Oaks anew before putting a placating paw on Harlan's shoulder. "We were just discussing this, Harlan. Keep your calm."

Harlan's ears flushed. "Calm? That owl's collar was priceless! And Theo just let it fly out the door." He turned a withering gaze on Theo. "Or maybe you just stole it."

"He didn't steal it!" Walnut protested. "Mr. Theo unlocked the collar!"

Harlan turned to Elder Yeth and Father Oaks. "You believe that? We all tried. You shouldn't lie like that, Walnut."

"It's not a lie!" Walnut protested. "He unlocked it with—" At Theo's warning glance Walnut bit back his words.

"With what?" Harlan's eyes narrowed. "It has something to do with the taboo, doesn't it?"

Father Oaks twitched his whiskers. "Be careful ye don't jump to wild accusations."

Harlan turned to Theo. "That's it. You broke your taboo and it somehow unlocked."

Elder Yeth's glare was enough to freeze fire. "Is that true, Theo?"

Theo tried to think of something, but his hesitation betrayed him.

Harlan shook his head. "Not only do you break your taboo, you let the greatest fortune Willago has ever seen walk out your door."

"That's enough!" Elder Yeth grumbled. "Harlan, if there is any judgment to be done, it will be done by the Elders. You're not an Elder yet."

Harlan scowled at his brother and touched the one thing marring his perfect appearance: a burn scar on his neck. Theo knew the gesture. It always surfaced when Harlan had the advantage.

"Very right, Elder Yeth. And I know you will perform justice in the meantime by locking Theo in the Dwelling of Isolation, since he may try and make a run for safety."

"The Dwelling of Isolation!" Theo repeated.

"The rules of Willago state," Harlan argued, "that someone who has broken a taboo of any sort for the third time will be confined until his punishment can be determined. Elder Yeth, haven't you caught Theo breaking his taboo twice now?"

"But all of Willago was trying to unlock it!" Theo protested. "All I did was figure it out."

"No one said that you should break your taboo."

"Harlan, don't be rash!" Father Oaks said. "Theo is not a threat to anyone! He needn't be locked away!"

Harlan shrugged. "Rules are rules, Father Oaks. And are not the Elder's rules very clear on this?"

Theo watched the Elder's face, dread spreading in him like unchecked poison. His gut twisted at the old rabbit's next words.

"I am sorry, Oaks. Harlan is right, we can make no exceptions. Theo will have to be confined in the Dwelling until we decide his punishment."

CHAPTER SIX

Ohenko the owl's eyes narrowed as he homed in on his target. His cry of relief at nearing sanctuary ricocheted off the cliff walls.

The stronghold of Mount Mahkah nestled in a mountainous cradle, its stone turrets blending into the surrounding rock. Even though he had left as a fledgling, the bird remembered his way well and banked to rush through the gathering dusk, towards a beckoning halo of candlelight.

The window was open, as if in wait for him all these years. Ohenko swooped into a large, domed hall that overflowed with light and the clamor of debating voices.

A long, oval table made of polished elm dominated the room. The owl alighted on a rafter that arced over the hall's far side, and surveyed the throng below. None of those engrossed in heated debate at the table took notice of him.

Except for Lord Noshi. His deceptive stillness betrayed how much the bird's homecoming meant to him.

The owl swooped to the man's chair and stepped up onto the man's proffered arm.

Oh Aktu, I had given up hope. Noshi examined the bird, his heart torn between faith and doubt. Was it the same one? Lord

Noshi had given up the owl as lost when year after year passed, with no word.

But it was indeed Ohenko. There were the moon shaped markings on the left wing, the hind talon smaller than its counterpart. And most telling, the prized object that the bird dropped into Lord Noshi's hand.

He lifted the collar in his palm. How light, he thought, for something whose cost and repercussions would be so heavy. Had he really found someone who might save what was left of Mankahar? Possibly the last of a kind that had been ruthlessly erased from these lands?

His plan, if he chose to put it in motion, would at best be dangerous, and at worst, fatal: if anyone discovered his intentions, his life would be forfeit. But it had to be done, and done now. Even Aktu had said so to him, in his prayers. Find one with the Forbidden Knowledge, and Aktu would show him the way. But would the Order let him?

Time was short. If he knew of this creature's existence, others might too.

He pocketed the collar and stood, motioning with his hands for quiet. At the sight of Lord Noshi they all fell into expectant silence. Never mind that he was a former Urzok, Lord Noshi had always commanded the most respect amongst them, partly because he had chosen to stand with the beasts of Mankahar rather than with his own kind.

"I know how this news of the princess has distressed all of us," he began, his gaze moving over the assembled priests. "I know more than anyone that out of the twelve she was one of our brightest hopes."

"Was?" asked a russet cardinal with a tongue as sharp as his beak. "Is she truly lost then?"

Lord Noshi raised his hand. "No, I have faith that Aktu shall protect her. She is a seasoned warrior, she will know what to do." He tried to believe his own words. She was but a young doe, and, warrior or not, no one could be a true match against the

Empire. Not yet. He pushed on, determined. "Now, it seems that when Aktu gives us adversity she also gives us good tidings: another apprentice has been named."

The assembled priests exchanged puzzled glances.

As usual, it was Lord Ibwa, a graying buzzard, who questioned this statement first. "Another one? Lord Noshi, there are twelve apprentices, no? The Council chose twelve."

Aktu help him, but Lord Noshi disliked Ibwa and his subtle attempts to undermine the High Priest's authority. Lord Ibwa had been a hard liner from the start, strongly opposed to trusting an Urzok who could betray them at any time. The only Urzoks Lord Ibwa trusted were ones that weren't breathing.

"After much communing with Aktu, I believe that there is another apprentice worth bringing to Mount Mahkah. Especially as we have lost several to the empire's forces. To confirm this, I sent Ohenko the owl to seek him out. He exists, and I will send a messenger to fetch him."

"What makes him worth bringing to Mount Mahkah?" Quiet and reserved, Tarq the wolf spoke little but his amber eyes missed nothing. The Order's Master of Combat Training insisted on ruthless criteria at every turn, refusing to take on anything he viewed as extraneous—including apprentices. Lord Noshi had expected this question, and had readied an answer.

"He has unsurpassed skills in strategy. No war has ever been won without the aid of skillful spies and immaculate planning."

As a swell of questions and disbelief greeted him, Lord Noshi sighed. *I no longer have their ears completely, Aktu.* The thought weighed on him, as heavy and unwelcome as age. Their trust had eroded over the years, chipping piece by piece—just when they needed unity more than ever.

Above all sins he hated lying, but he closed his eyes and prepared to do just that. *Forgive me for not telling them the whole truth.*

CHAPTER SEVEN

The rabbit drew her head deeper into her muddied cowl and tried not to give way to self-pity.

Outside her meager shelter under a levee of rock, the clouds vented their full wrath, puddles of mud exploding under fat droplets of cold water. She blinked back tears, her eyes raw from too much fear and too little sleep.

It took all her willpower to wrest her thoughts from her fallen companion and focus on the task ahead. If she let her thoughts stray to Kuno, she knew she would be in danger of crying. And then the Urzoks would catch up with her in no time. She reminded herself of her royal heritage and duty. Though she had only seen fifteen summers, she was no stranger to responsibility.

If she could just reach Jaipri and Queen Mercusa, she would be safe. Kuno had told her so.

To comfort herself she closed her eyes and thought of home: the wrestling games she played with her sisters, the feel of her servant's paws massaging sage oil into her fur, the smell of magnolias blooming in spring.

Perhaps next summer, Aktu willing, she would return home a heroine and be entitled to choose a husband by hanging a wreath of magnolias on his door. She knew whose door she would choose. The sword smith's son Nodin, with his mahogany fur and jade-flecked eyes, had long made it clear that he would welcome her attentions. The thought warmed her even as the rain began to seep into her pitiful shelter.

While night enshrouded her world, the princess allowed exhaustion to spirit her to dreams of home. Lost as she was in her memories of the past, her usually keen ears failed to detect the whinnying of horses and the muted thundering of hooves through the falling rain. Nor did she perceive the telltale clink of metal bridles, an Urzok device. These sounds came from less than fifty paces away, yet the rabbit princess slept on, oblivious. Gradually, the hoof beats faded into the night, as destruction bypassed the princess and moved on to another unsuspecting target.

CHAPTER EIGHT

Ostracized on the north side of Willago, the Dwelling of Isolation was a cold, grim affair only a few paces wide, windowless but for a crude hole in the roof.

Through that opening, he'd watched the sun come and go nine times now. Theo sat on an uneven wooden stool, one of the few pieces of furniture in the drab prison, and did the only thing he could: think of escape.

How had he come to this? Just over a week ago life was as it should be: harvesting iris roots and secretly reading his stories. Now, he was accused of breaking taboo, exercising sorcery, and had been locked in this damp, dismal space for what was beginning to feel like an eternity. His one comfort was when Father Oaks visited daily to bring him blankets, food, and what little else he could. No one else was permitted to visit the prisoner, though Theo supposed only Pozzi or Walnut would have tried. Theo had lost count of how many times he'd promised Kalmac that if he could be freed, he would never catch words again.

He heard footsteps outside and the creak of the bar. The door opened, revealing Father Oaks with a basket over his arm and Dill, the guard.

Dill's expression showed his unease. "Father Oaks—I don't

want to be doing this, you understand." Theo found it incomprehensible that Dill, a former playmate, was now his captor.

"I know, Dill." Father Oaks said. "Leave us now, will you, lad?"

Dill closed the door behind him and slid the bolt.

Father Oaks lifted the cloth on the basket. Inside nestled a jug of almond milk, along with carrot bread, plum jam, and a bowl of steaming oat and artichoke pudding. The old rabbit watched Theo pick at it.

Theo knew Father Oaks had brought these offerings to try and tempt his appetite. As hard as he tried, he couldn't contain his tears and hated himself for it. He rubbed them away while Father Oaks rested a comforting paw on his shoulder.

"What news today? Will they let me out?"

"No," Father Oaks said after a pause.

Theo sat back, crestfallen. "What more can I do except say I'm sorry? I swear to you by Kalmac I know I was wrong, I regret it, I shouldn't have disobeyed you!"

Father Oaks looked at him long and hard, and said, "I know, Theo. And I don't blame ye fer what ye did."

"You don't?"

Father Oaks smiled, though the sadness in it told the young rabbit he wouldn't like what he was about to hear. "I blame meself. By tomorrow they will hold a vote."

"A vote? For what?"

"They're discussing whether to ...." The old one's voice trailed off.

"What, Father Oaks?"

"They're talking of expelling ye."

Theo felt the bit of food he'd just eaten turn to cold clay in his stomach.

"Harlan has convinced the town that ye're using sorcery behind their backs, and that ye're a danger to them all."

Expulsion was the harshest punishment Willago could

impose, and Theo couldn't remember when it had last been applied.

Theo's voice came out small and frightened. "What am I going to do?"

Father Oaks tried to hide his worry, but the trembling in his whiskers gave him away. "I'm still trying to convince Elder Yeth t'show some leniency. If I can't stop 'em from expelling ye, perhaps it can be temporary."

The door swung open, and the light from a torch fell in on them. Dill stood in the doorway.

"Sorry, Father Oaks," he said, looking at his feet. "But I was given the strictest instructions."

"Yes, of course," Father Oaks replied. "Keep yer hope up, m'boy." He gave Theo's paw one last squeeze, then picked up the used dishes and hobbled out. Dill avoided looking at either of them as he pulled the door closed.

Theo listened to the sounds of Father Oaks's retreating steps, then leaned against the stones of his prison, dejected. Expulsion was as good as death. Though years of being the odd rabbit out meant he was no stranger to being alone, this was different. Without shelter, food, and the protection of other rabbits, how would he survive? Wandering alone beyond Willago's borders, he would be prey to countless predators and elements.

The crush of questions about his future was too daunting, and he realized that he was exhausted. He lay on his makeshift bed of moldy hay and curled into a ball. Cradling himself, he managed to make his way to a cold and fitful sleep.

~

Snuffling. The sound of claws on stone.

Theo sat up, ears erect.

Dawn had not yet arrived. The Elders wouldn't have him dragged from his prison in the middle of the night? He stood, apprehensive, and backed against the far wall.

There followed a moment of silence, then a shadow moved under the crack of the prison door. The bolt slid across, and the door swung open.

All Theo could see beyond it was darkness.

"Hello? Father Oaks?" he whispered.

Silence answered him. He took a step forward, then another.

"Dill?" Theo stopped, uncertain. If they had come to sentence him, why wouldn't they answer? But an open door was an open door, and leaving his prison would be a relief, even if just for a few moments.

Theo stepped out. The fresh night air felt chilly, but welcome. He turned to peer into the dark, looking for signs of Dill or Father Oaks.

"Hello?"

Something black and heavy dropped over him, fast as a shadow, then pulled taut and closed. He cried out, struggling against the burlap sack that now held him. Impossibly large paws twisted the bag's throat into a knot.

Theo managed a muffled scream before a paw smothered his mouth with the sack. He wriggled and kicked in his captor's invincible grip, then felt himself being carried off into the night.

CHAPTER NINE

Lord Ornox was in a foul temper.

It took a close servant such as Yod to know the myriad shades of the man's wrath, but this one, Yod knew, was one of the most dangerous kinds. It was a deep, seething anger, one that was quick to ignite but slow to express itself, like a coal left unattended beneath damp wool.

His master stood obediently still for the head tailor, arms spread, his only movement a tick in the lower lip that betrayed creeping displeasure. His dark hair hung in a thick braid down his back, while black eyes dominated a nose carved from authority itself.

The tailor had eyes for nothing except his work. He pinched and pinned the luxurious cascade of ivory-colored rabbit pelts to better fit his employer's angular, war-forged frame. A box lay open next to him, full of neatly arranged scissors, awls, needles, and spools of thread.

The object of Lord Ornox's anger stood simpering before him. Vorko was a darty eyed vulture with unkempt feathers. Yod sniffed in distaste. He hated vultures. But not as much as Lord Ornox hated this creature at this moment.

"... east, northeast, towards the Blackwings." The vulture

squinted rust colored eyes. For a moment there was nothing but the sound of the tailor's scissors as he sheared an offending piece of thread or pelt. Snip. Snip snip.

"So," Lord Ornox's voice rolled calm, controlled, and soft. Like a caress. "After sending you away, you have brought me a piece of rabbit's clothing and the assurance that you killed a messenger."

Vorko nodded, a trace of pride in his eyes.

Lord Ornox turned to his servant. "Yod, do you recall what I asked Vorko to bring to me?"

"You asked him to bring you the two of them alive, m'Lord."

The vulture scratched one leathery leg with a cracked claw, his eyes scampering from Lord Ornox to his servant, and back again. Yod could almost see the rusty wheels of his brain creaking in thought.

"So I did," Lord Ornox nodded, as if just remembering. "Instead," Lord Ornox continued, "I now have a dead messenger, an enemy apprentice loose and free, and no further information on the Order's next move."

Vorko's neck feathers fluffed in a defensive ring around his scrawny, mottled neck. "But the messenger—one more dead, that's—"

"That's useless!" Lord Ornox roared. The tailor jerked back, almost dropping his scissors. Lord Ornox lowered his arms, square fingers clenching.

Vorko pulled his wrinkled head into his body.

"To say you have disappointed me would be honoring you."

Vorko's beak opened in defense. Lord Ornox took the scissors from the tailor's hands and drove the spread blades into the vulture's head. Once, twice he thrust in precision, as if finding his stride, then launched a flurry of frustrated stabs. The spatter of blood fanned across the floor and onto Lord Ornox's robe.

The tailor cried out, as if he had been gouged instead of the vulture.

"They were specially bred ... all twenty ... ruined ...."

Vorko's feathered body slumped to the floor, his lacerated head leaking like a flask of overturned wine.

"Then buy another twenty," Lord Ornox said, cleaning the weapon on his destroyed robe before shrugging it off and letting it crumple to the floor. "I'll see that you're paid."

This only upset the tailor more. He gathered his ruined masterpiece to himself with trembling hands, whimpering like a broken child. Exasperated, Lord Ornox turned to Yod.

"Draw me a bath. And find my daughter Agacheta. Tell her it's time to stop her games. We need to see about these Blackwings."

~

Agacheta drew a breath and waited. Life could be divided into two parts: waiting, and action. Waiting was always the hardest, a seemingly endless test of endurance. But then came the exquisite, hair's breadth of time in which action changed everything. Irreversibly.

As it was about to change for the young pheasant hen stirring beneath the rock outcrop that jutted from the surrounding heather like a broken bone.

Agacheta tried to ignore the prickle of sweat near her hairline. She had her father's luxuriant dark hair, pulled back from her pointed, wolf-like ears into a traditional warrior's knot. Any hints at femininity were kept under rein beneath her loose hunting garb. She held the primed bow with calloused hands.

She could just spy the tail feathers of the blood pheasant, visible in tantalizing pinpricks through the underbrush. She imagined the imperial red feathers, fletched and proud, on the arrows she had commissioned. Imagined anything that would distract her from the numbness spreading through her hand, born from holding her bowstring immobile since dawn.

The hen risked a step forward, one russet foot raised and curled. A pause, a dart of the neck, and then the foot lowered, soft as down. Agacheta didn't breathe. Anticipation hummed in her veins.

And there it was. The hen shifted its weight forward, the body clear of the underbrush. An exhaled breath, the whisper of wood against wood as the arrow shed the bow, and then—

"My General!"

The hen twisted, but not fast enough. The wooden shaft pierced her in the lower back, pinning her to the earth and sending blood soaking into the feathers. She flapped against the ground, lurching to one side.

"My General, I disturb you hunting?"

The vulture perched on the branch above blinked at her with polite deference before his eyes drifted to the pheasant.

Agacheta strode forward and with the heel of one boot crushed the neck of the dying hen. It shuddered and then went limp. She examined the tail feathers. Snapped in some places, crooked in others. Actions. They changed everything. She sighed and turned to glower up at the vulture. She hoped he brought news that would make up for his blunder.

"Did you find it, Morkin?"

The vulture shook his head. Agacheta scowled. "Then what are you grinning about?"

"A village, General," Morkin's eyes narrowed. "A helpless village."

She glanced back at the pheasant. Perhaps the old saying "When the gods shelter a hare they flush a deer" was true. She had never believed the rumors about refugees fleeing the battles between man and beast by braving the Sea of Petrified Waves. Her advisor Caldrik's hunch had proved valid. He would never let her live it down, no doubt. But why would a messenger owl have come here?

"Defenses?"

The vulture shook his head. "None, General. Farming village, primitive. All rabbits."

"How many are there?" General Agacheta squatted by the pheasant and wrapped her fingers around the arrow's spine.

"Five hundred, six hundred, maybe," Morkin replied, his eyes fixed on the pheasant.

Six hundred? She did the calculations, and even at a conservative guess realized that would fetch a considerable sum. More than enough. Perhaps as much as the collar that owl had. She yanked the arrowhead out from the hen, bringing bone and a string of gut with it.

"Go tell Kotori we ride into the village at dark. Alert the troops and have all the units ready." Agacheta cleaned the arrowhead with a handful of dirt. "Also have one of yours fly to my father to let him know that we will be returning to Vyad at dawn."

"Yes, General!" The vulture bobbed his head. "Shall I have Caldrik prepare the Pacification?"

"Yes, do that. He won't need much to tackle a bunch of rabbits." Agacheta waved him off in dismissal. At his hesitation she sighed and motioned at the pheasant with her arrow.

"Thank you, General!"

Morkin swooped and speared the hen by the neck before setting off for the main camp in the northeast.

As she made her way back to where she had tethered her mare, Agacheta mulled over the vulture's news. This was it, she realized. This was what she had spent fitful nights waiting for.

She thought back to Caldrik's words when they had sighted the bird: *Follow the owl, and the Emperor will have to grant you the glorious position you seek, my Lord.* She could never quite tell whether he mocked her; referring to her in that fashion before she'd earned the title would have seen him lashed if they'd been in the capital.

But never mind. The title would soon be hers.

She hadn't needed much urging to change her regiment's course from their routine patrol of the southwestern steppes. The troops had become soft and restless from lack of action, their attempts to find unpacified animals had been laughably fruitless, so that tracking the mysterious bird and its priceless ornament to the western borders offered a welcome mission.

Her mare whickered in recognition when Agacheta reached the fallen oak where she'd tied her. She slung her bow against the pommel and pulled the hide stirrups down, mounting with an absentminded swing of the leg. She let the mare find her own way back as she contemplated her next move.

If she didn't find the bird, she would still be able to reach the allotted number of prisoners necessary for promotion. And if she captured the owl with its collar, she would be wealthy besides. The prospect thrilled her, for this was precisely why she had taken the post of Imperial Patrol rather than stay in Kalyuneh, the capital. She knew her father's ambitions for her, but she would rather cut her own throat than marry that decrepit old dog, emperor or no. She had greater ambitions: becoming a warlord. No, not just a warlord. The first female warlord.

Life was, indeed, about waiting and action. This particular wait was over. By dawn she'd have earned her dream. As well as her father's respect.

CHAPTER TEN

When he was set on solid ground again, Theo had managed to figure out three things: it was nearly dawn, he was a good distance from Willago, and whoever had abducted him was large, strong, and smelled of musk and pine.

"I'm going to let you out, but you have to promise you won't scream." His captor spoke for the first time, deep and authoritative.

The rabbit nodded.

"I can't see, is that yes?" his captor growled.

"Yes."

Rough paws untied the sack. Theo blinked, his eyes adjusting to the pre-dawn light.

At first he had the impossible notion that he was looking at a mountain. But it was worse: he was staring into the broad face of a towering brown bear.

Theo tried to tame his fear. "Are you … going to kill me?"

The bear stood at least three times the rabbit's height at the shoulder, a great hulking figure with a rich tawny coat that looked black in the last vestiges of night. On his head sat a metal helmet complete with nose bridge, while strapped to his back was a mean looking battle axe, its curved blade as sinuous as a cat's spine.

The bear harrumphed. "Not quite. Brune is my name. I'm a friend."

"A friend?" Theo repeated. "What kind of friend abducts someone?"

"It looks like you've got your tail stuck in a hornets' nest, as my father would say. I'm sorry I couldn't explain right then and there, but you would've screamed and woken everyone."

"Why would you free me?" Theo asked, confused. "You have to take me back."

"Take you back? Why? So you can be expelled?" Brune asked, amused.

"How did you know I was to be expelled?"

"I know a lot of things. I was sent for you, you see. I'll explain later, but for now, we're long on risk and short on time. Climb on." Brune turned and gestured towards his shoulder.

"Wait, why should I go anywhere with you?"

The bear leaned down and looked straight into Theo's eyes, making the rabbit flinch despite himself. "Because you're in more danger than a mouse at a minx party. Besides, even if you go back, Theo, you'll just be expelled. I'm here to protect you."

Theo's confusion grew. "How do you know my name?"

"As I said, I know a lot of things. But we haven't much time. Now are you with me?"

Theo hesitated. What the bear said made sense—he was as good as expelled, since how would he explain that he hadn't tried to escape? Whatever leniency Father Oaks had pleaded for would now be forfeit.

With a sinking feeling he realized he had little choice. If the bear was going to harm him, he would have done so by now. He gripped Brune's outstretched arm, and the giant swung him onto his shoulder and helped him find his balance.

"Grip tight now," Brune advised, as he began loping at a fast run. From this height Theo saw that they were on the hill northeast of Willago, where the thatch roofs etched an outline against the brightening sky. A few smudges of smoke unfurled their sleepy way from the occasional chimney. Willago was starting a new day. Without him.

As the dwellings he had known all his life slipped out of sight behind them, Theo realized that the bear was heading towards the River Tithe.

"Where are we going?" Theo asked.

"To the east, to Mount Mahkah," the bear replied, never missing a stride.

"What's at Mount Mahkah?"

"Your future. You're to train as an apprentice to become an Ihaktu warrior, so you can fight against the emperor, rot his bones and curse his hide."

"A warrior?" Theo repeated. "I can't become a warrior!"

"Why not?"

"Because—I'm just a rabbit. Rabbits don't fight."

"I assure you that they do," Brune chuckled. "Some of the greatest warriors I know are rabbits. Almost lost my eye to one once, he was fiercer than a bull with burrs in the backside. You, Theo of the Forgotten Lands, have been chosen for the army against the Red Emperor, rot his flesh and curse his pelt."

"The Red Emperor?"

Brune shook his head. "The Forgotten Lands are truly untouched. You've never heard of the emperor or his enslavement of Mankahar? This is not the time for details, but take my word for it: there is a very powerful force that has something worse than death planned for all of us."

"But what does any of this have to do with me?" Theo asked.

"It has everything to do with you, rabbit. You and several others have been chosen by Aktu, the goddess of all things." Brune glanced behind them, peering through his helmet. "That's how I am here now, rescuing you from a mob of angry rabbits who would like nothing better than to pound you into paste, no doubt. Speaking of which ...."

Theo turned to look back. They had climbed up the cliff edge that bordered the River Tithe and now stood at the brink of its descent into swirling waters. Up the stone slopes behind them clambered a group of roughly twenty rabbits, armed with clubs and slings. Though Theo recognized neighbors and fellow villagers, the way they carried staves and pitchforks in clenched paws made them menacing, unfamiliar. Leading the pack, with a thick coil of rope in one paw, was Harlan.

As if feeling his brother's gaze, Harlan looked up, and his slate grey eyes locked onto Theo's. Theo saw the resentful animosity there, and in that moment, Theo realized that the bear was right about at least one thing: he couldn't go back.

CHAPTER ELEVEN

"Hang on," Brune said, his muscles bunching. The bear plunged forward onto a rough path that snaked down into the gorge, through sparse shrubs and copses that clung to the sandy slopes. They slid down the hill face, soil and pebbles tumbling their way down ahead of them.

Theo chanced a look behind. Harlan and his group had paused at the top of the gorge to peer down at the fleeing pair.

"We're safe now. They'll not come any further. Our laws forbid it."

Brune snorted and paused in his descent, panting. He began picking his way to the left, testing with his back paws for firm ground and stable rocks.

Theo looked down the gorge and caught his first glimpse of the River Tithe. The mist from its waters hovered just above it, a roiling cauldron caught between the green-black of the gorge's slopes. On the far side of the river, imposing granite cliffs pierced the sky, their jagged teeth sharpening with the dawn.

"The Sea of Petrified Waves," Theo murmured, wide eyed.

A shower of pebbles rained down, some bouncing off Theo's head. He twisted and looked up. Harlan's dark silhouette was making its way down the gorge.

His companions reached forward to grab his arms in an attempt to stop him, but he shook them off and started down the path.

"They're coming after us!"

Brune glanced back at their pursuers and growled. "I'll give you rabbits this much, you've got determination." He picked up his pace.

A cloud of swallows swooped over their heads, hunting insects. Brune's front paw slipped, throwing his body forward. Losing his balance, Theo slid down Brune's bent neck before grabbing hold of his fur.

Brune grimaced as Theo hung there.

"I'm going to fall!" Theo cried, feeling his hind legs peddling air. If he lost his grip now, he'd tumble down the gorge face.

Brune bunched his haunches to get a firmer foothold, then raised a paw and grabbed Theo, pushing him back onto his shoulder. This delay allowed Harlan, and the few rabbits who dared follow him, to gain on the fugitives. They were only fifteen paces behind.

"Hurry!" Theo cried.

Brune bared his teeth. "I am! Now hang on tight and no more stunts."

Brune pulled out his battle axe, hefting it in one giant paw, and launched himself onto the slope.

They slid at a dizzying rate down the gorge, rocks and earth flying behind them as Brune buried his axe head in the soil like a crude rudder, trying to control their descent. Several times they rammed unchecked into thorny shrubs, which left stinging welts on their hides. The sound of the river flooded their ears as bear and rabbit at last tumbled and rolled to the bottom of the gorge in a cloud of dust.

As they picked themselves up from the ground, Brune looked back up the gorge face.

"By Aktu, they're not far behind."

Sure enough, a few smudges of dust pinpointed where

Harlan and his followers were sliding their own way down the gorge face.

"This way," Brune headed towards the trees that girded the river.

"Are you mad?" Theo asked. He hurried after him, for the bear had broken into a run. "That river is certain death! I can't swim!"

Brune frowned through his helmet, returning the axe to his harness in one smooth motion. "Can't swim? We'll have to fix that. But we need to cross it. And your neighbors will have to see you doing it."

"Why don't we head north, to the forests? They won't be able to find us there; or south, there must be another way!"

Brune shook his head, stepping over a fallen tree. "We must head east, over the river and to Mount Mahkah. This is the only way. They have to see you die."

Theo stopped in his tracks. *See him die?*

Just then the trees thinned, and they found themselves standing on the bank of the River Tithe. It was a dark, living mass of water, churning up everything in its path like a hungry beast, its back a roiling pelt of whitecaps glinting in the dawn.

Theo gazed at it in awe.

"Over here!" Brune called. The bear stood next to a large rock pool that adjoined the roaring river. Here the water swirled in a brisk dance, trapped in its confines of rock. Something bobbed on the water surface. Theo clambered down after Brune, who was craning his neck into the pool.

The bobbing object was a raft made of willow wood and lashed together with vines, anchored to a wood stake buried deep in the riverbed.

"Quick!" Brune called above the river's roar. "Help me untie this!"

Theo stepped into the pool, the icy water numbing his legs. He grasped the wooden anchor and began working it out of the pebbled bed. By the time he had it free his hind legs had lost all feeling.

"That's it, now get on!"

The rabbit hesitated again, but Brune grabbed the back of his jerkin and hauled him onto the raft. With a mighty heave of his shoulders the bear pushed the craft away from shore, then stepped back and began climbing the embankment.

"Where are you going?" Theo asked in panic. The raft shuddered like a scared bird as it neared the main stream of the river. It would be a matter of breaths before it was swept into the tributary's arms. Spray from the water stung Theo's back.

A shout sounded from above. Harlan stood at the embankment. He pounced, aiming for Brune's back, and the bear took a running jump.

To Theo, time slowed down as the bear flew through the air towards the raft, a hurtling mass of muscle, fur and axe.

"Grab hold, and don't let go!" Brune shouted.

The raft lurched with the impact of nine hundred pounds of bear. Theo grabbed hold of one of the vines as the raft submerged under the weight, then resurfaced like a leaping fish and spun out of the pool into the main waterway.

The last thing he remembered seeing before the icy water engulfed him was Harlan standing on the shore. This time it wasn't the look of anger in his brother's eyes that scared him. It was the look that said he was watching a rabbit as good as drowned.

CHAPTER TWELVE

Late morning light straggled through the smoky shroud lying over Willago.

Cries of anguish could still be heard, like ghostly disembodied voices through the thick air. Most of the warrens, torched during the morning attack, had been reduced to smoldering piles of sod, brick, and charcoal. The smell of singed flesh, fur, and fresh blood rode the morning breeze.

From her saddle, General Agacheta fidgeted with her mare's reins. Caldrik sat astride a spotted tan gelding, his hood pulled back to reveal a long, pockmarked face that was handsome once.

"Whose idea of restraint was this?"

Caldrik's voice, unlike his face, was smooth and supple. "Every dog will eat pheasant while he can. You must let them."

Her pageboy appeared, as if he had heard their conversation. "Food, my General?"

She glanced at the skewer of rabbit leg he proffered and turned away. She would rather bathe in coals than admit it to anyone, but she found the thought of eating unpacified meat repugnant. She recognized the wisdom of Caldrik's words, but it was time to put an end to the killing. Even though she could return now with slaves in tow and claim her title, the thought of the tracks she'd discovered here nagged at her. Since she hadn't found the bear that had made them, she needed information. Information only living, talking rabbits could give.

"Pacification spoils their meat. You should try it, wild rabbit is hard to come by nowadays," Caldrik observed, taking the skewer from the page and biting off a piece.

Agacheta ignored him, focusing instead on her approaching commander.

"What news, Kotori?"

"We found another group, General. Returning from the river. They were gone during the attack."

"Any signs of what we're looking for?"

The commander shrugged. "Hard to say. Seems they've their own religion out here. They've never heard of the Forbidden Goddess. We interrogated several, even the young ones. They know nothing of the Order, or of the War."

"That may be, but tracks do not lie," Agacheta said. "He's been here. Let's find out why."

~

General Agacheta surveyed the line before her. They were roped together, shivering in their tattered robes from fear more than cold. Commander Kotori stood next to her, impassive.

Her eyes settled on one paunchy specimen, who flinched as if struck. Such spineless animals, these. How did any of them expect to withstand the empire? "There has been an unusual visitor in these parts."

Her eyes raked over the lot, noting that another of the prisoners jumped.

"There's no point in lying," Agacheta continued. "My soldiers have found the tracks, very fresh, heading towards the river." From the corner of her eye she saw an older, grizzled rabbit stealing glances at a honed but nervous companion down the line.

The time was ripe to set the trap. "I should mention that the whole reason we are here is because he has something of ours." She offered a reassuring smile. "We just want to get it back."

The general moved down the line, scrutinizing each furry, petrified face. "If one of you would just come forward and tell me what you know, we will spare you any more killing."

Her eyes bored into her target, who took a deep breath before stepping forward.

"We didn't take the collar!" He tried to stand tall and look General Agacheta in the eye.

"Harlan!" the grizzled one barked.

So the bird had been here. "Be quiet, rabbit, and let the good creature speak. Go on. Harlan, is it?"

"Will you really let us live, if I tell you what I know about the bear and Theo?" Harlan asked.

Theo? First an owl, then a bear had come here, and he had not left alone. She looked at Caldrik across the line of prisoners. She was sure her tutor was having the same thought.

"Of course I will," Agacheta replied. "Ask any of my men: the general always keeps her word."

"Don't be a fool, Harlan, she'll kill us anyway!" the older rabbit cried. At a signal from Agacheta, a guard cuffed him with the handle of his wooden club.

"You were saying. Theo," Agacheta prompted.

CHAPTER THIRTEEN

"Theo! Theo! Wake up! That's it!"

He tried to open his eyes. His head felt like pounded dough.

Icy water swirled at Theo's waist, while his jerkin bit at his neck. The fabric had snagged on branches overhanging the river, and Brune was trying to disentangle him.

"Theo! Wake up!"

He began coughing, deep coughs that rippled through his belly and gripped his chest. Warm water rushed up his throat and nose, spilling over his drenched front.

"There you go, you're all fine now." Brune pulled him out of the water with one giant paw and slapped the rabbit's back.

Theo crouched against the pebbly beach, feeling like his lungs would split open. His legs shook with the cold, and the roar of the river still rang in his sodden ears.

The bear dropped a woolen blanket over Theo and a small cloth pack by his side.

Brune pulled off his helmet, then fell to all fours and shook himself, sending droplets flying like scattered seeds.

Theo clutched the dry blanket, his wet ears plastered to his back, his teeth chattering in his skull.

"Where'd this come from?"

Brune clapped his helmet back onto his burly head. "Ill prepared is ill perished, as my father always said. No point being soaked as a frog in a bog from our little swim. Come on, let's pick up the rest of the supplies."

He turned and began plodding along the bank, whistling. Theo opened the pack and looked inside: flints, a well-honed knife, a water flask and a digging stick were tightly packed amongst what looked like morsels of dried foods wrapped in waxed leaves. Theo shouldered the pack, hurrying to catch up. His cold began to give way to wonder at his near brush with death.

"I'll bet no one in Willago would ever believe we'd made it alive across the River Tithe!"

"Let's hope so, Theo. It's best that everyone thinks us dead."

~

By mid-morning they were deep within the Sea of Petrified Waves, a place more desolate than Theo could have ever imagined.

They found a narrow corridor that tunneled between the high walls of stone, its floor covered in coarse white sand. Once the rock structures closed around them, the corridor became a netherworld, darker than the thickest forest. Here and there patches of light straggled through from ruptures or holes in the rock ceiling above where time, ice and heat had done battle with the stone fortress.

The walls did indeed seem like water frozen in time, with wave-like swirls and petrified mollusks embedded in the rock. Theo heard the cawing of birds from nests perched high on countless outcroppings. Suspicious eyes peered down at him.

As they trudged through this world of sand and rock, the sun's warmth steadily waned. Brune seemed not to notice, whistling as he strode ahead. Theo struggled to keep up with him on his shorter legs, but didn't want to stoop to the ignominy of asking the bear to slow down.

"It's gotten a bit foggy, hasn't it?" he asked instead, shivering as tendrils of moisture clung to his fur.

"The Sea of Petrified Waves has always been a place of fog and mist." Brune stopped so his companion could catch up. "Some say it's always fighting to return to its liquid state. Many enter the Sea, and many never come out." He grinned. "Stay close, rabbit. This is no place to get lost. Follow my voice if you can't see me."

Theo nodded. Brune continued on, his whistling a ribbon of sound through the thickening fog. Gradually Theo could only make out his silhouette as he fought to keep pace.

They walked on for a league or so before Theo noticed that Brune's whistling was growing more distant. The bear was moving too fast.

"Brune!"

There was no answer except for the fading whistling. Cursing under his breath, Theo hoisted his pack and broke into a run.

After several dozen paces, he noticed Brune's whistling getting weaker instead of stronger. Confused, he turned about in the dense sea of white.

"Brune!" He called out at the top of his lungs, the cry bouncing furiously off the walls. Silence closed in again once the echoes sank into the fog. He strained to hear a paw fall or responding shout, but there was only the sound of his own labored breathing.

He reached out and scrabbled blindly until he felt the cold stone wall. He followed it back the way he had come, calling out regularly and trying to feel for a break in the rock where Brune might have turned off the path.

After retracing his steps for a good hour Theo had to admit that he was lost.

He stood still and tried not to panic. Brune would notice he wasn't behind him and come looking. But if he couldn't find Brune, how was Brune going to find him?

He was just about to try renewing his search on the other side of the path when he heard the sound of rushing air.

He looked up, in time to see a bird materialize from the fog, wings and razor-sharp talons outstretched.

Theo threw himself to the ground, sand flying into his mouth. The bird screeched as its talons snapped inches above his neck. The air from its wide wings filled Theo's ears as it rose to circle and try again.

He scrambled to his feet and began sprinting, the pack bouncing wildly on his back. He heard the telltale scream of the bird's return. It had no trouble finding him despite the dense fog, and Theo's lungs seared in his chest.

Just as he heard the ominous sound of feathers beating air, he slipped the pack from his back and burst into as much speed as his legs could muster. The pack might divert the bird's attention, but for how long?

Theo began to regret abandoning his one form of protection, but then he spied a hole in the rock. *Thank Kalmac!* He threw himself into the opening, ignoring the pain as his shoulder scraped against the jagged rock.

He sucked in his breath to fit better in the narrow space and worked his way along the wall until he was clear of the entrance.

The bird's yellow eye appeared, angry and sinister, at the opening. Theo backed himself further into the rock as the hunter's pupil first dilated to adjust to the dark, then fixed its hungry gaze on the rabbit.

The bird turned its head sideways and tried to reach into the crevice, snapping its beak. Theo cringed. The bird's breath reeked of rotting flesh.

After several failed attempts, the bird withdrew. Theo listened to the scrabble of claws against sand before silence descended. He heard a soft punching sound. Having failed to hunt down the main game, the bird had settled for second prize: the pack.

Theo breathed a sigh of relief, then wondered whether the bird would wait at the rock entrance until he came out.

Perhaps there was another way out of this stone prison. He managed to turn his head and saw that behind him the passageway widened into a cave. Peering into the gloom, he tried to determine how far the passage went, but could see nothing.

The cawing faded. Apparently it had lost interest in the pack. Theo debated whether to venture out, but then saw a glow emanating from the darkness.

The rabbit squinted. There had been nothing there before. But, sure enough, the glow persisted, even flickered.

"Hello?" he called out. His voice echoed down the cave.

Theo managed to turn himself around in the tight space and take a few steps towards the light. He had to scrabble with his paws to squeeze himself through the tunnel, but by sucking in his belly he made it to the other side.

The faint scent of oil and smoke hit his nostrils, and with it the tension melted from his body.

Fire! Where there was fire there was life, and warmth, and safety. Maybe even someone who knew how to get out of this barren piece of rock.

He felt his way along the corridor until he found an entry covered by a piece of rough and tattered cloth, behind which the fire flickered and cracked a merry invitation.

"Hello?" Again there was no reply.

He pulled back the curtain and stepped into a spacious cavern with a floor of dry sand. A dug-out in the middle held the cheerful fire of driftwood, moss, lichens, and dried sea brush.

A giant rock sat against the far wall, as tall as Theo's waist and twice his arms' span across. What caught his eye, however, was not the rock itself, but what was on it: a bottle full of liquid and a platter heaped with food.

Moving towards the rock, he tried one last time to announce himself. “Anyone here?”

Only the crackling of the fire replied. His stomach rumbled at the sight of thick slices of dried cranberry cheese, a bowl of currant and apricot pudding, squash filled with spiced cabbage, and a fluffy biscuit that beckoned with melting apple butter. A crude earthenware pot held a dark liquid, the crisp aroma of crab-apple wine unmistakable.

The feast was too tempting for a rabbit who had just fled the jaws of death and hadn’t eaten since sunrise.

Theo began nibbling on a corner of the biscuit at first, unable to resist the apple butter. Soon he had finished that off and licked his paws clean. His stomach growled at the interruption. Looking around and seeing no one, he decided that the slices of cheese were really very small and insubstantial.

Before he knew it, he’d ploughed his way through all the cheese, cleaned off the bowl of pudding, and eaten all of the stuffed figs. He was wiping the telltale remains from his mouth when he heard the voice.

“Eaten your fill?”

Theo whirled about. There was no one there. He eyed the fire, for it was the only movement in the entire space. It cackled a mischievous laugh at him.

“I said, have you eaten your fill, rabbit?”

Still seeing no one, Theo replied, “Yes—who are you?”

“Why, I’m the dweller of this cave, rabbit,” came the voice again, from behind him. He turned to the table, where the empty dishes and wine pot stood. There wasn’t a living soul in sight.

Unnerved, he asked, “Where are you?”

“Right in front of you, rabbit; right in front.”

The table heaved, first one way, and then the other. The empty plates and wine jug slid to the sandy ground. Two stout, leathery legs emerged from the left end, followed by two similar limbs on the other. When the “table” at last stood on these sturdy appendages, a large head emerged from what Theo now realized was a giant shell, not a stone. A leathery face gazed at him with watery grey eyes. The eyes blinked, and then the thin lips parted in a pleased smile.

"Welcome to the Sea of Petrified Waves," said the creature.

Theo swallowed. "I … I apologize for eating your meal, I … I thought there was no one here."

"Not at all," the creature huffed, shifting to better face his visitor. "Food is meant to be eaten, and there's more where that came from." He winked. "And you were obviously famished. Well, little rabbit, what brings you into the den of a tortoise such as me? Hmmm?"

"I got lost," Theo said.

The tortoise raised one eyebrow. "Lost? Lost isn't so bad. Unless, of course, you hope to be found."

"Perhaps you could help," Theo said. "I'm from Willago, over the River Tithe."

The tortoise frowned. "Well my dear rabbit, how could you have gotten here? No one crosses the river."

Theo drew a breath. "This bear brought me—"

"Why would you be with a bear?" the tortoise asked, perplexed.

"It's a complicated story."

The tortoise smiled. "Is it ever not? Why don't you tell me, young rabbit? I don't get companionship often."

And so Theo told him everything, from the owl arriving to washing up, half dead, on the other side of the river. He glossed over how he had freed the bird, leaving out his word-catching.

Theo sat down by the fire and stared at its flames. "And now I'm lost. I don't suppose you could tell me how to find my way out?"

The tortoise nodded his head in sympathy. "Yes I could. But everyone's path out of the Waves is different. You are lost because you don't know your path."

"How can I know my path if I don't know where it leads?"

"Well, little rabbit, I do like you, and you're ever so muddled about what you should do. I might be able to help you."

"Really? How?"

The tortoise's eyes twinkled like a conspirator's. "Don't you know that a tortoise's shell can tell the future? Perhaps we should see what lies at the end of your road."

"You could do that?"

"Oh, reading your destiny is easy. But it comes with a price."

"What do you mean?"

The tortoise's voice grew soft. "Knowing your destiny can be a dangerous thing. You must be prepared for the consequences, and face it no matter how terrifying it may be. But I sense that you're no ordinary rabbit."

And with that he motioned towards the fire. "Go and look under that stone, and bring me the box of shells."

Theo did as he asked, and found a flat box buried beneath one of the fire pit's stones. He opened it and discovered a pawful of green and brown shards, so old and worn he could barely make out that they were tortoise shells at all.

"Go ahead now, and cast them," the tortoise urged.

Theo poured the shells into his paws, then cupped them for a moment. They felt warm and alive against his palms. At his host's urging, he tossed them.

They fell against the sand, their polished surfaces winking in the firelight. The tortoise craned his neck, his gaze roaming over the shells.

"Interesting. I have never seen a future quite like this before."

Theo waited, watching the tortoise's leathery face, then looked back at the shells. Some were turned up, some faced down, and they were all of a different shade and shape.

He couldn't contain his curiosity any longer. "Well?"

The tortoise sighed. "I can tell you what awaits you back home. That is very clear."

"What's that?"

The tortoise indicated, with one cumbersome toe, a cluster of small dark pieces. "Only death awaits you if you go back."

The rabbit's heart sank. "And if I go forward?"

"That's where it becomes interesting. Now just give me a moment."

He squinted at various pieces, his eyes crinkling at the corners as he mumbled, "Ah, yes, a choice!"

"What do you see?"

The tortoise smiled, but it was carved from sadness. "Well my little friend, you do not have an ordinary or easy destiny, but it is an important one. I see a great secret surrounds you, a heavy secret, which will cause you great suffering and no little danger. But I also see a love, a royal's love. And last, I see a great battle, one that will require a hefty sacrifice, one in which you will need the utmost of bravery."

"I'm not very brave," Theo admitted. "I don't even know how to fight."

The tortoise chuckled. "Bravery is not always proven with swords and arrows, little friend."

"Will we win the battle?"

"Battles are never won. No side ever entirely wins or loses. But I have something that may help you."

At Theo's puzzlement, the tortoise motioned towards his back. "As I said, tortoise shells have great power. Choose one."

Theo hesitated. "Any one?"

"Yes. Listen, do you hear it?"

Theo closed his eyes. He felt something pulling at him, and his paw moved as if of its own will. He opened his eyes. The shell he touched was darker than night's underbelly, and just as smooth.

"Pry it loose."

Theo felt along the edges of the shell, and he pulled it out easily. It was smooth and warm, and when he turned it over he saw a murky surface. "A mirror?"

"I suppose you could call it that. It shows what is within."

What is within? "Thank you," Theo said, though it was the most ineffectual mirror he'd ever seen: its surface barely reflected his outline.

"That," said the tortoise, "is no ordinary mirror. Use it in your darkest hour, for it will bring out your deepest fear."

"Why would I want to do that?"

"Because sometimes, what you fear most is what you need most." At his confusion the tortoise grinned. "Worry not, little rabbit, I think you will find the strength to use it. Guard it well, for it has great power if it should decide that you're worthy."

Theo couldn't see anything special about the ordinary looking shell, but felt it would be rude to show his doubt. "How would I prove I'm worthy?"

The tortoise smiled. "All in good time, my friend. All in good time. But first, rest is the key."

No sooner had he said these last words than Theo felt an overpowering drowsiness. The wine, mixed with a full meal, had had its effect.

"So sorry," the rabbit apologized, rubbing his eyes.

"And I have just the remedy, my dear fellow," the tortoise replied. "You just lie down by the fire and have yourself a sleep, and when you wake up, we'll go looking for that Broom of yours."

"Brune," Theo muttered, lying down and curling into a ball.

"Yes, Brune, that's right ...." His voice faded off into darkness as the rabbit succumbed to sleep, though even behind his eyelids he could still see the beast's watery eyes, blinking at him.

He dreamed of a great expanse of water; it glittered in shards of gold, blue and green, and rushed on gentle feet to the shore. The smell of raw salt and wind hung in the air, and swathes of clouds brushed across the sky's blue face.

As he watched, the green of the sea darkened, and he heard

something else breathing. Something much larger. As he squinted into the mist, two eyes the color of burnt ochre seared the gloom. Before Theo could run, the thing lunged, the mist parting like a shredded nest.

The Griffin.

It pulled him to the ground, grinding the breath from his chest.

Theo lay frozen by fear, wanting to move but unable to. The Griffin's claws drew skeins of blood.

What are you?

Theo tried to answer, but his voice hid somewhere with no doors or windows.

What are you?

With a shriek the Griffin lay into his ribs, cracking Theo open like a soft-shelled egg.

CHAPTER FOURTEEN

When the remnants of his dream sank away, Theo saw he was in a sandy clearing, the moon's light spilling through chinks in the rock above. It took him a while to remember he was in the Sea of Petrified Waves.

Brune sat on a nearby rock, examining Theo's discarded pack. It had several punctures, but the food and tools seemed untouched.

"Blasted kawa birds," he muttered, before putting it down and yawning. The bear pulled off his helmet and scratched his head.

"How'd you find me?"

"Easy. The fog lifted and I followed your paw prints to that hole you were hiding in."

Theo held a paw against his forehead. He was hot with fever, and yet felt chilled, and his bones ached. "Where's the tortoise?"

"What tortoise?" Brune asked, yawning.

"A giant tortoise was in the cave, and I ate his food. He was right there."

"Perhaps you've been listening to too many tales. Don't tell me you thought you were dining with the Grey Rock?"

At Theo's confusion Brune chuckled. "When the Petrified

Waves were still an ordinary sea, its king was a giant tortoise with magical shells. Some say Aktu turned the sea into stone to punish him for some offense or other, until the day he atones for it." Brune shifted onto his back and settled his great arms over his belly. "Get some sleep, it's a long journey out of this Sea."

Theo was about to ask more about the Grey Rock, but soft snores gurgled from the bear's throat.

Theo lay back down and wondered if he had imagined it all. He ran a paw over his jerkin and found the mirror in his inner pocket, its face secretive in the moonlight. The tortoise had been real after all, which made the whole thing even more unsettling. He turned the object over in his paws. What power could such a piece of shell possibly hold? He replaced the gift in his pocket and tried to shut out the questions that crowded in on him, as oppressive as the stone bluffs that arched overhead.

~

Two days after being separated in the fog, the travelers emerged from the Sea of Petrified Waves. The edges of the stone sea ended in a wooded valley with a brook carved through it. Theo made straight towards the water, grateful for a chance to slake his thirst.

As the rabbit drank, Brune pulled the pack and axe holster from his back. He leaned against a scaly oak and began rubbing his shoulder against it, causing the tree to shake and creak in protest.

"Ah," he sighed in bliss. "That's better. Great contraption, but the thing itches like a shaved bum in ivy!" He squinted into the sky. "Winter will come early this year. We'll have to hurry if we're to reach Ralgayan before the empire's forces cut us off."

Theo was simply grateful to have a rest and pulled off his coat to stretch his aching limbs. Myriad scratches and welts on his legs reminded him of their clumsy descent to the River

Tithe. For the hundredth time he wished he had his medicine chest with its array of salves and tonics.

He hefted the digging stick from Brune's pack and began heading upstream, knowing that comfrey root favored moist areas near water. Brune grunted behind him.

"Don't go far. We should head off soon."

His search proved difficult. Though the moist ground did support certain straggly leaves, he only managed to dig out a few withered and stunted tubers.

Theo tucked his findings in his belt and retraced his steps to the clearing. He found Brune swinging his pack onto his shoulders.

Theo held up the tubers. "Slim pickings but enough to ease these cuts of ours."

Brune looked up and frowned. "Who's that?" He pointed.

Theo turned. Standing there, some paces away, was a rabbit.

Theo's first thought was delight and relief to see his own kind—there *were* other rabbits beyond the Sea of Petrified Waves! But something about her checked his excitement. She was naked, with dirty brown fur and mud-flecked paws.

Theo turned. "I don't know, I didn't even ...." He looked back at the stranger, trying to hide his embarrassment. She was a fine looking doe beneath the grime.

Theo touched an ear in traditional greeting. "A peaceful day to you."

When she didn't respond, he picked up his coat. He held it out to her, trying to keep his eyes on her face. "Here, you'd best cover yourself. My name's Theo."

He started to move towards her, hesitant. Was she mute? Lost? Perhaps she'd wandered too far from her warren and been hurt while she was bathing.

Just as he was about to wrap the coat around her shoulders, she twitched her nose again and reached out a paw. She began to sniff his face, and gave his ear a lick.

"What in Kalmac's name—"

"Get away from her, Theo!" Brune's cry was stern and urgent.

There was nothing appealing about her beauty now. Theo was desperate to get himself out of her clutches. She pawed his neck, no matter how much he protested and tried to stop her.

He managed to break free and fell back from her, panting. Theo rubbed his neck where she had clutched it. She looked straight into his eyes, and that's when he noticed it. There was something wrong about her eyes, something vacant. There was no ebb and flow of emotion or reaction, only a dumb look of—of what?

"Is she ill?"

Brune strode to Theo's side. The rabbit backed away, looking at him with clear suspicion and raw fear. Her ears flattened, the whites of her eyes half-moons beneath her irises. She crouched to the ground as if preparing to flee.

"She isn't ill," Brune said, his voice quiet.

Theo looked from him to the rabbit in confusion. "She's clearly not well. She's out here alone, naked, and mute!"

"She isn't ill," Brune repeated. "She's been pacified."

The rabbit had backed away even further, looking from Theo to Brune. Cautiously, she stretched her head into the air and sniffed, her nostrils flaring.

"This is Dorgun's power. He can suck the soul out of a creature and turn it into what you see before you." Brune's voice burned with anger. "This is his future for Mankahar."

"You mean she was once like us?" Theo watched, dumbstruck, as she dropped her snout into the earth, feeling safe again. She began snuffling about, eating the raw grass and whatever seeds her digging revealed.

Brune nodded. "She would've once been a thinking, talking creature, just like you. But she's come into contact with Dorgun's poison. And now she's homeless and hapless, wandering around with no rational thought other than fear, hunger, and instinct." His voice hardened. "You see why the Red Emperor wants to make everyone just like her: mindless, mute, as capable of logical thought as a stump. Once he's made us into this, there won't be a field mouse left to challenge him."

He turned to look at Theo, and the sudden movement made the young doe bolt into the dense underbrush, her white tail flashing in alarm.

"Can you now understand, Theo, why saving Ralgayan and defeating the Red Emperor is so important to us?"

CHAPTER FIFTEEN

General Agacheta watched the last of her soldiers emerge from the Sea of Petrified Waves, trying to control her exasperation. Slowed down by armor, chained prisoners, and dense fog, it had taken two days for the long caravan to wind its tortuous way, single file, through the narrow faults in the rock.

Luck, it seemed, had fled along with her patience. First there had been no trace of the bear after the river, and then Caldrik's assistant had allowed the Pacification containers to get wet in the crossing. She'd never had to transport this many unpacified prisoners, and if she was to reach Nyatha's market before the slavers left she'd need to make better time.

She turned in her saddle and shaded her eyes against the setting sun. Scanning the valley, she noted the plentiful groves of cottonwood and alder that fringed the cliff bases.

Digging her spurs into her mare's sides, she galloped down the long line to where Commander Kotori was barking orders for the captives to hurry.

The commander looked up at her. He had served with her long enough to know that only cowardice irked her more than inefficiency. "What are your wishes, my General? Shall we divide the army?"

"Not yet. Order a halt. Tonight and tomorrow we build wagons to transport the prisoners."

As she spoke a dull brown rabbit passed by, his mother holding his paw and his neck stooping with the weight of the collar fastened around it. He looked up at Agacheta, his cheeks stained with tears. The general looked away. She didn't like dealing with unpacified young ones. Like many of her generation, she was used to pacified animals providing her with meat, transport, and clothing. She couldn't help but find their ability to speak abhorrent. It felt unnatural.

The rabbit's mother snatched her offspring close.

"Don't look, Walnut!" She murmured, hastening him.

Agacheta pointed her sword at the nearest swathe of alders. "Start with those and work your way through them until we have four carriages. Make sure they're light enough for the pack horses. I want all the animals loaded and ready to leave by sunrise tomorrow."

Kotori grunted. "As you wish, my General." He mounted his bay mare and rode off, shouting orders as he began re-organizing the soldiers into teams to bring down the trees.

Agacheta scanned the line of prisoners trudging before her. The dun-colored one looked at her with accusing eyes.

"You said you'd let us go," Harlan called to her. He cringed as the general's horse cantered up to him, its eyes wild and its mouth frothing from the bit that tore at its pink gums.

"I said I'd let you live," Agacheta corrected. "And I suggest you save your breath for walking."

The rabbit's mate clutched at his arm, pulling him away from the mare's hooves. Agacheta watched them for a moment before she noticed that Caldrik had pulled his horse alongside hers.

"He may have been lying," Caldrik suggested.

"They're not smart or brave enough. That one would have sold his own child if he thought he could live another day."

"Then the conclusion is the same. The bear is alive."

"It's possible they drowned. Likely, even."

"But you don't believe that," her tutor said, making her feel she was being tested.

"I don't trust any corpse that I haven't been able to sink my sword into," she replied. "You taught me that."

"I taught you well then," Caldrik smiled, pride warming his granite-colored eyes. "So we continue the hunt?"

"How? The trail is cold. Best to take them to the camps at Nyatha, get them pacified and sold." She paused, thinking. "That's not to say you shouldn't perhaps open a few ears."

Her teacher rubbed the patterned ring he wore on his thumb. "The ears are always open, my Lord."

CHAPTER SIXTEEN

"Have you seen many creatures like that one?"

It had been two days since they'd come across the pacified rabbit. Tonight they'd found shelter by a rock outcropping on a densely treed hillside. The encounter had left Theo shaken, and he'd spent the last day mulling over what he'd seen.

Brune nodded. He tossed the branches into the cooking pit, then hunkered down to start lighting the fire. "There are vast lands of them, Theo. Lands where you could travel for many moons and not encounter another living—*truly* living—creature." He nurtured a flame into a timid fire.

"You've lived a sheltered life, rabbit, in remote lands untouched by the war." He removed his helmet and ran a paw over his head. "But I know kingdoms and entire races that have fallen to Lord Dorgun, curse his mother and rot his loins. Places where Dorgun's allies and servants hunt for pleasure instead of just for food, where they set up game rings to pit these mindless creatures against one another, to fight to the death. For amusement. They have no respect for the laws of Aktu."

Theo stared into the fire in silence. He would never forget

the look of that creature, its empty eyes. What if Willago became that, too?

"Who is this emperor anyway? How did he become so powerful?"

"It started many generations back, when the first Urzok King stole the Book of Ills."

"The Book of Ills?" Were these Urzoks word-catchers? Like him?

Brune swallowed his bread and wiped the crumbs from his mouth. "The Book told him how to rob creatures of their ability to reason and speak. Since then the Urzoks have tried to enslave all of Mankahar, or pacify us, as they would say. The emperor won't rest until we're all like that rabbit you saw back at the stream."

"Isn't there anything that can stop him?"

Brune smiled. "We're hoping you and your fellow novices can, Theo. Twelve disciples have been chosen to go to Mount Mahkah to train as warriors of Aktu. The Ihaktu army will have the power to bring down the Red Emperor, curse his beard and rot his tongue. Which is why he's so eager to find you before the Order does. And why Lord Noshi himself assigned me the task to make sure you arrive safely at Ralgayan."

"What happened to the Book of Ills?"

Brune shrugged his great shoulders. "No one knows. Some say the first Urzok emperor had it destroyed so that no one else could use its power."

"Perhaps there's a Book of Cures."

The bear snorted. "The Book has been the source of all Mankahar's misery. Speaking the language of the gods is a blasphemy, and we're still feeling the sting."

Theo pretended to be absorbed in his food so that Brune wouldn't see his curiosity. Father Oaks had been right: the Old Lands hated word-catching even more than Willago did. It felt strange keeping a secret from someone who had become his only friend. But did he have a choice?

"How far is Mount Mahkah? And where does Mankahar end?"

Brune grinned. "Indeed, I've been remiss. It's time we gave you a geography lesson of these parts." With one paw he cleared a rough space near the fire pit's ash, then began collecting bits of stone and wood lying nearby.

"Willago is here, see," he said, placing a stone down with his great claw. "It's in the west, and we've passed through the Sea of Petrified Waves." He placed another stone some distance to the upper right hand corner. "This is Mount Mahkah. To get there, we will have to pass through the Jaipri Forest, where we'll meet with my brother, Kuno, and the disciple he's escorting to Ralgayan; together we'll go north of the Blackwing Forest, cross the Yharu passes and the Plains of Fire, before reaching the port city of Ralgayan, the passage to Mount Mahkah."

Theo watched in wonder as his new tutor dropped pieces of wood or stone in each place as he named it, and little by little a rough map emerged. Even with little to give scale, it was obvious that the breadth of Mankahar was greater than anyone in Willago could have imagined.

"The Red Emperor is preparing his armies to push north and attack Ralgayan before the first snows," Brune said, pointing at a pebble he had placed just northwest of Mount Mahkah. "If he takes it, Mount Mahkah and the Order are lost, for Ralgayan is the only free port guarding the entry to Mount Mahkah now. All the others—Velbind, Oerskel, and Illieth—have fallen and are under Urzok control. Without Ralgayan, the free beasts of Mankahar will have lost their last refuge."

Over the following days, they hugged the shady, forested strip of land that Brune explained ran from the Petrified Sea to the Jaipri forests. They avoided any open scrubland and exposed terrain to the south where Dorgun's agents could spot them. They met few other living creatures, only once startling a pacified deer by a stagnant pond. It ran in panic at their approach.

Twice the two travelers passed through the ruins of small

villages. There were few remaining tokens of normal life. Broken shards of pottery or a chipped, rusted tool embedded in the earth stood like silent markers of another time.

"Are there other towns in Mankahar that are as big as Willago?"

Brune laughed. Theo realized it was the first time he'd heard the bear make the sound. It was a deep, rumbling bellow that sent the birds scattering into the skies, their raucous calls seeming to echo the bear's mirth. "The cities of Mankahar are over fifty times the size of Willago, rabbit! But their allegiance lies with Dorgun. Otherwise, they are razed to the ground."

"Are you from a city, Brune?"

At this, Brune looked away. "You could say so. I was born in a place called Hegg, just before it was destroyed by the Urzoks. Both my parents were slain there, and if it were not for Lord Noshi, I and my brother Kuno would have died there, too."

"I am sorry," Theo said, feeling the inadequacy of his words.

Brune huffed. "I was one of the lucky ones. My brother and I have each other at least." He shrugged his massive shoulders and grinned. "If it hadn't happened, I wouldn't have met Lord Noshi and you. So you see, as my father always said, there's a tasty grub inside every rotten log."

He began walking again, his great swinging gait making the axe bounce against his back. He started to whistle a tune as Theo hurriedly followed behind him.

"Even so, I don't know anything about fighting," the rabbit mused, kicking at a piece of broken pottery as he followed Brune's track.

"Take heart, rabbit. Lord Noshi says Aktu has named you as one of the novices. And Lord Noshi never lies, you can bet your carrots on that. Aktu willing, we'll make a warrior out of you yet."

"What if I fail in my training at Mount Mahkah?" Theo asked. All these expectations of him made him nervous.

Brune clapped a reassuring paw on Theo's shoulder, rattling

his shoulder blades. "You worry too much, Theo. As my father always said, why worry about bee stings when you haven't even found the honey?"

CHAPTER SEVENTEEN

The fortress of Kalyun-eh loomed like a crouched cat on its impregnable cliff over the surrounding lands, a menacing testament to the power of the Dakus Empire.

Lord Ornox stared at the fortress, deep in thought, as his retinue wound its way through the military camps. They neared the moat that coiled like a choke hold around the fortress base. His guards' warning trumpet calls signaled the passage of a great lord, and most prudently melted away before the entourage's horses.

They passed a butcher straddling a bucking calf, pulling its head up by the muzzle to draw a blade across its throat. The calf's eyes rolled as the blood ran from its severed jugular. Several calves in a rough metal corral awaited a similar fate, their cries lost in the melee of horses' whinnying, and the clanging of the metal smithies. Ornox returned his attentions to the fortress on its hill.

With luck, his flesh and blood would rule over this fortress within two years. The idea had come to him some time ago, but he'd kept his thoughts to himself, for Lord Ornox knew better than anyone that timing was of the utmost importance.

The emperor Dorgun was in dire need of an heir and had

been trying to beget one for decades now. In whispered conversations just out of the emperor's hearing, it was rumored that the ruler couldn't conceive. Some blamed it on his advanced years. Others said it was because he had murdered his own father for the throne, an act no god could leave unpunished.

The emperor was convinced that it was not his seed that was the problem. The problem was that an emperor should beget children by someone worthy to bear such an important task, and that he had not yet found the right royal. Therefore the emperor turned to more unorthodox means.

Lord Ornox spat onto the street. Most feared the group of four witch doctors led by the one called the Child, but Lord Ornox had nothing but contempt for them. What were they but a bunch of semi-mad, failed priests who dabbled in hallucinatory herbs? But the emperor had become convinced that these four wizened swindlers could divine the reason behind his failures to produce a son.

There could be no doubt that the emperor was growing unhinged. But, Lord Ornox knew, an unhinged ruler with absolute power presented infinite opportunities for those who knew how to handle him. And Lord Ornox planned to make sure that when the time came he would be there to step in. But first, he had to marry Agacheta to Dorgun.

Of course for the time being there was the war to deal with, and the traitor Noshi must be crushed, along with the pitiful army he was assembling. But once that was accomplished and Mankahar was ruled entirely by Dorgun … an empire needed a bloodline, after all. And Lord Ornox had been blessed with a very capable, if somewhat soft-hearted daughter, who would share his ambitions. Eventually.

A smile flickered across Ornox's face as they reached the castle's drawbridge. It creaked and groaned in its sluggish descent to the landing, while news of his arrival was shouted across the ramparts of the fortress. His fortress.

~

"His Lordship Ornox of Vyad," the Imperial Herald announced, prostrating himself.

He backed out on his hands and knees and closed the great double doors to the audience chamber, leaving Lord Ornox on one knee in his formal regalia.

For a moment there was only the sound of the flames flickering in their torches. Across from him stretched an open balcony, tiled in smooth granite with pillars carved from the bones of tusked elephants, a balcony that had a complete view of all the lands around the fortress.

No enemy could approach this castle unseen, Lord Ornox thought with admiration. It was an impeccable fortress, suitable for grandeur as well as war and siege. The architect, along with his main crew, had been buried under the last flagstones.

"Death and life abide in the tongue, and those who love its words will sing on," a voice drawled.

Lord Ornox bowed his head. "The poet Calgornan, from *The Ballads.*"

Near the balcony there came the sound of rustling robes. "Who taught you the old writings, Lord Ornox? Stand."

Lord Ornox straightened.

"He wrote good poetry, no?" Emperor Dorgun sighed. As he blinked, only one eye closed in his sallow face. His other eye was a limpid white orb, diseased by some unknown, incurable ailment. "Pity he had to be executed with the others, in the end. And yet, though he died hundreds of years ago, you still know his work."

The emperor motioned with one bony finger for Lord Ornox to follow, then turned towards the balcony. They looked out over a rectangular stretch of playing field, demarcated by a low stone barrier on one side and the imperial stables on the other. Players, marked in either red or green feathers in their helmets, were readying for a game of horseball, adjusting their gloves and checking their horse's bridles. On either end of the field were staked a row of four hoops made of stiffened leather, in descending size. The riders mounted and kicked their steeds into action, shouting taunts to opponents and encouragement to teammates. Lord Ornox could not see the ball.

"How I miss this game," the emperor murmured, his eye roving over the mounted players. A guard standing watch at the far end of the field looked up at the emperor, expectant.

Dorgun gave a slight flick of his fingers, and the guard whistled in the direction of the stables. Two burly prison guards emerged from within, half carrying, half dragging what appeared to be a mass of black and tan fur between them. As they approached the field, Lord Ornox finally saw it for what it was: a badger, beaten but alive, all four paws tied behind his back so that his spine was forced into an arch and his belly was exposed.

"This particular fellow had over five original copies of Calgornan's anthologies," the emperor said. "Priceless."

"He couldn't understand it, surely?"

The emperor grimaced. "Of course not. But as dearest Father always said, if the beasts start understanding the Forbidden Language, where would the empire be?"

The players gave a shout to assume places. Red and green separated, lining up on opposing sides. The guards abandoned their prisoner in the middle of the field and retreated. A sharp horn blast heralded the game's start, and the players spurred their mounts forward, whooping and brandishing their ball-headed clubs. The first blows brought agonized screams from the live game piece, as bones splintered and organs ruptured. When a resounding crack to the skull cut short the badger's last cries, the emperor turned away, bored.

"You obviously felt you couldn't wait for the war council tonight." The emperor scrutinized his most infamous general.

"I've received word from Agacheta about the Forgotten

Lands to the west. She's found an isolated village beyond the Petrified Sea."

"What of it?"

"She learned that a messenger had been there. The Order had an interest in someone."

"She has excellent instincts, it seems," the emperor said.

"Her one allegiance is to her emperor. She serves you with all her mind and heart," Ornox replied, careful to leave his tone light. "She's captured the inhabitants and will be bringing them to the camps for pacification."

"Very good," Dorgun nodded. "However, you wouldn't have asked for a private audience to tell me of our successes. A public airing of your daughter's exploits in front of the War Ministry would've been much more to your liking, I imagine."

Lord Ornox tried to ignore the barb. "I'm trying to be discreet, Your Excellency. She's not captured them yet. She's tracking them down as we speak."

"Hounds can track, Lord Ornox," Dorgun snapped, his eye boring into the warlord. "Even those disgusting vultures we use can track. What we need that fine daughter of yours to do, is *find* these little vermin, and their messengers. Wipe them out, exterminate them, you understand. We don't need my brother's silly prophecies gaining traction."

Lord Ornox bowed his head in agreement. He waited while the emperor calmed himself.

"The Child tells me that you also found another messenger, near the Blackwing Forest."

"That is correct, master," Lord Ornox said, silently cursing. How did that bastard know so much? "However, the novice escaped. The messenger is taken care of."

"This novice is the so called Princess of Alvareth?"

Lord Ornox nodded.

There was a pregnant pause. "Find her, my dear Lord Ornox. Find her." His white opaque eye turned like a waxing moon to his chief commander. "The Child tells me that she is the one."

Lord Ornox started. "You surely don't believe in the prophecy? Your Excellency is invincible."

"Of course I don't believe it!" the emperor barked. "But the Child says that without a doubt she will be Empress. Her line will rule Mankahar, Ornox. And that line must be mine. She's the only one who can produce my heir."

He was not quick enough to stop his initial reaction. "You're speaking of crowning a beast Empress?"

Dorgun trained his liquid eye on the vassal, making Lord Ornox flinch.

"You doubt me?"

Lord Ornox felt his pulse shiver, and hated himself for it, but he kept his face impassive. "Of course not, my Lord. I will see to it that she is found and brought here. Alive."

~

It took Lord Ornox several days to see to all his duties in Kalyun-eh. Once he had reassured himself that there would be enough pacification available to deal with Ralgayan, and that the bulk of the imperial army could be ready to join his battalion by mid-autumn, he took his leave of the emperor and set out from the castle walls.

As his retinue wound its way through the choked streets of the capital, Lord Ornox allowed himself to tackle the problem that had been uppermost in his mind: the emperor's new notion of marrying himself to a rabbit.

The emperor had truly lost his wits if he was now fixing his sights on one of the animal warriors as his chosen bride. Perhaps it had been a good thing, then, that the princess had escaped their clutches. And if the vassals of Mankahar heard of their feared emperor engaging in such ridiculous activities, they might decide that the dynasty had weakened enough to wrest power for themselves.

For now, the throne was still safe for Agacheta. But he would have to find a way to make the emperor come around to accepting Agacheta as his bride. He would have to find a way to have the princess killed, and convince Dorgun that she had succumbed to wild beasts.

His retinue wound its slow way through the crowded, twisting streets. Merchants, metal and bone smiths, slave mongers, healers, musicians, scribes, jewelers, bakers, weavers, brewers and whores—they all flocked to the capital to try and scrape out a living. The streets had become a melting pot of haphazard shanties and shops selling everything from woven cloth from the east to the unparalleled glass of the west, from exotic fruits of the south to fresh meat culled from pacified animals, farmed on various tracts of land outside city walls.

His lips curved at the memory of those who had claimed that altering other creatures for their benefit was at least unfair, perhaps immoral, and certainly unholy. They'd been silenced along with their precious priests and philosophers, and now most of the population couldn't remember a time when they weren't the rulers of Mankahar, to do with other life as they saw fit. Dorgun's inherited powers, along with his notorious penchant for cruel punishments, ensured that even the strongest supporters of the empire feared the one who ruled it.

Lord Ornox was brought out of his thoughts by the sight of someone in a white cowl, following his retinue.

The figure wove through the throng at a discreet distance, but Lord Ornox knew he was being tracked. He patted his horse's neck in an understood signal.

Yod was there in an instant, his eyes fixed straight ahead. "Yes Master."

Without looking towards the figure, Lord Ornox said, "We have an unwelcome friend. See what his business is."

With a quick nod of his head Yod fell back and disappeared into the crowd, making his steady way towards the follower who had stopped by a shoe cobbler.

Lord Ornox never slowed his pace, but kept his retinue moving, looking straight ahead.

Soon Yod was back by his elbow, his head down as he spoke in a low voice.

"He refuses to give a name, but says his master would like to see you about something of the utmost importance and secrecy."

Lord Ornox hissed in annoyance, his thick brows knitting. "I have no time for silly games with those who cannot even give their identity."

"He said to give you this," Yod passed up a small ring, about the size of his thumb. Lord Ornox took it. His breath quickened when he saw the engraving on the dull metal surface. He looked around, but the figure had already disappeared into the faceless crowd.

As if reading his thoughts, Yod said, "He said to meet his master at the Blood Hound, near the southern Dorgun temple, at the hour of Clouds tonight."

Lord Ornox's mind raced. "We will make the appearance of leaving the city tonight. Have the guards continue as planned, but find a nearby inn. We will wait for the hour of Clouds."

CHAPTER EIGHTEEN

By the time the bear and the rabbit had crossed the rolling grasslands and come upon the fringes of Jaipri Forest, their supplies were almost gone.

Brune proved an adept forager, and along their travels showed Theo edible, though unfamiliar, vegetation. The plants he recognized all had to do with healing. He'd never had to learn what might be used for food, having depended all his life on the tended plots in Willago.

"That's the difference between a life at peace and a life at war, Theo: farms are a peace time luxury."

They stumbled upon such a farm on a grassy embankment wedged between two brooks, half a day's journey from the Jaipri Forest. But unlike other settlements they had seen, this was no crumbling marker of a long-abandoned home. Theo stared at the fresh scars: layers of ash piled between the jagged remnants of house beams, like spittle gathered between teeth; crumbled stone fences blackened with soot that sagged in defeat around plots of once-tended earth. Several crows sat on the few remaining high perches, looking down on them with judgmental eyes.

Theo stepped past a doorframe and into what had been a pantry. Fire had eaten away all the thatch roofing, as well as the doors and most of the shelves, but Theo found cracked clay jars amongst the ash. He opened one and sniffed.

"Look, Brune! Sunflower seeds!"

The bear joined him. Soon they had uncovered several jars that still held an assortment of charred but edible foodstuffs: a pawful of chestnuts, two jars of hazelnuts, a cask of pumpkin seeds, and enough cranberry beans to feed them for two or three days if they were frugal.

"Can we carry it all?" Theo opened his pack.

"Leave it," Brune growled. "We're not safe here."

"But it'd be a waste," Theo protested. He was loath to continue on Brune's helpful but unappetizing diet of dandelion shoots and nettles. This find was a delicious banquet in comparison. Before the bear could protest, Theo slipped out to find a bag to carry their plunder.

He scoured the perimeter of the main house, looking for a tool bin. He spotted a shed off the rear, its roof lined with crows that shrieked and squawked at each other.

He began to jog towards it, then slowed, unnerved. What was that poking out? Just behind the shed, like a beckoning arm?

It *was* an arm. Tied to a post.

Theo wanted to stop himself but couldn't. Something drove him to keep walking until he saw the thing for what it was.

The crows barely acknowledged his arrival. They rested on and near their meal, voraciously tearing chunks of flesh from the sagging body of what had once been a badger. Their violent feeding caused the arm to jerk in a macabre dance. The creature had been tied, limbs splayed, to a crude cross. His paws had been severed—not by the crows, but by a sword. His eyes were also gone, though the healer in Theo made the sickening realization that they had not been picked out by crows, but burned out: the bone sockets showed scorching.

Theo tried to take deep breaths of air but found his body

wouldn't obey him. He turned to run, and stumbled into Brune's solid mass.

"What did they do to him?" Theo managed to say once he had controlled his breathing.

"This is the Urzok punishment for having banned materials," Brune said.

"Banned materials? Like what?"

"Something with the Forbidden Language of the gods on it, Theo. Trapped words, like what was in the Book of Ills." Brune nudged at a piece of wood that lay half buried in the ash, its surface charred but still bearing the telltale outline of script. "Looks like they burned it with him."

Theo felt his stomach give a dangerous turn. Had the badger been a word-catcher?

"It's been many a year since I've seen this punishment." Brune growled. "Poor bugger. Come on, we best get away from this place. I fit what I could." He tossed Theo his traveling pack, then sheathed his axe and turned to walk away.

"We're just going to leave him like this?" Theo asked.

Brune stopped. "That's exactly what we're going to do, Theo. We have enough trouble without burying a criminal."

"A criminal? Because he possessed a few pieces of wood?" Theo protested.

Brune's face turned dark, and his voice was flinty. "Theo, what you see here is Urzok savagery. Our kind would never do such a thing. But make no mistake, keeping materials with the Forbidden Language on it is not just dangerous, it's sacrilegious. He knew he was dancing with fire."

Theo looked back at the badger's frame, at the fat, sleek crows that gorged at their leisure. Who was this badger? Had he been a word-catcher? Whoever he was, he had risked and paid the ultimate price to keep a few caught words. He deserved dignity, and where would he get it except from another who could understand?

"No matter what, he didn't deserve this," Theo said, shedding his jerkin.

He chased the crows, shouting with a ferocity that surprised him. They resisted at first, and Theo received vicious pecks to the arms and ears before Brune ended the dispute by wading in and crushing a few bones with his paws. The crows retreated to a grudging and malevolent distance, but hovered in hopes that the two intruders would change their minds.

"Thank you," Theo said.

"If you're going to be stubborn as grits to do right we might as well do it fast."

~

It was nightfall before they'd managed to dig a hole deep enough for the badger's mangled remains. They piled a crude covering of stones as protection against the crows. Theo's shoulders and back ached from hauling rocks and working the spade, but he felt a measure of satisfaction in the physical exertion. It helped ease a gnawing question.

"You said this was Urzok savagery. What would his punishment have been with the Order?"

Brune's eyes flickered, as if in memory. "It's very rare to find someone breaking the ban. But anything with the Forbidden Language on it would have to be confiscated and destroyed. As for the guilty one, it would be exile at the least. The Urzoks don't spare anyone they find with the stuff, Theo. They kill your entire family if you're lucky, and your whole village or city if you're not. I've never seen anything but sorrow and death come to those who dabble in Aktu's Forbidden Language. Now get some sleep or we'll be slow as turtles in tar tomorrow."

Father Oaks had, as usual, been right. At best he could hope for banishment, and at worse he could meet the badger's fate. Unless he could find other word-catchers, the best thing to do was to follow Brune to Ralgayan and on to Mount Mahkah, learn to become a warrior if he could, and hope that no one found out his secret.

CHAPTER NINETEEN

As they neared the Jaipri forests the following day, Theo found himself growing uneasy, and not just from the badger's death. Brune had told him Jaipri was serpent country, which turned his blood frosty. Serpents and rabbits were not an ideal combination. Then again, some would have said the same of rabbits and bears.

Sensing his discomfort, Brune grinned. "Jaipri's ruler, Queen Mercusa, is an ally. Besides, many folks would never dream of eating you if they found out you were a disciple of the Order."

But if they found out I was a word-catcher, being eaten would be a merciful death. The thought rose like bile.

A barely discernible trail, no more than a pace across, led them deeper into the heart of Jaipri. Theo had to struggle to keep up with Brune's long strides. The underbrush slowed the rabbit more than the bear, since his sheer bulk could snap all branches that dared infringe on the narrow pathway.

By mid-morning Theo was out of breath and wincing from the blisters on his feet.

"Why don't we rest before—"

"Shh!" Brune raised a paw in warning.

The bear stared ahead. Vines and tangled elderberry formed a dense wall through which something glinted.

"Passage, in the name of Aktu." Brune's voice was quiet but authoritative.

Neither of them moved. The silence stretched, taut and brittle.

Theo thought Brune had been mistaken. Then came a soft rustle, like leaves scuttling over wood.

Brune drew his axe in one fluid movement, gripping its handle in both meaty paws as he crouched, ready.

The dense green wall in front of them seemed to dissolve, then reform. The emerald and yellow-striped head of a giant serpent, wide as a tree trunk, emerged from the cover of the forest. An intricate blood red tattoo between the eyes made him even more intimidating. Behind him were at least five other serpents, though none similarly marked.

The bear gave a whoop of joy and wrapped the tattooed serpent's head in a vice-like grip. "Lyusa, you old bag of scales, what are you doing sneaking up on me like that?"

The serpent writhed in Brune's affectionate clutches, before drawing enough air to rasp out a greeting. "Brune, good to see you—though gentler, please. My bones have gone brittle in my old age."

Brune laughed and batted the serpent's cheek. "You'll still be young and spry long after I've gone to my eternal hibernation! By Aktu, it's good to see your sly old face." As if just then remembering, Brune gestured towards Theo.

"Where are my manners? Theo of the Forgotten Lands, meet Commander Lyusa. He has more war stories than he has scales, isn't that right?"

"Ah, you were forever the bear with the honeyed tongue." The Commander didn't even look at Theo. At his expression Brune's jovial smile faded.

"What's the matter, old friend?"

The Commander's voice was soft. "It's Kuno. We found him two days ago."

~

A tense silence escorted the party to the Palace of the Serpents, which turned out to be a labyrinth of underground tunnels and chambers set into a cypress-crowned hill.

Brune had to stoop to enter, and his helmet scraped along the stone-lined ceiling, causing sparks to fly from the aggrieved metal. He didn't seem to notice, but hurried on, his jaw clenched.

They wound their slow way down several tunnels before the passageways opened into a wide hall domed in veined marble. The lamps in the alcoves made ominous shadows against the walls. The air stank of sweat, mixed with the sharp aroma of mulberry stewed in vinegar—the healer's common antidote to poison.

Theo saw several red-furred monkeys, all of them half his size, bent over a basin stirring the concoction over a flame. Their paws turned the ladle in a smooth rhythm, while others ground mulberry leaves in wooden mortars. The chief healer was a wizened monkey with sharp obsidian colored eyes and a purple robe, who stared at the two arrivals with naked curiosity.

In the middle of the room lay a pallet of wild grass, on which a great black mass breathed in jerky, irregular spasms. Next to him, coiled in thick ropes of amber and scarlet scales, was a giant serpent.

At their approach her triangular head angled towards them, her eyes the same deep blue as Lyusa's. She had a royal, dignified aura that identified her as a queen without introduction.

"You've come at last," she said, her voice relieved yet pained. "He has been calling for you."

Brune drew the helmet from his head and approached the

pallet. He knelt and reached out to touch the black figure lying there.

"Kuno," Brune said softly. "Kuno, it's me. Brune."

The patient stirred and raised his head with great difficulty. Eyes that had once been a lively brown were now sunken and discolored. The bear managed a smile.

"What happened, Kuno?"

The black bear swallowed with pain, and his voice struggled in his throat. "I've failed, elder brother. I failed her. And I failed you." At this tears welled in his eyes.

Brune knelt and cradled Kuno's head in his paws. His voice, when it came, quavered. "No, you did not fail. You did well. So very well."

"We were ambushed, but I made sure she escaped. She's still alive, I know it. You must find her, Brune, and bring her with you. To Mount Mahkah."

Brune bowed his head. His voice held the threat of tears. "Never mind that now, we'll find her later. We need to take care of you first. Come, bring the healers, there must be something!"

"Brune," the invalid protested.

"Hurry, why are you all standing around doing nothing?" Brune shouted, so that the attendants jumped.

"Brune of Hegg," the chief healer said, stepping forward. "We've done everything we can. He goes to Aktu now."

"My royal healer, Eluk, speaks the truth," the queen added.

"There's nothing you can do about me. But you can still save *her*!" the dying bear whispered.

Brune bowed his head, and the tears broke through. At last he nodded.

"Do you know where she is?"

"We were ambushed near the Blackwing Forest. The southern side."

Brune ground his teeth. "Of all places. If she doesn't fall into the Urzoks' clutches, she will fall to the Blackwings."

Kuno swallowed and his words came out as an urgent whisper. "I know, Brune, but you must find her. I promised I'd take care of her. I cannot die knowing I failed Noshi." He winced. "Help me atone for it." His voice wavered as he looked at Brune. "You've loved her as I have, from her infancy. Find her, bring her to Mount Mahkah. Glory will be yours if you do so."

Brune clutched at Kuno's fur. "Never mind the glory. I shall do it for you. I swear it."

Kuno closed his eyes, as if his pain had disappeared. "Thank you. I know you will." His breath rattled as he tried to form his next words. "I have another favor to ask."

Brune gazed at his brother, then shook his head. "No, do not ask that of me."

"Who else?"

"I cannot—do not make me. There is a way. You can come with us. Noshi will understand—"

"I will not be remembered as a dumb, mute beast, Brune. You know I cannot."

Brune turned his head away.

"Promise me, Brune." His brother pleaded. "I have been in agony for days. But I waited. Because this is how it should be."

Brune rubbed at his eyes with one angry paw. There was a pause as he sat and struggled, before his head sank in resignation. "So be it."

The queen motioned for her attendants to give them space. Eluk watched, his paws folded respectfully in his robes.

Brune stroked his brother's head, and Theo saw what a great effort it was for the bear to keep his paws from shaking. At last, he placed them around Kuno's forehead with the gentleness of a parent holding a newborn.

Brune and Kuno looked into each other's eyes. Kuno's glazed with pain, while Brune's raged with something more than grief.

Kuno smiled. "Do it."

"Walk with Aktu, my brother."

Brune's paws twisted hard, the movement so fast and decisive Theo wasn't sure what had happened, until he heard the unmistakable crack of vertebrae snapping. Kuno jerked, then lay still.

For a long moment time held its breath. There was the sound of the fire cracking beneath the cauldron, the hiss of steam as mulberry overflowed and ran into the flames. Then the stone chamber reverberated as Brune threw back his head and howled forth his agony.

CHAPTER TWENTY

The Blood Hound squatted, ugly and dilapidated, a few paces from the Dorgun temple by the city's southern wall.

Lord Ornox watched the run-down inn from the shadows of the temple's statue, his face hidden in an oversized hood. It had begun to rain, and the water was soaking into his cloak, creating deep pools of mud and grime beneath his cured leather boots.

He'd been watching the comings and goings for some time, looking for signs of imperial spies or other suspicious activity. But so far the Blood Hound looked like it was servicing its usual patrons: degenerate thugs and petty thieves, swindlers and hired mercenaries, here to drink away their earnings and find some cheap lass or lad for their other cravings.

Lord Ornox fingered the ring in his pocket. The grooves in its sides had become as familiar as those of his hand. There was no doubting its authenticity, but he knew he couldn't afford to be careless. This was the capital. The emperor, for all his half-crazed beliefs in witch doctors, was very much in control of his information network. The statue of a deified Dorgun looming over Ornox from the temple steps heightened his unease.

But he had been careful to make sure the guards at the city

gates had seen his retinue passing through, heading west for Vyad, before he donned the clothes of a common foot soldier and snuck back into town.

Ornox glanced up the street to make sure that Yod was in position, squatting like a beggar amongst the tanning barrels piled near a closed leather stall.

Satisfied that his slave was keeping a close eye on everything, Lord Ornox pulled his hood further over his face and stepped out.

Inside the Blood Hound, the night was in its customary full swing. Dirty oil lamps hanging from the rafters lit up the grime-smeared interior, where ragged patrons huddled over their tankards at the ale-soaked bar. A fight between a muscled, wine-sodden soldier and a group of bodyguards had broken out in the far corner, providing the evening's entertainment. Standers-by shouted encouragement and placed bets, swilling ale and trying to fondle the passing waitresses. A barmaid in a gaudy, unlaced bodice wandered from one customer to another, luring buyers with her painted lips.

Behind the bar, the innkeeper stood wiping glasses with a greasy cloth while shouting abuse at the patrons who were trying to wheedle him out of a free tankard. His wife, an equally ill-tempered matron with hair and arms that stank of blood and fish, was gutting a still squealing piglet on the counter for a waiting customer. Several other piglets hung writhing by their hind trotters from a hook behind the bar, their high-pitched screams drowned out by the general hubbub of the inn.

Lord Ornox's nose wrinkled at the overpowering reek of regurgitated ale, pig guts and blood. There was also the lingering stench of urine, testament to years of patrons relieving themselves in some dark corner while the innkeeper and his wife weren't watching. His eyes surveyed the mix of men, apes, vultures, and various other creatures gathered there for the night. No one seemed likely to be the one he sought.

He moved towards the back and chose the last booth, its

table littered with empty tankards and half-gnawed pig bones. A wiry patron in tattered rags, one eye puckered shut from some caper involving fire, peered at him with his good eye, sizing him up as a potential target. A deft movement from Lord Ornox, showing the dagger at his belt, made the would-be attacker sullenly turn back to the bar.

Lord Ornox let the robe fall back. The door opened and a short, portly figure entered. He was bundled in robes and a head scarf so that only his eyes showed. He surveyed the throng before maneuvering around the screaming spectators who were still engrossed in the brawl between the soldier and the hired brutes.

Lord Ornox watched with wary eyes as the figure slid into the chair opposite him. His wrap obscured most of his face, and his arms remained hidden in his billowing sleeves.

A scrawny barmaid approached. "What's it t'be then, sirs?"

Before Lord Ornox could send her away, the figure opposite him pulled out a fat, slippery toad from one sleeve, letting the thing fall to the table with a wet plop.

The thing blinked up at them from a face smothered in warts the color of rotting lime. "A pig," the toad rasped. "And two tankards of blue wart ale."

The stranger tossed two coins on the table, which the barmaid's bony hand snatched away. When the new arrival looked up at him, Lord Ornox found himself staring into two pale eyes, so pale that the irises would have disappeared completely into the whites if those hadn't been bloodshot. The veil wrapped around his small head marked him as out of place: the fine weave of the wool could have paid for every debt in the house that night.

A boyish giggle escaped from within the veil, and a child's voice asked, "He's a wonderful conversation piece, isn't he?"

The Child! Lord Ornox didn't need to wait for his new companion to remove the veil to know that the emperor's chief advisor sat opposite him. He had only heard of the Child's face, and never seen it, but there it was: soft skin unblemished like fresh cheese, a smooth brow eerily untouched by his sixty some years, lips firm and unlined as an infant's. A rare illness had kept the boy named Brel from growing or aging normally. Only his eyes, those pale flat discs the color of washed stone, hinted at the Child's infamous history of debauchery and excess.

Lord Ornox felt a prickle of unease. He hadn't expected the Child himself. Was it the emperor who had set this up? Was this an attempt to test his loyalty? He would have to concoct a good story, and his hand reached for his dagger.

"Relax," the voice piped, while one hand urged the toad back into a hidden sleeve. "I know what you want, and I can make it happen."

Was this a trap? An attempt to make him admit something treasonous? He decided that the best tactic was to put the Child on the defensive.

"If this token is genuine, you should be wetting your britches. This could be considered highly suspect should the emperor know of this."

The face opposite raised a delicate, ginger-colored eyebrow. "Of course, if you'd like to tell the emperor yourself, that's up to you. But I have a feeling you won't once you hear me out."

Just then the barmaid arrived, unceremoniously dropping rough wooden plates in front of them. The Child shielded his face with his veil, whether to avoid the stink of pig or to hide his identity, Ornox couldn't tell. The barmaid held a wriggling piglet in one hand, its liquid brown eyes streaming tears of terror.

"This one do?" she asked in a voice that could grate stone, turning the piglet to show off its soft, pink belly. The Child's eyes glistened as he nodded his approval.

The barmaid pulled the short carving knife from her belt, its hilt already stained with the blood of numerous other meals.

The piglet managed a high pitched "No!" before the blade severed its vocal chords. Ornox and his companion watched as the barmaid bled the pig over a wooden basin. The dark blood pooled, thick and wet, at the bottom.

As she took the dying pig away to be gutted, the Child turned back to Lord Ornox, the corners of his eyes wrinkling as he smiled.

"I enjoy places like this. They still slaughter the unpacified beasts. This generation has gone soft, they don't know what it is to kill for their supper."

"You didn't lure me here to talk preferences in food, Brel," Lord Ornox deliberately used the Child's name. He wasn't going to be intimidated by some aberration with a toad.

"You're brazen, Lord Ornox," the Child trilled in his sing-song voice. "Though it's of no importance, for as I said, you won't be telling the emperor of our meeting."

"And why is that?" Lord Ornox asked. He would have to be careful not to commit himself and to tread warily.

"What do you know of omatjes and their powers?"

Lord Ornox's eyes narrowed. "Accounts differ. But I know the usual things, their ability to decipher the Forbidden Language. He or she would be the key to Ak—the library of the forbidden religion."

"So you do know the old stories," Brel said, like a teacher congratulating a pupil.

"And that's what they are, stories," Lord Ornox added.

Amusement lit the cloud-colored eyes. "Oh Ornox, if you believed that you wouldn't be sitting here, risking your good favor with the emperor."

"Perhaps I'm looking out for the emperor's well-being," Lord Ornox replied, "ferreting out those with traitorous thoughts."

"Sometimes even the emperor is afraid of things more powerful than himself. That doesn't mean that an intelligent, ambitious general with foresight cannot use these powers to his own ends."

Despite himself Lord Ornox felt his pulse quicken. The roar of the inn receded into insignificance as his ears strained to catch every nuance in the innocent sounding voice, probing for traces of a trap. The emperor's advisors had always spoken in riddles. This directness intrigued Ornox yet made him suspicious. "What are you saying?"

"I've reason to think the fabled Library of Elshon wasn't destroyed." The Child studied Lord Ornox for a reaction. "But of course, without an omatje, a library would be useless."

"Are you saying that omatjes still exist?"

The Child held up a young, plump finger. "Ah, do I detect interest now? During the chaos of the Pacification, man and beast fled far and wide—who's to say some omatjes didn't flee with them? Imagine, he who controls an omatje, a key to deciphering the Elshon Library, could control more than just Mankahar ...."

Lord Ornox exhaled a breath he hadn't realized he'd been holding. What the Child was suggesting made treason look like mere jest. These were ambitions beyond even emperor Dorgun: the attainment of absolute rule, the conquering of unknown, half-mystical lands beyond Mankahar, even. He was talking of acquiring powers that defied imagination, for no one knew what secrets were locked away in the Libraries of Elshon—or even if it really existed.

"Dorgun isn't interested in conquering the lands beyond the eastern seas," the Child continued. "He has grown weak, obsessed with killing that turncoat brother and breeding himself with a beast."

Lord Ornox's eyes scanned the room. Spies could be anywhere, and this frank talk of treason could put them both on the block.

As if reading his mind, the Child patted Lord Ornox's hand in a gesture meant to be reassuring. Ornox pulled away, unnerved by the smooth, infantile fingers.

"Who do you think the spies of Mankahar report to, Lord Ornox? For that matter, where do you think Dorgun got the notion that this rabbit would bear his son?" At Ornox's expression the Child's face wrinkled with mirth. "Give us the omatje, and we will make sure the emperor marries Agacheta."

"Why? How does that profit you?"

"It's time for a new emperor, one who isn't afraid of powers he doesn't understand. Dorgun is too trapped in his own obsessions. But you," here the Child leaned in, and Lord Ornox could smell the sickly sweet incense he bathed in, "you, I feel, can be Mankahar's future. You can make the empire even stronger than it is now. Invincible, in fact. The Library of Elshon holds infinite power, but the key to it, the one who can unlock its secrets, is the omatje."

And then I could be emperor myself. Lord Ornox pulled himself back from that thought. "You're forgetting a few details. For one, where would you find an omatje? They've been purged to extinction. Second, no one knows where the library is. Legend has it several omatjes tried and failed."

The pale eyes twinkled with proud delight. "Ah, you underestimate me. To your first question. I have an extensive network of spies throughout Mankahar. Very little happens without my knowing about it. Our spies have gleaned some very reliable gems."

"And you're telling me that you've found him?"

"I have my hunches. Did your daughter not find evidence that the Order sent a messenger beyond the Sea of Petrified Waves?"

"How do you know?"

"Did I not say I have an extensive network of spies?" The young voice turned peevish. "Now unless Noshi's lost his wits and cannot count anymore, he is recruiting thirteen apprentices, not twelve."

How he had not noticed that before? It was so obvious. "We know the Order chose twelve."

The Child tapped the table with one pudgy finger. "Which is why it's so interesting, is it not, that another one, who just happens to be from beyond the known lands, has been summoned to Mount Mahkah? Either the Order is hedging its bets, or they know something we don't. The thirteenth is an omatje, I am sure of it."

Lord Ornox tried to keep his thoughts from overrunning each other.

"As to your second question, about the library," the Child pulled out a leather scroll. "This was found amongst a peasant badger's belongings during a routine raid. I believe you last saw him participating in a game of horseball."

Lord Ornox reached for the scroll but the Child held it just out of grasp.

The Child grew animated, like a fisherman who senses a catch. "I am positive this is a map to the Library of Elshon. If we find an omatje to unlock it, then we will be standing on the brink of discovering the fabled fount of all power."

"I still don't understand where you see me in your plans," Lord Ornox said, trying to keep his voice noncommittal.

"You and your daughter are in a position to intercept the omatje, and use him to your—our—purposes. Dorgun's plan is to capture all of the summoned warriors and kill them. But if you capture the omatje alive, and we help you find the library ...."

Dorgun would have to bow before me, Ornox finished silently.

"The timing is ripe," the Child added. "With the emperor so obsessed with begetting an heir, he has no time to worry about a coup from the inside."

"And what do you want in return?"

"Simply the auspices of your new majesty's good graces," the Child's voice dripped with fawning subservience. "Ah, our food."

The barmaid slid the platter of fried pig slices onto the table and clapped down two overflowing tankards of bluish-black ale. The pig's skin was now a crisp parchment of dark brown, its eyes staring sightlessly out of its cloven head.

Lord Ornox watched, thoughtful, as the Child reached out with his small hand, plucked the piglet's open eye and held it to his sleeve.

"I'd ask you to think about it, but I trust that you already are," the Child said. The toad emerged, sniffed at the proffered eye, and wrapped his sticky black tongue around the morsel.

"Emperor Ornox—now that does have a certain ring to it, doesn't it?"

CHAPTER TWENTY-ONE

Across the plains, always towards the Nyatha ranges, the army drove their rabbit charges. The Willago rabbits watched from their wheeled cages as their captors bullied small communities of weasels, stoats, hedgehogs, possums, and squirrels, ransacking their houses for food and drink, taking tools or small trinkets that they fancied, killing or beating anyone who resisted—though there weren't many who did.

The look in the inhabitants' eyes told Pozzi that this wasn't the first time they'd experienced Man passing through, and that they'd learned from bitter experience to keep their mouths shut and endure as best they could. Which also meant doing nothing to help free the prisoners.

They stopped for a day's rest at a farm, where the soldiers helped themselves to their host's recent harvest and livestock. The rabbits tried to block their ears to the screaming of lambs at slaughter, but it was impossible to avoid the smell of fresh blood, fear, and bowels loosed in death. The soldiers spitted the lambs and roasted them, while the farmer served his guests what ale and bread he had on hand.

The killings they could now understand in a way, if only because they'd seen it before. But what confused Pozzi was the presence of a shaggy grey and tan wolfhound, who, unlike the sheep, still had the spark of soul and reason in his eyes. Pozzi watched the hound throughout the evening as the beast followed at the farmer's heels, occasionally winning scraps from the soldiers' dinner.

Late that night, a mother fox wandered close to their pens, drawing panicked shrieks from Keeva and the other females who had been huddled in the corner trying to sleep. Before Pozzi or anyone else could act, the wolfhound was baying up a storm, fangs bared and eyes flashing as he drove the intruder back into the night.

"Are any of you hurt?" the wolfhound asked, once he'd made sure the fox was gone.

Pozzi helped Keeva survey the still traumatized group of rabbits, and confirmed that no one was hurt. Others gathered around to comfort their companions and stare in unabashed curiosity at the wolfhound.

Pozzi turned to their benefactor. "Thank you ... sir?"

"Ulfrid," the hound replied. "Though the master of the house calls me Ulfi."

"The master of the house being that ... Urzok, they're called?" Keeva asked.

Ulfrid grinned. "Aye, that's the one. Though they call themselves Man, and you better too if you want to avoid a beating."

"We appreciate the help," Pozzi said, trying to phrase his next question. "But why'd you protect us? Aren't you on their side?"

The wolfhound glanced at the farmhouse, where the owner and the soldiers slumbered on. "Protecting you is helping them, my friend. You're now property of the empire. And if anything happens to you lot while you're in the master's care he'll be punished sure as pups follow mating season."

"How come you're allowed your freedom?"

Ulfrid snorted. "I wouldn't call it freedom, but I guess you could say I have it better than some. I guard his stock, and in exchange he leaves me and mine alone and makes sure we're fed well. It's better than having to hunt for myself."

"Can't you let us out?" Keeva pleaded, hopeful. "They destroyed our homes, killed our friends, our family."

The wolfhound shook his head in regret. "Not a chance, pretty one. They would flay me and all my pups as well. I'm sorry, but there it is."

Keeva's face folded with disappointment. "Why don't you help the little ones get back to sleep?" Pozzi suggested.

She nodded, finding comfort in the comfort of others, as Pozzi knew she would. When she had herded her charges to the other side of the pen, he turned back to the wolfhound.

"What will they do with us?"

Ulfrid's eyes probed his. He checked to make sure Keeva was out of earshot, then nodded. The wolfhound looked towards the sheep pen, where they could hear bleating. The sound was empty, a noise stripped of all its meaning, nothing but the random crash of air upon the ear. Pozzi sank his head against his wooden prison, trying to wrestle the cold panic that coiled in his stomach.

"How long do we have?"

"A few days, a week. Fort Nyatha is where they send prisoners for pacification."

"Everyone? Even the young ones?"

"These are cruel times," Ulfrid said softly. "May the Ihaktu army rise soon. But who knows when that will be? Anyway, I'd best be going."

"Wait, what is the Ihaktu Army?" Pozzi asked.

"Don't you know about the Order? They're building an army from the best warriors in the land to defeat the Urzok Empire. The empire will do anything to crush the Order. How is it you've not heard this?"

Something in Pozzi's mind clicked. "Does that have anything to do with us?"

The wolfhound darted a glance at the house, where a light

had been lit. "The soldiers are keeping tight lipped, but I overheard something about them hunting one of yours who escaped —Theo?"

"He's alive? What can they want with him?"

"I don't know," the wolfhound mused. "But the empire wouldn't go to this much trouble for a rabbit unless it's mighty important." A commanding whistle emanated from the farmhouse, and Ulfrid leapt to his feet. "Have to go. May Aktu be with you!"

Pozzi watched as the wolfhound loped off towards his Urzok master, his hopes of escape dashed.

CHAPTER TWENTY-TWO

Kuno's final rites took place beneath the grim smile of the new moon.

Torches of fresh evergreen blazed in a ring around the funeral pyre, which had been built on the Jaipri forest's sacred rock. Several red-furred monkeys were dressed in white robes of mourning, while the serpents had white patterns painted against their scaled throats.

Theo stood next to Brune, whose eyes were locked to Kuno's coffin. Brune had laid his brother within his final bed, cushioned in pine to symbolize everlasting life and wreaths of white crocuses to represent his purity of heart in entering the afterlife. Now the open coffin lay upon a high mound of juniper and cedar logs. Their sweet aroma mingled with the oils that Brune had applied to Kuno's body.

On the other side of the pyre stood the queen, her chamberlain Eluk, and General Lyusa. Theo couldn't look at the queen's chamberlain without a flicker of unease, for he constantly sensed the monkey's hostile eyes on him.

Most of the Palace inhabitants had gathered to honor the fallen warrior, and the area surrounding the funeral pyre glinted with countless scales and the misty eyes of the hundreds of attendees. The priest, a wizened monkey who stooped with arthritis and the burden of his years, stood at Kuno's head. His gnarled paws were raised to the sky as his chanting floated across to the assembled guests.

"In Aktu's balance
Nothing is created
Nothing is destroyed
Through death shall be born life
And through life shall be born the balance

Though you walk in the shroud of death
I know you walk next to me
Though I cannot hear your voice
I know it sings in the wind
Though I now seal your eyes
I know they shall open in wonder on the other side

Leave in joy and return to the earth
May you re-enter Aktu in peace."

At this the gathered throng repeated, "May you re-enter Aktu in peace."

Brune stepped forward. An attendant handed him a small earthenware jar, its top sealed in green wax.

Standing over Kuno's body, Brune hefted the vessel in one paw, then smashed it against his unprotected head. The jar shattered, sending fragments of ceramic scattering around the funeral pyre, while the thick honey within leaked over Brune's bleeding brow and onto Kuno's still form.

"Walk safely, my brother." Brune wiped the honey and blood from his face with one great paw, then smeared it over Kuno's eyes and mouth.

Brune stepped back, while a ring of palace monkeys emerged

from where they'd been waiting. Each held a blazing evergreen torch. At a signal from Brune they thrust their flames deep within the maze of kindling beneath the coffin, and soon the entire pyre was alive with destruction.

The priest made the signs of Aktu over the flames before hobbling away with his walking staff. Theo noticed Eluk appraising him again with those unnerving black eyes. Most of the monkeys and serpents followed the priest's example, filing silently by Brune on their way back to the Palace.

When the last of them were gone, only Brune, the queen and Theo remained. Mercusa's scales glimmered like liquid amber in the pyre's light.

"Theo, go and join the funeral feast," she urged. "I wish to speak with Brune alone."

Theo glanced at Brune, who nodded. Though he was a little put off at not being included in their conversation, the rabbit reluctantly left them standing in the firelight.

The new moon did little to ease the darkness, and the stars were bathed in black clouds. The way back felt longer than he remembered, but he put this down to anxiety. When he saw the bobbing of torches through the trees he hurried on, thinking he must have reached the edges of the palace.

Only when he was almost upon the clearing did he realize he had lost his way. This was not the sacred rock of Kuno's funeral, but a smaller one below the hill. The sound of Eluk's voice froze him.

"... suspicious about that rabbit. Lord Ibwa was right to warn us."

Theo's ears pricked. He hunkered down and crept closer, careful not to make a sound. He could discern Eluk in the fire-light, conferring with several unfamiliar serpents.

"This whole business about the thirteenth disciple has been strange from the start," one of them grumbled. Theo made out a faded tattoo that marked him as a general. "Has anyone but Lord Noshi endorsed the thirteenth apprentice?"

There were murmurs of agreement.

"He's not even a warrior," another sniffed. "Have you ever seen such a fat rabbit?"

"Cowardice wrapped in blubber." The general whipped his tail back and forth in derision. "If that's what our beloved disciples are made of, Aktu help us."

"There must be some reason Lord Noshi wants him at Mount Mahkah," Eluk mused.

A nearby monkey shrugged. "I've heard he's learned something of herbs."

Eluk shook his head. "What need does Mount Mahkah have of healers? The place is full of priests and herb witches. No, there's something Lord Noshi is hiding. Lord Ibwa, I fear, is right. Trusting an Urzok is like entrusting mice to a cat." He turned to the general. "Go back to the palace, make sure the little glutton is stuffing himself at the feast. Then search his things."

The general scraped his scales together. "We could take him down to the dungeon and use a little ... persuasion on him."

"No," Eluk said. "We mustn't raise suspicions. If we do, word might get back to Noshi that Lord Ibwa is asking questions. Lord Ibwa was clear: we must catch Noshi red-handed in whatever scheme he's brewing. Only then can we persuade the Council to depose him."

As they dispersed for the palace, Theo remained crouched in the underbrush. His anger at being called cowardly and plump gave way to confusion, then fear. He knew as little as they did about why he'd been summoned to Mount Mahkah. But now he knew he was in danger, even amongst supposed friends.

CHAPTER TWENTY-THREE

"Theo, aren't you supposed to be at the funeral feast?"

He was holed up near a dilapidated wall when Commander Lyusa found him, too apprehensive of Eluk and his cronies to enter the palace. Theo gazed up at bright blue eyes that shone even in darkness, with the moon nothing but a curled wood shaving in the sky.

The commander's smooth head towered above the young rabbit, whose throat went dry. What he'd overheard in the clearing had evaporated any trust in these serpents.

Commander Lyusa touched him gently on the shoulder with his tail. Theo jumped.

"By Aktu, you look like you've encountered the legions of Lost Souls!"

When he still did not reply, the commander said, "Come, let me show you something."

Wordlessly Theo followed him back through the dense underbrush towards the palace.

They traveled a roundabout way, skirting the main entrance where the subdued chatter of sentries signaled the changing of the guard. They came to a low stone portal half obscured by curtains of moss and damp lichen, which the commander swept aside so Theo could pass.

The rabbit hesitated. Could Lyusa be part of Eluk's plan?

The serpent's tongue flicked between his lips. "Outside of my sister the queen, my greatest loyalty is to Brune. I could never harm him or his."

Reassured, Theo stepped in.

They entered what appeared to be the underbelly of the Palace. Theo heard the occasional patter of feet or slither of scales against stone from above. They were soon in a maze of rock and earthen corridors, none of them straight. Most branched off in uneven angles from main antechambers. They headed downwards, into the earth, the sound of Lyusa moving before him guiding Theo through the dark.

"This is the Old Palace." Lyusa's voice floated back to Theo from the darkness ahead. "It's been abandoned for years."

The floor evened and the space widened. Theo heard a rummaging sound, then a soft hiss of satisfaction.

"Did you bring a flint and stone, Theo?"

The rabbit dug in his pockets for his flints. He struck them together and soon they had a wall torch blazing.

The light fanned out, uncovering a wide stone chamber. The commander passed Theo his torch, then plucked another off the wall with a deft move of his tail.

"The queen tells me you know little of Mankahar's history," he said, touching his torch to Theo's. The light burst against the chamber walls, illuminating swathes of mosaics and painted scenes that extended to the ceiling. "Such ignorance won't do for a novice entering the Order."

A visual feast of ochres and kingfisher blues, vibrant yellows and smoky browns covered every surface of the chamber walls. Depicted was a vast city where vendors and cobblers mingled with priests in flowing robes, bejeweled badgers and hares flocked to temples and silk merchants, and old grandfathers whiled away time playing board or dice games in the shade of spreading oaks.

What made Theo stare in disbelief, however, were the scenes related to word-catching: in one corner a portly matron badger read from a book to an eager group of toddlers. In another, various attendees clasping open books and ledgers debated with each other. Another wall showed a market that sold only books—carts and shelves and makeshift bins piled high with scrolls and volumes, while crowds swarmed around them, haggling, buying, examining, and comparing the goods on offer.

"You've not heard of Elshon?"

Theo shook his head.

"Legend has it that Elshon was renowned as a place of learning in Mankahar, a center of great knowledge and wisdom, a place of sages." Lyusa's eyes roamed over the painting. "Legend also says there was a large library there, along with a great school where one could learn anything under the stars: philosophy, botany, the military arts, the heavens, music and dance, medicine and geography, the great literature of those times.

"Of course all this is so long ago we don't even know whether it's true anymore. You would've liked it, I imagine."

"What happened to it?"

"Well, Aktu bestowed the knowledge of speech—spoken and written—upon Mankahar. Those who devoted their lives to the art of the Language were called omatjes. When the Urzoks began enslaving the rest of Mankahar with the knowledge they'd learned from these books, Aktu became angry and said that Mankahar had made this gift into a curse. The library—indeed, the whole city of Elshon—sank into the sea and was never seen again. But the truth is just that the Urzok King felt threatened by this power, so he rounded up the omatjes and killed them all."

"Why would the word-catchers—or omatjes—be a threat?"

"Knowledge is power, rabbit." The serpent turned away from the murals, his blue eyes somber. "Knowledge is spread through many things, but even I, a military beast down to every last scale, know that it's spread furthest through words. And caught words, those that can be heard not just by this generation, but the next, and the one after that, have a very long life. The first Urzok king didn't want his name sullied." The commander's scales rasped against the stone floor. "So he banned these things, he killed those who could catch or release words and denounced those practices as evil. Over time, the creatures of Mankahar themselves came to believe that this knowledge was a curse, because it had started their persecution."

"Brune said that, too."

"Did he? It's understandable, seeing as he's lost so much. His city, Hegg, was destroyed because they were rumored to have harbored omatjes."

So that's why Brune was so cold towards the badger and his fate, Theo realized.

"Are there any other such great libraries?"

The commander shook his head. "The first Urzok king was very thorough in burning them all. Though some—very few, mind—say that if the Library of Elshon is ever found, it may bring back Mankahar's Golden Age."

Never could Theo have imagined a library full of caught words, or even that there might have been a time when word-catching was a gift.

"But even if it's found, who would be able to read the books? Are there any omatjes left?"

The commander laughed. "Ah, young Theo, you have strong curiosity for a rabbit. Who knows? It's said that Mankahar has no omatjes, that if they exist it's only beyond Mankahar's furthest reaches."

At Theo's crestfallen expression the commander smiled. "But Aktu always rights her balance. Come, I'd like to show you something else."

He slid to the far corner of the room, to a heavy wooden chest covered in dust. Lyusa passed his torch over the top, the flames sending several fat-bellied spiders scuttling away.

He unlatched and lifted the lid. Inside was a rolled leather pouch, oiled and inlaid with amber buttons. He motioned for Theo to lift it out, and Theo stroked the smooth cover with his paws.

"Go on, open it," the commander urged.

Theo unclasped the leather lip and peered inside. Lying nestled in special compartments were small bottles of fluids, as well as pouches of dried herbs and medicines. Already his nose detected hemlock, rose hip, and milkweed.

As he unfolded the last flap of the pouch, something fell to the floor. Theo bent to pick it up, but once he felt its shape, he pulled back as if burnt.

Lyusa picked up the leather-bound book and held it out to Theo.

"What is it?"

The serpent's tongue flicked out between his lips. He placed the object on the chest.

"That's for you to find out," Lyusa said. "Brune tells me you've skills in healing. This belonged to one of our shamans many generations ago. Use it wisely, and perhaps one day you'll even heal the wounds of Mankahar." He turned and began sliding his way towards the door.

Theo hesitated. "I wouldn't know what to do with it."

Lyusa rasped his scales together. "Perhaps. Even so it's yours, along with the choice of whether to use it, Theo of the Forgotten Lands."

CHAPTER TWENTY-FOUR

To Harlan, life in Willago felt like an unimaginable distant past. The last weeks were a bewildering and senseless horror that he still had trouble comprehending.

He was sick of it all: the barren plains, mud choked from the last summer storms; Keeva's weeping; the smell of vomit and raw fear; the shiny, hairless faces of those accursed soldiers; the stink of the packhorses. He was exhausted from the barrage of thoughts he couldn't shut out: Why were they doing this? Where were they taking them? What would happen to them? Most important, how could he escape?

He always reached the same conclusion: Kalmac had once again favored his runt brother—death by the River Tithe was preferable to this. As usual when he thought of Theo, he felt the scar on his neck tighten.

Everyone, especially the young ones, had sunk into traumatized silence. At night they huddled together for warmth, and by day each little rabbit clung to its mother or father as the rough wagon wheels jolted along.

At nightfall their captors halted the day's march and unbarred the wagons. The prisoners stumbled out into the mud and rain, their legs cramped and trembling from hours spent crouched on the wagon bed.

The soldiers booted the confused and bedraggled throng into a line, snapping at those who did not move fast enough. Harlan had never cared much for the young, but even he felt a twinge of compassion seeing the useless Walnut clinging to his mother's fur. The soldiers passed out chunks of moldy bread. Like his fellow rabbits, Harlan fell upon the pitiful dinner with famished gusto, stuffing it in his mouth before it turned soggy. Meals came but once a day, and already rabbits that had been plump and sleek now had concave bellies and protruding ribs. Harlan felt a stab of anger seeing Keeva's dull fur and bony body.

Walnut's mother offered her son her own bread ration. The little glutton began stuffing it down.

Harlan swallowed the last of his food and smirked as he saw Pozzi the Bucktooth offer part of his own bread to Walnut's mother.

"You're a fool, Pozzi. She won't survive two days."

Pozzi glared at him. Walnut dropped his bread, his hunger forgotten.

"Don't say that!" Walnut's eyes brimmed.

Harlan shrugged. "It's the truth."

"Aye, and don't you know everything all of a sudden?" Pozzi snapped. "If you hadn't decided to open your carrot hole and tell 'em about the collar, we wouldn't be here, would we?"

"No, we'd be dead!" Harlan snarled. "That what you want, Bucktooth?"

Pozzi shook his head. "You're a black-hearted coward, Harlan."

In an instant Harlan was on him, pummeling and scratching. The rabbits around them skittered clear as Harlan and Pozzi rolled in the mud, an interlocked ball of flying fur and gnashing teeth. Harlan was by far the stronger, having grown up fighting, and managed to rip a gash in Pozzi's ear before they were pulled apart.

General Agacheta held Pozzi to the ground, while several guards rounded up the prisoners. She roughly examined Pozzi's ear, making him cry out in pain.

"There is to be no fighting, is that understood?" she barked. "If you can't keep your tongues in check I'll do it for you." She pulled her knife from her boot and began to pry Pozzi's mouth open.

A grunt of surprise from her guard, a blur of tanned hide, and someone screamed "Walnut!"

Agacheta watched the assailant tear past her glove and skin, settling his teeth into her flesh with jagged determination.

A sickening silence descended. Eyes closed, ears braced, rabbits and captors alike waited for the general's wrath.

Instead, she let out a short laugh. Releasing Pozzi, she turned to free her hand from her attacker. Pozzi swept Walnut up and held him close.

Agacheta pulled her glove off and examined her bloodied fingers. "Give the little biter a loaf of bread. A fresh one." She grinned. "It seems rabbits do have teeth."

CHAPTER TWENTY-FIVE

Inside her scarlet tent, Agacheta listened to the vulture's message. Then made him repeat it.

The messenger had arrived when most of the regiment was already slumbering. The talon insignia on his collar marked him as bearing a missive of the utmost importance. A missive that could not be leaked. Once Agacheta had arranged the vulture's execution, she sat for several moments in silence, pondering this new piece of information. How would her life change from this night on?

She debated what to do and, as always, sought out the one whose advice she disliked but never ignored.

From the sounds in his tent she knew her timing wasn't ideal, but she didn't care. She threw open the covering and let her lantern light announce her.

The youth had the shame to scramble to his still booted feet, pulling the bedclothes over his shock of light reddish hair. But Caldrik merely rearranged his expression from furious into annoyed, leaving his wiry, pitted body in full view.

"Leave us."

Caldrik's assistant shot out into the night like a pale cat. Agacheta grimaced.

"The army is no place for this."

"The army is the best place for it, my Lord," Caldrik replied. "They're just trying to get promoted, like you."

"I will flog you myself if you call me that again," she snapped, then drew a breath. "What do you know of omatjes?"

Caldrik's languid body tensed. "Lord Ornox has told you then."

Her eyes strayed to his hand and the ring. "What other secrets have you been keeping, besides your working for the Child?"

Her tutor pulled on a robe, unhurried. She felt she was looking at a stranger, a manipulator who used her as a pawn. Just like her father. He saw her expression and rose to his feet.

"Before you decide to punish me and ruin your one chance to rule Mankahar with your father, perhaps you'd like to hear what my ears have been gathering?"

~

She hated to admit it, but her tutor's advice had proven its worth several times over. Food and drink loosened Harlan's tongue in a way that intimidation never would.

After she let him ravage a flask of wine and a hearty plate of mushroom and chestnut stew, she decided to launch her offensive.

"Your grandfather has a strange way of choosing favorites."

Harlan let out a soft belch. The wine had loosened his manners along with his tongue. "He's nothing but a fool."

"Why did you not become his apprentice, Harlan? You are obviously clever." She was surprised that she meant it. For all his cowardice, the rabbit was not stupid.

"What do I care?" Harlan smirked, pouring the dregs of the wine into his goblet. "He wouldn't teach me any of it. Not the healing, nothing. Instead he sends me off to Gaweld the brewer, and keeps Theo. Gaweld the Belt, everyone called him." Harlan scowled and touched his neck.

"Was it Gaweld who gave you that scar?"

Harlan dropped his paw.

"Why would your grandfather do that? Toss you aside in favor of your brother? You are eldest, are you not?"

"It was all Theo's doing. He convinced Oaks that I would never make a good healer, that 'the paw was strong but the heart was weak'," Harlan said, shrugging with practiced indifference.

"Unlike your brother?"

"My brother doesn't have the strength to turn barley to beer. He'd never have survived a day at Gaweld's, but does he treat me or anyone else with any respect? Never! No matter how many times he disobeyed the taboo, he never got anything close to the hiding I got every day."

"The taboo?" Agacheta plucked the word and held it.

"The one about his word-catching," Harlan said. "I saw him catching words several times and told Elder Yeth. He got many a beating for it. Father Oaks was a fool for teaching him."

"So your grandfather can catch words too?"

"We're not supposed to say, but it doesn't matter anymore," Harlan muttered, wiping his mouth of stew.

"What about the other rabbits?"

"Word-catching? Never."

Agacheta stood to fetch another flagon of wine, her mind working. This her father didn't know. She had an omatje right here with her, and another one was on the road to Ralgayan, according to Caldrik's sources. Imperial law dictated that she execute the old rabbit, but the two most important men in her life were commanding her to flout the rules.

"Harlan, what you lot need now is a leader, someone who knows that to protect the many it's necessary to sacrifice the few. Someone who can keep them from panicking and fighting amongst themselves. Someone with a 'strong paw', as you put it."

She refilled his goblet, watched his nose twitch in anticipation. "We'd thought of asking your grandfather, but I say you're a better choice. And if you do well, there would be many opportunities for you in the empire."

"I thought you were letting us go back to Willago?" The rabbit's voice held suspicion.

"Of course, if you choose to return that's up to you." Agacheta shrugged. "However, if you stay, and work with us, you'll find that you'll be rewarded. Amply. We want to see you and seed like yours flourish."

At his hesitation she changed course. "I suppose you'll need to consult with your fellows before making a decision. And if you'd rather refuse, I can find someone else."

Agacheta could see the pieces falling into place in Harlan's mind.

"What kind of rewards would there be, exactly?"

~

Pozzi had smelled the bag of sugared persimmons and roasted chestnuts brought to the commander's tent. Shortly afterwards two guards had come to the prisoners' enclosure and grabbed Harlan by the scruff of his neck, pushing him off towards the ominous red tent.

Pozzi left a sleeping Walnut with his mother, then pressed his face to the pikes that marked their prison. He of all the rabbits would've felt a measure of guilty pleasure to see Harlan come to some unhappy end. But something about this meeting of Harlan's felt odd.

Staring out at the camp, he barely registered the presence next to him. He glanced across and was surprised to see Keeva.

Her beauty had been marred by the events of the last weeks. Her eyes, once so bright and liquid, had become sunken and red from crying. Her once lustrous fur was caked in mud and dust, and she looked as thin and hard as one of Harlan's short arrows. Pozzi felt an unexpected stab of sadness.

"Is your ear all right?"

Pozzi twitched his whiskers. "It'll live."

"I'm sorry. Harlan has always had a bit of a temper ...." Keeva's voice trailed off.

"You would have been better with Theo, y'know. He's no Harlan—but then again, enough said."

Keeva's ears flushed and Pozzi instantly regretted his words.

"It's just that ... everyone said Harlan would be a good provider. And Theo was always odd."

"He was just nervous around you, Keeva." Pozzi made his tone light to try and cheer her. "We all were, you know."

The doe gave him a shy smile before her expression returned to concern. "Why are they doing this to us? Is it because of Theo? Did he bring this on us?"

Pozzi twitched his whiskers in thought. The question gnawed on everyone, he supposed. As the shock of being enslaved had eroded, it had been replaced by a burning desire to know why this had befallen them. As if a reason were all that was needed to endure this existence.

"They do this because they can. They're more powerful than we are."

"Harlan says there's something Theo has that they want." Keeva's voice wavered between doubt and loyalty to her mate. "That golden collar, most likely."

Pozzi was about to make an unflattering remark about Harlan's powers of deduction when he saw the tent entrance open. An inebriated Harlan tottered out between two guards, who half supported, half dragged him back to the enclosure.

Keeva sighed with relief as they unlocked the rough-hewn gate and pushed him in. Harlan collapsed, laughing and hiccuping, in Keeva's arms. Pozzi could smell the giddy aroma of thick stew and wine.

One of the guards rattled the cage pike to get their attention. "Oy, the general said to give you this. Can't have you catchin' chills, she said."

With that he tossed in a woolen blanket, small and threadbare but *clean* and *dry*. Pozzi tried to contain his distaste as he watched Keeva wrap the covering around her drunken mate.

"So what were they wantin' with you then, Harlan?" Pozzi asked, hunkering down beside Keeva. She rubbed Harlan's arms and paws with the blanket.

Harlan sneered drunkenly at him. "Ah! Now wouldn't you like to know, Pozzi Bucktooth!"

"Harlan!" Keeva turned an apologetic eye towards Pozzi. "He's had a bit of ale. He didn't mean that."

She had some learning to do about her husband, Pozzi thought to himself.

"You and Theo, you'll both learn some respect," Harlan muttered.

Pozzi felt a tingle of unease. "What did they want with you? They tell you what they're going to do with us?"

Harlan pushed at Pozzi, trying to get up and brush his query aside, but Pozzi reached out and gripped his arm. "What did you promise them?"

By now Harlan's return, and Pozzi's raised voice, had drawn the curiosity of the rabbits around them. Long ears stood up off sodden backs and some craned their necks to better hear Harlan's answers.

"Mind your own carrot patch, Bucktooth," Harlan snarled, his temper turning malignant.

"Not all of us had the pleasure of eating stew and guzzling ale," Pozzi replied softly, pointing at the dry blanket around Harlan's shoulders. "We deserve to know what you know, or what you traded for a hot meal."

At this there were murmurs of disgruntled agreement. By now everyone had realized that Harlan had a full belly, while they'd been penned here with nothing but scraps of hardened bread to keep the blood warm in their veins. Harlan glared at Pozzi.

"You bought your hide at the expense of mine."

Everyone turned to look at Father Oaks, sitting bent and broken in the corner. A silence fell.

"It's true, isn't it, Harlan? You told her I taught Theo his word-catching." Father Oaks's face sagged. "And look, here they come now."

The rabbits turned to see three figures approaching with knives at their waists and ropes in their hands. One of them said something and the other two laughed.

"Kill me," Father Oaks whispered to Pozzi, clutching at Pozzi's arm and pushing a small rock into his paw.

Pozzi thought he had misheard.

"Kill me, before they take me away," Father Oaks snapped, desperate now. "It's best for everyone."

"Father Oaks, this—"

"Please!"

The guards opened the door. Pozzi could still hear the old priest's beseeching cries to kill him as the guards dragged him away, leaving the remaining rabbits more frightened and confused than ever.

CHAPTER TWENTY-SIX

Theo shivered in his cloak, rubbing his paws together and folding his ears over his head to try and keep them warm. He watched the swarm of monkeys scurrying about packing foodstuffs, flints, and repair tools into packs. The autumn morning's drizzle blanketed the landscape, and already he could feel a cold tendril of water working its way down his collar.

He stole a glance at Brune. The bear gazed ahead, his eyes seeing none of it. His shoulders hunched against the wet, and his arms were crossed over his chest.

Father Oaks had taught his grandson to deal in words and healing herbs, but for once Theo felt helpless to ease another's suffering. There was no magical root or fluid to deaden the bear's pain, he knew, even amongst the rare and precious medicines Lyusa had given him.

All morning he had debated about whether to tell the queen or Brune about what he'd overheard the night before. Would the queen believe him if he told her Eluk wished him harm? But how plausible would that sound? She'd think him a spineless child, running to her and tattling on her chief chamberlain.

As for Brune, he was still lost in his own world. Theo had

barely spoken to him since the funeral, and he knew there was a gulf between them. He was about to say something when he noticed the queen approaching, followed by the commander and Eluk. Eluk's shiny eyes brimmed with animosity, and Theo tried not to fidget under their gaze.

"I've made certain that you have all the supplies you'll need," the queen said. "The commander will guide you through our forests to the ridge that marks the beginning of the Blackwing condors' territory. Then he'll be unable to follow. Take care in your search for the princess."

Brune's jaw tightened. "And I cannot change your decision?"

The queen exchanged looks with Lyusa and Eluk, who wore a smug air like a mantle.

"Ralgayan could use your help. But I've done all I can." The bear moved forward and hefted the supply packs onto his broad shoulders, handing a smaller one to Theo.

"Travel well, novice," Eluk said, his voice silky.

Theo bowed his head in a polite reply, but felt his tail stiffen under the chamberlain's scrutiny. He knew Eluk had had his pack searched, though someone had been at pains to replace everything as they found it. Theo knew that there was nothing to find—he'd slept with Lyusa's gift under his head.

As Brune and Theo started out behind the commander and his group, the rabbit could feel the chamberlain's eyes on him, as if the monkey could see through Theo's cloak and jerkin and straight to the forbidden object that lay tucked into his belt.

When they'd put half a day's distance between themselves and Eluk, Theo felt safe enough to examine his smuggled prize.

He made an excuse about watery bowels and ducked behind a thicket of ferns while Brune waited. Hunkering down, he slid the book from his belt and gazed at its cover. Its worn edges and grime-seamed spine told of years of long use, and the parchment within had bucked into ridges here and there from water, but the curling symbols still marched down and across in neat, clear rows.

The Miraculous Cures of Zo the cover said to Theo.

He turned the first few pages, his eyes flying over the script. It was some sort of medical instruction, with examples of exotic ailments and treatments that the shaman had tried and found effective.

"By Aktu, rabbit, are you passing a stone in there?"

Theo hastily closed the volume and tucked it back into his belt.

"Don't you have something you can use for those bowels of yours?" Brune commented when Theo emerged from the thicket.

"I'll mix something later when we stop."

They continued in silence through the thick forest, with its dense undergrowth and clinging thorns, until Brune conceded to lunch. Theo gratefully dropped his pack onto the mossy ground.

"Do you know much of this princess we're seeking?"

Brune stirred himself out of his thoughts. "I knew her, but it's been a long time. A promising warrior, from what I hear."

"What does she look like?" Theo blurted.

For the first time since Kuno's funeral a smile tugged at Brune's lips. "I haven't seen her for years, Theo. Why?"

"No reason." The rabbit quickly turned his attention to lunch. When he reached into the pack containing their food supplies he felt a sharp pain in his paw. "By Kalmac!" He jerked back and saw that one of his digits was bleeding. "Something bit me!"

Brune grasped the pack and upended it. Out tumbled dried apples, digging tools, bandages … and a monkey.

His red fur was disheveled, and a wild fiery mane framed his wrinkled face. His eager gaze scampered from Brune to Theo.

"Who are you? What are you doing here?" Brune demanded.

"Manneki! I called Manneki. I wanna come and train at Mount Mahkah, be mighty Ihaktu!" He gestured with his furry red paws.

Brune growled. "I don't have time to care for some runt of a monkey!"

Fast as a blink the monkey snatched a stone and flung it, hitting Brune on the softest part of the nose. Brune cried out in pain again.

"I not a runt! Manneki is son of Shodo the Warrior. And you see, I can fight, I can help!" The monkey shook his fists, refusing to be cowed by a beast several times his size.

"If he wants to come, what's the harm?" Theo said. "We can use help."

"Yes, Manneki great help!"

Brune shook his head in irritation. "The more mouths to feed, the more food we need. The more food we need, the heavier we travel and the more time it takes. And we don't have time!"

"But I want to fight Dorgun!"

Brune sighed and patted the monkey's head. "I understand. But the Blackwing Forest is no playground. Scamper off, this is no journey for a young thing like you."

Another stone flew, and again Brune cried out, clutching his nose with one paw. "By Aktu! He hit me in the exact same spot!"

Theo had to resist laughing. The monkey's aim was indeed enviable; there was a red flush on Brune's snout.

"We can't take him back, it's over a morning's journey. We might as well let him come," Theo reasoned aloud. He didn't add that he hoped to never cross paths with Eluk again. He'd become a firm convert to Brune's argument of making all speed.

"I've had enough of young, hot-headed youths sacrificing themselves!" Brune said through clenched teeth, his eyes roiling with anger. "Take the advice of someone older and wiser: get back to your parents, who are frantic at your disappearance."

Theo sighed. “We can’t send him back by himself. It’s too dangerous, and he’s too young. Let’s just have a bite to eat and then talk, all right? He must be starved.”

At this Manneki brightened. “I cook!” He dove into their supply packs with gusto, pulling out cheese, nut bread and wheatgrass, all the while keeping up an incessant chattering.

Brune glanced at Theo, both of them sharing the same thought. Their new companion might be enthusiastic and helpful, but their journey onwards would no longer be dominated by long silences.

CHAPTER TWENTY-SEVEN

It wasn't long after they entered Blackwing Forest that Theo understood why Brune had described it to Manneki in such bleak terms. The bear never missed an opportunity to stress the horrors of the infamous area—the Blackwings flayed and disemboweled their enemies, their favorite food was monkeys small enough to swallow whole, the forest floor crawled with stinging beetles the size of crab apples—all in hopes that Manneki might change his mind and head home. But the monkey was stubborn, and two days of listening to Brune's warnings had done little to cool his enthusiasm.

The Blackwing Forest, a dark mass of towering junipers and fungus-encrusted oaks, all draped in blankets of moss and twisted vine, occupied most of north-central Mankahar. No sunlight pierced these depths, and the damp smell of rotting vegetation soon worked its way into their clothing and fur.

By their fourth day in the forest, the ground below had turned boggy, and unseen frogs and birds called out eerie warnings. The forest floor soon became so impossible for Theo to navigate, weighed down as he was with his packs, that Brune had the rabbit climb onto his back. With his height and thick, sturdy legs, the bear could navigate the clinging mud more easily. Manneki was the only one who had no trouble with the environs at all, leaping nimbly from branch to branch above their heads.

"And we couldn't have just skirted this horrible place?" Theo asked, pulling at strands of slime covered moss that caught like cobwebs between his long ears.

"You think I enjoy trekking through this accursed bog?" Brune grumbled. "If we skirted the Blackwing Forest we'd still be at its southern tip by winter. We haven't the time if we're to find the princess."

Theo tried to keep his mind off the miserable surroundings as well as Manneki's off-key tunes. The smell of wet rot was so overwhelming that their meals tasted like mold. Afraid of the damp eating into the packets of herbs or worse, into the pages, he wrapped Lyusa's medicine kit and the book in a food cloth.

He tried to conjure images of warm log fires, toasty warrens, and mugs of steaming cider on stovetops. But he couldn't shut out the suction sounds of Brune's legs in the clinging mud.

Theo frowned. Something was wrong. He couldn't hear Manneki's incessant half chatter, half singing.

He searched for the monkey in the thick mess of shadows and branches above. Had the young imp decided to abandon his wild notion and head home after all?

Fuuut!

The sound was close, and something grazed by faster than he could see. Brune's legs gave out beneath him, the entire world tilted, and he soared.

His arms rotated like useless wings before he felt the sharp punch of the ground knocking the wind out of his chest.

Close behind came his pack and the medicine pouch, which hit him on the back of his skull, and sparks blossomed before his eyes. He couldn't tell which way was up, and he sank in the swampy mud of the forest floor.

Something tore through his shoulder and he instinctively

opened his mouth. Dank, fetid mud rushed into his throat, and everything went dark.

~

He awoke shivering.

The cold was so palpable it felt like it lived in his bones. Opening his eyes, he could make out a cell with damp wooden walls and floor, though he was on a thin reed mat. He put a paw to his nose—the cell reeked of urine, blood, and mold.

As he sat up, a thick metal cuff on his ankle, attached to a heavy chain nailed to the wall, scraped along the floor.

He couldn't tell what time of day it was, but his head felt too heavy for his neck and his tongue too thick for his mouth. There was a sharp pain in his shoulder where someone had done a butcher's job of trying to staunch what appeared to be an arrow wound.

"Hello?" he called out. He tried to remember what had happened. It had been so fast—where had they been? Why did Brune fall? Where was he and, more important, what was going to happen to him?

Something clanged and scratched in the hallway outside the cell door. Perhaps alerting the captors to the fact that he was awake hadn't been a good idea.

The hole in the cell door went black, and Theo had the briefest glimpse of a ruddy eye before it disappeared with a heavy grunt. There was the sound of more scratching, and then silence.

He twisted his ankle this way and that, trying to pull it out of its manacle. But it was no use. He tugged on the chain, but it remained firmly attached to the wall.

All of a sudden the door burst open, and several giant figures holding torches entered. He caught a glimmer of jet-black feathers and wild red eyes before a rough, rancid bag was clamped over him and closed tight. He heard the sound of a chain being unlocked as he was swung over a massive shoulder.

As he bumped along upside down in the stinking bag, he tried to control his rising panic.

Think, Theo, think, think think think! The blood rushed to his already pounding head. Just as he'd made up his mind to try and chew his way out of the bag he was turned right side up and dropped, with a heavy thud, onto a rugged plank floor.

Someone yanked his leg chain, and with a yelp he was dragged several paces. His eyes smarted in pain as large slivers detached themselves from the floor and slid into his back, like knives under the skin.

He looked up. He was in an expansive hall woven out of thatch and saplings, with a hole in the roof to allow for some sluggish forest light. His captor, a giant looming creature, hooked the chain into a ring on the floor.

The first thing he noticed about the Blackwing condors were their eyes. The irises were the color of day-old blood, peering from their leathery pink faces. They had hooked beaks, the length of which equaled a rabbit's torso. Winged and hideous, their bodies were covered with black feathers, which did little to hide the mottled gray skin underneath. He'd never seen anything so repulsive, and this one was made even more loathsome by a chipped upper beak, which gave him a permanent sneer.

The creature's beak opened wide, and to his horror Theo spied a snake-like tongue inside, wriggling its way towards him. Just as he was preparing himself to be snapped up, a shrill cackle ripped through the air. Chipped Beak snapped to attention and retreated to the sidelines.

There was a shuffling at the far end of the hall, and four torch-bearing Blackwings entered. Behind them came a large figure, who walked with a limp. As he came into the light, another Blackwing scurried forward with a stool carved of bone and placed it in the pool of light from above. He was given a sharp stab of the beak by his master for not moving away fast enough, and then the Blackwing who seemed to be in charge sat down on his bone seat.

If possible, this new figure was more repulsive than Chipped Beak. Wrinkled and fat, the creature's sparse gray feathers stuck up in tufts from his chest. All this was not as hideous, however, as the severe ringworm running rampant across his flaccid grey belly, to the point where his crown feathers had fallen out to give way to scaly patches of dried, fungus-eaten skin. A gold and bone pendant, marking him as king, hung down his neck and onto his wrinkled belly, which rose and fell with each breath.

Reaching down, the enormous Blackwing grabbed the rabbit's chain and gave it a vicious yank. Theo found himself an inch away from that frightful, shining beak, looking up two chestnut-sized nostrils and feeling the creature's fetid breath against his face. He was sure the bird could hear the thunder of his heart.

The Blackwing king cocked his head to one side and chuckled, while one claw scratched at his ringworm.

"Heheheph …." He poked Theo's belly with one reptilian claw, then scratched Theo's head, leaving a long welt along the rabbit's skull. "We will throw him to the Game!"

His words elicited a hearty cheer from the surrounding Blackwings. Theo didn't know what the Game was, but the hysterical cackling all around him boded ill. Chipped Beak lumbered forward to grasp the rabbit's chain.

Through the hubbub, Theo noticed the king was still picking at his ringworm with one grimy claw to ease the itching.

"To the Game! To the Game!" Chipped Beak's eyes glinted with anticipation as he unhooked Theo's chain and gave a vicious tug that Theo knew would leave an impressive bruise. He dug in his paws and mustered his courage.

"Your Highness, I can cure that within three days."

The king eyed Theo with disbelief. He raised a wing and the

hall fell silent. All the Blackwings craned forward, turning to one another as they murmured amongst themselves.

"What did the vermin say?"

"He says he can cure the king's fire warts!"

"Impossible! Nelafar the magician himself could not rid the king of his curse!"

The king glared at the gossip mongers so that their murmurings squeaked to a halt.

"You can make these fire warts go away—for good?" he asked, his eyes narrowed in disbelief.

"Your Highness," Theo replied, willing his voice to stay even. "No one can promise that it won't come back, but I can cure it, and make you a preventative for it."

He could see the king weighing these words, and, as the Blackwing thought about it, he reached up a claw to scratch his scalp. That tipped the balance.

"Three days," the king growled. "And if you haven't cured me, you'll wish you'd been tossed to the Game today."

In the king's chambers, he accepted his medicine pouch with incredulity. It hadn't been lost in the mud, but had been retrieved almost whole as a curiosity. That hadn't kept the Blackwings from rifling through everything and making a mess, however, and Theo felt sharp disappointment cut through him when his paw fell on the third flap, where the book had been. Empty.

"Looking for this?"

Chipped Beak held the leather book by its cover, so that the script on the parchment was clear for the king and the gathered Blackwings to see. The birds squawked and cawed as they clustered around for a better look, their suspicious gazes alternating between the rabbit and Chipped Beak's prize. The king speared Theo with a look of mistrust.

Theo felt his insides turn to ropes of fear—they knew! He looked at Chipped Beak's cruel eyes and tried to scramble for an explanation that wouldn't see him thrown to the Game. Or worse.

Chipped Beak jerked the book up and down with one claw, so that the pages flapped and slapped against each other. "What do you do with it, rodent? Is it a fan?"

"It's pretty. Let me see!" One of the Blackwings lumbered forward.

"It's skin on the outside. It's for eating! Give it here!" another cackled.

They didn't know what it was. Theo could have laughed with relief.

"Stop! It's a magical healing tool. Your Majesty, without it I cannot cure your fire warts."

At this the king bellowed for the object to be brought to him. Chipped Beak snatched the book back from a Blackwing who had wrested it from him, and half hopped, half hobbled forward to present it to the king.

Theo held his breath as the king lifted the book in his claws, peering at its spine before flicking it open with a dirty talon and holding it upside down. He shook it a few times, but when nothing came out he tossed it at Theo's feet with a grunt of disinterest.

"Enough delay! Get to the cure!"

Theo spent the rest of that afternoon soaking strips of dried moss in apple vinegar and mixing a thick mud paste. He made sure to occasionally pass the book over his ingredients and murmur some gibberish. The king and his entourage watched Theo's every move with naked suspicion that slowly yielded to curiosity. They craned their necks as Theo opened a vial from his supplies and began sprinkling salt on the king's infected areas. Living in a bog-ridden forest, they'd probably never seen salt, or knew what it was. The king winced and hissed in discomfort, but let him work on.

After Theo had rubbed the salt in, he applied a thick mud layer to the king's scabby scalp and belly, before removing the whole mass and laying the vinegary moss strips over him.

"Three times a day, for three days, and the fire warts will clear."

This prediction, along with the lessening of his itching, launched the king into a much jollier mood.

"Hehehe—maybe rabbits are not just good for eating, eh?" he cackled. He slapped the top of Theo's head with a wing in a rough gesture that neared grudging affection. "Come, let us take our little friend to watch the Game!"

The king's servants fastened a chain around Theo's neck and dragged him headlong with the other Blackwings through the king's chambers and out onto a wide platform. Here the Blackwings took flight down to the forest floor, and before Theo could protest two of the king's servants gripped his arms and pulled him up into the air.

After a dizzying flight during which Theo thought he'd be sick, they landed at an enclosure hemmed by high mud walls, where the screeching and cawing of thousands of Blackwing voices seemed to shake the ground itself. His captors dragged Theo with them as they followed the king through a high arch made of bone and wood, into an arena a hundred paces wide and two hundred long, its floor comprised of hardened, blood-stained earth.

Theo's eyes squinted against a sudden burst of light, for this patch of the Blackwing Forest had been meticulously cleared of any foliage, allowing the sunlight unhindered access.

The surrounding tiers seethed from all the Blackwings turned out to watch the spectacle. In the middle of the arena stood a stoat, his fur mud caked and bloodied. He warily circled an armed and helmeted Blackwing who towered at over twice the stoat's height.

At the sight of their king, a mighty roar of greeting erupted from the spectators. The guards pushed their prisoner along until their king took his seat in the royal viewing box. The king perched on his throne, while the rest of his entourage stood flanking him.

Theo stared in macabre fascination at the spectacle being played out to thunderous cheers. They were watching a fight to the death, the pitting of a captured stoat against a fully armed Blackwing. Brune had told him of this, but still Theo was unprepared for the sight of it.

In a few minutes it was all over. The Blackwing managed to back his opponent against the wall, then delivered a crippling blow with his beak to the stoat's shoulder. With a scream that was swallowed by the approving roar of the crowd, the stoat went down and the Blackwing hacked it to pieces.

As Theo watched hulking Blackwing guards dismember and drag the body away, he wrestled the nausea and fear in his belly. This was the Game. The stoat's fate could have so easily been his if he hadn't spoken out to cure the king's fire warts.

The crowd's renewed cheering brought him out of his thoughts. At the far end of the arena, a wooden prison gate was lifted by ropes. Could there be an encore to the last bloodbath? His fears were confirmed as a figure appeared out of the gloom. When the wooden gate fell closed behind it, his breath caught.

She was dressed in a simple linen shirt and torn breeches, and the late afternoon sunlight lit her, her fur glowing a dusky ivory. She stood, alert and wary, her tattooed ears swiveling as she absorbed the lusty cries of the audience. Even from this distance Theo could see that this was a creature of unusual beauty, but she was also the first rabbit he had seen since that pacified one so long ago. And he was about to watch her die.

The king gave a signal. The tiers erupted in shouts and whistles, snapping Theo out of his daze. At the other end of the arena a similar wooden gate creaked open. A towering Blackwing stalked out, ugly as a nightmare, one claw dragging a sharp-toothed mace behind him. The crowd roared its approval as the

Blackwing began swinging the mace to show his strength and skill.

With no warning the Blackwing lunged, beak agape and mace hissing through the air like a deadly serpent. Theo shouted, but his cry was lost in the cheers around him. The rabbit, quicker and more agile than he expected, rolled to the side as the mace pulverized the ground where she'd been standing. The two circled each other, the rabbit wary, the Blackwing menacing.

For a moment they stood, sizing each other. Even the king shouted encouragement to the Blackwing, his eyes bright with bloodlust.

"Cowards," Theo muttered, unaware that he'd spoken until he noticed the king's furious eyes fastened on him.

"What did the rodent say?" The guards surrounding Theo flinched.

Somehow he found the courage to repeat himself. "I said it's cowardice, this Game."

The guards around him sucked in their breaths, their eyes widening at this impertinence from a prisoner whose life was now surely over. But he pressed on. "Is your warrior so afraid of a rabbit that he has to fight a female fully armed, while she doesn't even have a stick to strike back? This isn't sport. This is cowardice."

The king's eyes shrank to hard slits. In the royal box all eyes fixed on Theo and the king.

"The Blackwings are not afraid of little rodents!" the king screamed, spittle flying from his beak. One grimy claw pointed at Theo's nose. "You will eat your words when you see that Blackwing warriors are the mightiest beasts in Mankahar!"

With a screech the king signaled for the Game to halt. In the arena, the Blackwing had cornered the doe. Theo could see bright red trails of blood where she hadn't been quick enough to avoid the mace's teeth. At the king's enraged roar the Blackwing paused and looked up. The doe's eyes filled with wary disbelief.

"You said she doesn't even have a stick to defend herself," the king retorted, looking at Theo out of one sly, blood-colored eye. "So we shall give her a stick."

He signaled to a guard on the wall who held a lance made of yew. The guard gave a squawk of incredulity but, at the king's glare, tossed his lance down into the arena. It landed at the rabbit's feet.

"Pick up your weapon, little rodent!" the king commanded. The doe's eyes narrowed in indignation, but she snatched the lance and gripped it. Theo thought he saw the ghost of a smile, which he wished that he could share. He'd managed to give her a weapon, but what use was it? Against the Blackwing's mace and size she might as well have been waving a leaf against a sword. Why did he feel so afraid for a rabbit he didn't even know?

"Begin!" the king screeched, and a drum beat reverberated around the arena walls. The sun had climbed to its noon post, turning the sport ring into a whitewashed patch of hardened, blood drenched earth. The cheers renewed as the two opponents again began to circle each other, the sun glinting off the Blackwing's ebony feathers. The brute was still confident. After all, what match was a female rabbit with a single lance?

The Blackwing charged with a cry. His clawed feet kicked up the dust and his mace whistled. But the rabbit was ready. At the last moment she leaped aside. The Blackwing recovered in an instant, reaching out to grab her. Again she was ready and used the lance as a vault pole. She leaped out of reach, swinging herself around it and slamming her wide back paws into her opponent's spine.

Taken by surprise, the Blackwing stumbled forward, and his watching comrades cheered. The Game had just gotten more interesting.

His pride wounded more than anything, the warrior whirled around to face the rabbit, who stood ready with her lance, ears flat.

The Blackwing tugged the mace into the air with one claw,

swinging it in heavy circles. The doe's eyes watched both the mace and the Blackwing, trying to anticipate the next move.

The mace flew, its hungry teeth shrilling through the air. With a roll and a dive so quick and deft that it was almost invisible, the doe unexpectedly ducked towards the Blackwing rather than away from him. She righted herself and thrust out her lance, catching the mace's chain. Arrested in mid-flight, the weight of the ball swung back around the lance pole and came hurtling towards its owner with brutal force.

The Blackwing managed to duck, but had forgotten about his claw, which still clutched the mace's handle. The toothed ball smashed into his leg like a boulder into a sapling. The crush of bones and flesh could be heard even in the royal box, followed by the Blackwing's ear-splitting scream of pain. His claw, pulped and shattered, now hung at an abnormal angle by his side, the bloodied mace still attached to his useless limb.

The king was on his feet, as was half the arena, shouting insults and urging the Blackwing to fight on. The rabbit gripped her lance, her chest heaving with exertion. For a moment their eyes met, and more than ever Theo prayed to Kalmac that she wouldn't die.

Just then, the Blackwing lunged.

"Behind you!" Theo screamed.

To his surprise she turned before the words left his mouth, as if she already knew. She sidestepped the oncoming blow from his beak, then fended a series of others with the lance. Theo feared the lance would break, but she managed to avoid letting him bite down on the wood.

The loss of his arm seemed to have invested the Blackwing with new rage, for he launched a terrifying onslaught. But his claw was still tangled in the mace handle, and when he pursued his victim too far the chain brought him up short.

The rabbit harried his wounded side, where he was defenseless. The cheers were still for the Blackwing, but he was tiring. At last the rabbit had the opening she needed, and feinting to the beast's left she spun on her hind leg and sank the lance deep into his right side. Theo shouted in triumph, for the blood came out frothed and foaming. She'd punctured his lung.

The Blackwing slumped against the lance, flapping his wings. His claws raked the ground, as if trying to stand, and then he lay still.

For a moment there was silence as the Blackwings absorbed what had just happened. It was clear they'd never had a defeat at the Game.

Theo felt a flood of relief, followed by a quick surge of foreboding. What if the king decided to take revenge? The prisoner might have just fought for her freedom to win her death sentence. Theo looked apprehensively towards the king, as did everyone else in the arena.

When the command came, Theo's heart thudded.

"To the dungeons with the vermin! Tomorrow, the vermin fights the bear!"

Brune. It had to be Brune.

CHAPTER TWENTY-EIGHT

Though he wasn't thrown into the dungeons with the warrior doe, Theo could tell the king felt seriously torn about his decision. Since the unexpected defeat in the ring he'd developed a foul temper, kicking and screeching at anyone in his way.

For all his ill humor the king had to admit that the treatment of his fire warts was working. He insisted that Theo be chained to a post in his chamber, the medicine pouch close by, so that Theo could attend to him.

At nightfall several small Blackwings swept into the king's high chamber, delivering baskets of food. To Theo's horror, he heard chirping and clawing in the baskets. He almost lost the contents of his stomach when he saw the king open one, reach deep inside with a claw, and pull out a large, squealing rat by its tail. Another Blackwing held forward a crude wooden cup with some sort of rancid-smelling fat, and the king dipped the rat in the cup, brought it out drenched and spluttering, and swallowed the creature whole.

Theo couldn't bear to watch, and huddled in a small space between two large baskets, his one thought to escape and somehow find Brune.

Suddenly the deep bellow of a drum echoed through the treetops. The king and his attendants stopped their feasting, and in a rush of feathers took flight out of the huts.

For several moments the deafening sound of hundreds of wings filled the air, followed by the sigh of feathers against wind, and then miraculous silence. Theo scrambled to the open doorway of the king's abode and peered down.

At a drop into nothingness.

As a ground dweller, what Theo saw over the threshold was enough to make his legs tremble. On his way up he hadn't dared to look down, but now he saw below an abyss that sloped away into the dark foliage of the forest.

"Pffsssst!"

He whirled around.

A grey paw extended out of one of the discarded food baskets. It was attached to the body of a possum.

"Hey, chum, don't just stand there, give a boy a paw!"

The speaker had a plump, open face, framed by bushy white brows and bristly chin hairs. His pointy ears flicked.

"What are you waiting for? The atonement of Grey Rock? Get a move on before they get back!"

Theo scrambled over to the basket and clambered on top, looking for the lock.

"Quick!" the possum hissed.

Theo found the latch and swung the top hatch open. The would-be-meal leapt out.

"By the hairs of Aktu's ears, thanks for that. What's your name, son?"

"Theo."

"Well Theo, don't stand there like a stump, help me get these other poor rascals out." The possum leapt nimbly onto another cage and started working at the lynchpin. The birds ensnared within chirped and fluttered.

Theo clambered up and helped him open the cage. A flurry

of birds emerged and rushed out the door, a streak of blue and green feathers calling out a hasty gust of thank yous.

The possum whistled as he jumped to the next cage and jiggled the lynchpin. Soon he had the remaining two baskets opened and was helping the little wood mice and lizards out the door.

"Well, I'd best be going." The possum dusted off his paws and gave a mock salute. "Thanks for yer help, Theo boy." He turned to head out the door.

"Wait!"

The possum turned, one eyebrow raised.

"You can't leave me here," Theo protested. "I just saved your life!"

The possum's brows knitted. "I suppose you're right, chum, but what do ya propose I do? Rabbits can't climb trees, and ya certainly can't fly! Besides, the king seems to think ya make too good a pet to eat ya."

Theo had to get out of there and help free the doe. And Brune, of course. It occurred to him that when the king came back and found all his food gone he'd assume (and rightly) that Theo had freed them. Any scatter-brained hare could predict what would happen then, gifted healer or no.

"You have to help me," the rabbit said. "I have to find my companions and get out of here!"

The possum's nose twitched, whether in sympathy or distaste Theo couldn't tell. Then he sighed. "I s'pose I should help ya out in some way. I can tell ya right now that any companions ya had are now in the bellies of the Blackwings."

Theo bristled at the possum's callous assessment. "Then help me get out of here! You seem to know the Blackwings' habits well, so you must be from around here. Think of something!"

"Now don't get in a twist about it, chum," the possum said, fluffing out his chest. Something in Theo's face made him soften, however, for he gave the rabbit a comforting pat on the shoulder. "Alright, looksee here, you're right. Ya did help out a chum in need and I should see what I can do." He paused and turned towards the doorway. He listened with pricked ears. There were distant sounds of activity, the sharp clap of Blackwings talking and, occasionally, the whisper of a wing.

"I have to go, chum. They're coming back," he said. "But I'll see what I can do. For now, make sure ya don't provoke them. The king has a wicked temper."

Before Theo could protest, his ringed tail disappeared over the threshold. And with him went Theo's courage, for he could hear the raucous caws of returning Blackwings.

He scurried back to his hidden alcove between the baskets, out of sight and praying that he would then be out of mind. He hoped that his knowledge of curing fire warts would preserve him.

The king and his attendants swooped back into the residence, squawking. As soon as the king spied Theo he shambled over and gave the rabbit's chain a sharp yank. He examined his prisoner through one blood-red eye, menacing and curious.

"Well little vermin, you fetch a high price from the empire for one so small and unremarkable."

Theo swallowed. The empire? Had the empire's forces somehow found him?

"What do the Urzoks want with you, I wonder?" The king scratched at a scaly patch on his arm.

"Don't scratch, Your Highness. It makes it worse."

The king chuckled. "Ah yes, we can't let the little healer go before he's cured our fire warts, can we?" He leaned so close that Theo could smell the stench of his breath. "What are you, besides a healer? Why do the Urzoks want to find you so much that they offer me many lands and an alliance in exchange for your little vermin head?"

Theo blinked under the Blackwing's hostile stare. "I'm nothing but a rabbit, Your Highness."

The king's eyes narrowed. "Are you now? We shall see."

CHAPTER TWENTY-NINE

Theo waited for the king and his attendants to settle down in their nests and fall asleep, the time dragging interminably. One Blackwing emitted deafening snores, while another sputtered periodically in his dreams.

He'd already tried picking the lock attached to his collar and pulling at the chain that held him fast. But he was no locksmith, and fiddling with the chains had only woken an irate Blackwing who threatened to peck out his eye if he didn't stop.

He finally conceded defeat and sat panting, exhausted.

A sliver of moonlight pried its way through a hole in the thatched roof. The night lay quiet and still outside, and Theo thought of Brune and Manneki. Tomorrow Brune would likely be pitted against that warrior doe. He had to find a way to save them. And Manneki? What had the Blackwings done to him?

A clammy paw clapped over his mouth. When he tried to scream, the paw clamped tighter and a voice hissed in his ear, "Shush, chum. Do ya want to wake the whole confounded forest of 'em?"

Theo twisted around to see the possum. And next to him Manneki grinned, flashing his white teeth in the moonlight.

Theo never thought he'd be so happy to see the monkey's wrinkled face.

Before Theo could speak, the monkey brought a finger to his lips.

The possum unsheathed a short sword from the woven belt at his waist. Its blade caught the moonlight, throwing it straight into one of the attendants' faces. They held their breaths as the Blackwing flinched, then tucked his head under another wing and resumed his soft snores.

Trying to keep the blade out of the moonbeam, the possum began to pick at the lock that held Theo's collar to the door pole. His arm muscles bulged as he grappled with the tough metal, but it proved no match for his sword and with a click he had the prisoner free.

His rescuers motioned for Theo to follow them to the doorway, but the rabbit shook his head. Theo ignored their frantic gestures and walked on silent paws towards the king's bed.

Manneki leaped forward on nimble feet and grabbed Theo's wrist. He bared his teeth in warning. Looking him straight in the eye, Theo pried the monkey's fingers loose. Before the possum could stop him, Theo reached below the king's bed.

When he felt the comforting shape of his pack, he drew it out, careful to not bump the wooden frame that held the royal nest. He then crept towards the door.

All three tried to keep the wood planks from creaking beneath them. Standing at the door, Theo's relief at being free was cut short by the second view he had of the cavernous dark spread before them. Here and there the shadows shrank from the light cast by metal lamps, suspended by chains from trees. He could make out sentries, shuffling as they moved along branches. Other than that all was still.

"How are we going to get down from here?" Theo whispered.

Manneki slapped a paw over the rabbit's mouth and shook his head. The possum pointed down the tree about fifty paces where a rope was tied around a branch. It hung straight down into the blackness below, partially disguised by foliage.

Theo's stomach somersaulted, and he pleaded silently with Manneki. *Anything but this!*

But already the monkey was pushing him forward. Placing his sword between his teeth so it wouldn't slap against his flanks, the possum made his way down the oak trunk towards the rope, as comfortably as if he was walking on level ground. There was nothing Theo could do but pray and follow, trying to find paw holds in the bark as he inched his way along.

Theo felt as capable of climbing down the oak as a fish was of burrowing into a hillside. Manneki silently scaled the tree beside him, grasping him when his grip faltered. Theo's arms began to ache from gripping the bark and trying to move without too much noise. To Theo, the rope felt as far away as the moon. His limbs quivered with the effort, and it occurred to him that it would be so much easier to fall and let the abyss have him.

When he reached the rope, it took all his willpower to not collapse on the branch and just stay there. But Manneki's grip on his arm left no room for argument.

"Slide down with the paws, and use your feet to stop yourself," the possum whispered. "And remember chum, try not to make too much noise. I'll make sure the way is clear."

And with that he was gone, leaving Manneki to motion him forward. Theo realized that the monkey had the same misgivings about the rabbit's ability. He felt a ripple of fear as he looked down at the endless rope. He forced himself to think of the Blackwings, what *not* going down would mean. With a deep breath Theo grabbed the rope and let his hind paws leave the tree branch.

He slid, the sudden rush downwards unexpected and terrifying. He clamped his hind paws, bringing himself to an immediate halt and sending the rope whipping in a crazed dance. He closed his eyes and tried to still his fear, waiting for the rope to settle before continuing.

The few times his swinging back paws snapped a twig, it sounded loud as thunder in the quiet night. Manneki would rustle the nearby leaves and make faint clucks, like a bird waking. Branch by branch they descended.

Theo could have cried with relief when he at last reached the forest floor and felt solid ground beneath his paws. The possum had been waiting for some time, his sword unsheathed, casting nervous glances. Manneki leapt down from the rope, while Theo tried to rub some feeling back into his arms and paws.

With the possum leading, the three fugitives made their way as quietly as possible across the forest floor. Most of the moonlight couldn't penetrate past the thick tree branches, leaving the area drenched in inky shadow.

They passed one sentry slouched over a flat stone, his drooping head nestled in sleep. The possum motioned for them to duck into a tree hollow at the sounds of an approaching Blackwing.

The patrol woke his slumbering comrade with a none-too-gentle poke and gave him a sound tongue lashing. The three waited until the argument subsided and both sentries had moved off.

Once he was sure the danger had passed, the possum whispered, "This is where we part ways, chum."

"Wait," Theo said. "You have to help me find the bear and get him out."

The possum swallowed a mirthless chuckle. "What do you take me for, chum? An oak tree short of acorns? You asked for my help, and I gave it. But breakin' into the Blackwing dungeon? Might as well fall on this here sword. 'Twould be faster!"

"I can't just leave them there! Tomorrow they'll be put in the Game together!"

The possum remained unmoved, his eyes hardening to pools darker than the night around them. "Aktu gave me a brain bigger'n a cranberry, and I know how foolish it is to try and rescue a prisoner from the Blackwings. Ya need to get your companions out, that's your nut to crack, chum."

His voice had risen, and they all shrank back behind the tree as a guard shuffled past. Once the rustle of his claws had receded, Theo gripped the possum's arm.

"Listen, that bear is a messenger from Mount Mahkah, and the rabbit that fought today is a princess, chosen to be a novice with Lord Noshi. If you help me get them out you'll be a hero!" He had no idea whether the doe was the princess, but he needed something convincing.

The possum's eyes widened. "By the sweet breath of Aktu, why didn't ya say so? I have a special fondness for princesses, that's true."

"So you'll help us?"

The possum nodded, then put a paw to his lips. His ears twitched to catch any surrounding sounds. Satisfied, he motioned for them to follow him.

They wove between trees, dodging the occasional Blackwing sentry. They eventually broke out of the dense scrub, and even in the dark Theo recognized the wall that marked the Game arena. They skirted its border for several paces before the possum darted into a hedge, grabbing his companions with him. Crouching down, he pointed at a rough entrance, its dark mouth twitching in the light of a fire at its entrance. Five Blackwing guards sat in a circle around the fire, tossing bones to pass the time.

The possum threw Theo a look. Even in the dim light the rabbit could read his expression as if he'd spoken: *so how d'ya think you're getting past that?*

Theo gritted his teeth and tried not to lose hope. Five clawed beasts against the three of them. *Think, Theo!*

He'd have to take the possum with him. He was armed and seemed to know the Blackwings' layout. That left Manneki.

There was no way to tell them his plan without alerting the Blackwings. It was now or never. Taking a deep breath, and praying for the monkey's forgiveness, Theo shoved Manneki out of the hedge, a squawk of surprise bursting from the youngster's throat.

All of the Blackwings stopped their game, their leathery heads snapping around to fix Manneki with hostile stares.

Manneki stood, his thin limbs and tail clutched to himself. Theo prayed to Kalmac that his companion would understand that he was supposed to be the diversion and not the sacrifice.

Just when Theo thought he had relied too much on Manneki's impish nature, the little creature pulled a face and made a rude gesture with his tiny hands.

The effect was immediate. The guards leapt up, snatching their pikes. Manneki spat at them for good measure, then made for the scrub. Their game forgotten, the guards raced off to pursue Manneki, leaving the entrance unprotected.

"Come on," Theo hissed, grabbing the surprised possum by the scruff of his neck and hauling him up. "He won't buy us much time."

They bolted for the dungeon entrance, taking torches from the guards' fire as they passed.

They hurried as fast as they could down a steep earthen staircase, straining to hear the telltale sounds of guards lurking behind the next corner. The stairs were slick with damp fungus and spilled slop, and Theo had to steady himself with thoughts of the doe. And Brune. He had to free Brune as well, of course—but first the doe.

The possum raised a clenched paw, stopping him short. From the light of their torches Theo saw that the staircase had given way to a cramped hall with dark corridors branching off in different directions.

"Which way?" Theo asked, dismayed.

His companion grunted. "How would I know, chum?"

"If you were the Blackwings, where would you keep a massive bear that was four times your size?"

The possum's eyes lit up. "Well now there's a thought. Only place that'll hold the likes o' him would be the mess pen."

"I'll meet you back here," the rabbit said, hurrying off towards the nearest corridor.

"Where ya going?"

But Theo was already halfway down the first tunnel, his hind paws slipping and sinking on the grimy floor. The torchlight, dancing as erratically as his pulse, threw warped shadows against the damp walls. On both sides he passed cell after cell, which were little more than cramped holes carved into the rock. Dark shapes and hollowed faces peered out from within, all chained by their necks to bars embedded in the rock. Theo hurried on, not daring to linger. His eyes and his torch sought only the flare of those defiant eyes.

After running the length of the first corridor and most of a second, he fought a rising panic. Manneki couldn't keep those guards distracted forever, and they'd already been down here a good while. It wouldn't be long before they were discovered. His torch was fading to embers, and still there was no sign of the doe. Just as he was about to retrace his steps and search a third corridor, two eyes the color of fresh basil glowed at him from the dark.

He held the torch up, the flames illuminating the feminine face. Though grime spattered and chained to the wall, her eyes burned with indignation.

For a moment he stared.

Say something, you fool!

"I'm here to rescue you."

She frowned, then glanced behind him. "With what?"

It dawned on him that he hadn't brought so much as a rock to help break her shackles. He felt so foolish he blushed to the roots of his fur, and hoped the dark would hide it.

"Stand aside, rabbit."

Brune loomed behind him. Somehow he'd managed to retrieve his battle axe and helmet. Theo was torn between relief at seeing him and shame that he needed the bear's help. This was not the heroic rescue he'd envisioned.

With his mallet-like paws Brune gripped the chains wrapped around the doe's arms, then grunted as he gave a mighty pull. The metal gave a groan as it detached from the rock wall, and soon the doe was free.

"Thank you," she said, rubbing the feeling back into her wrists. "Though who are you, and why're you helping me?"

Brune grinned through his helmet. "Were you too young to remember your Uncle Brune, Princess?"

The doe's eyes sparked with recognition. "Brune bear? Did you find Kuno?"

Brune's grin contorted into a grimace, the answer undisguised on his face.

Just then the possum thrust his bewhiskered face into the light. "If ya don't want to be making pretty designs with your blood in the Game tomorrow, we'd best get our hides going."

As if to prove him right, the sounds of caws and angry squawks echoed down from the dungeon's entrance. The guards had returned and were coming down the stairs.

"Is there another way out of here?" Theo asked the possum.

He gripped his sword. "It's a one-way dungeon, chum. If we hurry we can surprise them at the bottom of them stairs."

Brune drew his axe. In the cramped space there was no room to swing it, but it could be used as a battering ram. "Let's hurry, then."

They ran back through the corridor until they reached the space where all the halls converged at the base of the stairs. Along the way, the princess managed to commandeer a short pike abandoned against the wall. Everyone was armed but Theo, who felt defenseless.

The stairwell soon darkened with the Blackwings entering the chamber, their red eyes gleaming and suspicious in the dim light of their torches. By the time they'd noticed Brune, the bear was already upon them. Fangs bared and axe blade lowered, he charged.

There was a screech and a burst of feathers as they tried to back their way out of the stairwell, but instead ended up falling over one another in their haste. Brune cracked two skulls with his axe handle, and the doe tripped another one with her pike before they were able to gather their wits. It didn't take long for the remaining two Blackwings to realize that they couldn't subdue an armed bear and three others. They started a hasty retreat up the stairs, shrieking in panic.

"Escape! Escape in the dungeon!"

Brune raced up the stairs after them. There was the scrabbling of claws and the frantic beating of wings, then a cut off scream as Brune silenced them.

The possum bounded up the stairs. The princess and Theo were close behind, and as they rounded a corner they saw Brune standing over the Blackwings' inert bodies.

"Do ya think anyone heard 'em?" the possum asked.

"If they did, they'll be here soon enough," Brune replied. "Let's get out of this stairwell before we're stuck like a pig in a rabbit hole."

As they moved into the passageway the princess stripped one of the Blackwings of his short sword and tossed it to Theo.

"I don't know how to use this." He mentally kicked himself. Why had he said that?

She took the sword back. "Stay behind me then. And try not to trip."

When they emerged from the dungeon entrance, they were greeted not by a horde of Blackwings but by the desperate chattering of Manneki. He was tied with rope to a roasting pole over the fire.

As Theo undid his bonds, the monkey's words tumbled out in a torrent of excited jabber. The Blackwings had decided to have him for a meal, and had gotten as far as singeing his fur when out of desperation he'd told them of the trespassers down in the dungeon. What possessed all of the Blackwings to go down together they couldn't imagine, but Theo thanked Kalmac that they hadn't thought to alert anyone else before investigating.

"There's no time for a tea social. We have to leave before they discover ye're gone." The possum was already peering left and right for signs of more Blackwings.

Brune dipped his head.

"Thank you. May Aktu reward you for your help." He turned to go, but the possum reached out a paw and grasped his fur.

"Hold on, chum, how do ya think you're going to get out of this cesspool of a forest without some sort of guide?" The possum squared his shoulders, one paw resting on the hilt of his sword.

"I know you're a messenger, bound for Mount Mahkah and the Order. Ya should get as much help as ya can, bless your hides. And you'll need to find your way out of these here parts fast, before the Blackwings send out a search party." He put a secretive paw to his mouth. "Rumors around here are that the Blackwing king already knows you two aren't just average visitors wandering through. He's made a pact with the Urzoks."

Brune frowned at the possum. "You're familiar with the forest, then?"

The possum snorted. "You familiar with your own privates?"

"Point taken," Brune grinned. "We must head north, sir ...."

"Pachua, chum. The name's Pachua."

CHAPTER THIRTY

True to his word, the possum led them straight and sure to the eastern fringes of the Blackwing forest, where the tentative warble of thrushes and wrens hinted at dawn. Throughout the night they hadn't dared utter a word as they navigated the dark forest, but having left the nightmarish trees behind them they all grinned with relief.

"Well this here's where I say goodbye." Pachua touched his forehead. "You'd best be hurrying along. The Urzoks have been lurkin' in these parts, a right mean mob. I'd bet my last apple they're looking for you lot. And no doubt the Blackwings have already found their comrades in the dungeon there."

He then saluted each of them in turn, until he came to the princess. He took her paw and made a gallant bow over it. "And may I say, 'twas an honor to rescue a brave and beautiful princess such as yourself."

Theo's ears flicked in indignation. He was the one who'd had to persuade the possum to help her, and here the rogue was claiming all the credit! Theo noticed darkly that she seemed flattered.

"Might I ask the princess's name?"

"Indigo of Alvareth. A pleasure to meet you, Sir Pachua."

Brune whistled, scratching his head with one broad paw. "Doesn't time pass like a winter's sleep! I remember when you were in swaddling clothes, Bobo—"

"Please don't call me that," Indigo interrupted, bristling. "I've been crown princess for some time, Brune."

"This is Manneki," Theo chimed in, pointing at the little monkey who was examining his singed tail. "And my name is Theo."

"Like you, Theo here will help defend Ralgayan before going to Mount Mahkah to be an apprentice," Brune explained. "And Manneki ... that's a long story."

Indigo looked Theo up and down with mild interest. She double knotted her sword's hilt to her belt, then said, "The possum is right. The sooner we leave this accursed forest the safer we'll be."

~

They weren't long with their new companion before it dawned on Theo that saving her had guaranteed him a good portion of misery.

Brune had a fond familiarity for the young rabbit. A bond, invisible yet as tangible and sturdy as the fir saplings around them, grew between the two. It had its roots in their shared grief over Kuno's death and Brune's having known the princess's mother. Despite his attempts to ignore it, Theo had to admit that jealousy hung like a black cloud over him. He hadn't realized how much he'd come to enjoy Brune's company, how he'd liked the bear's easy confidence towards him. Now that it had moved to the princess, Theo felt he'd lost his place in the sun.

What made it worse was that the jealousy was twofold. However much he wished to have Brune's favor again, he craved Indigo's attention even more. He felt shy and ungainly next to her, for everything about her was strong and self-assured: from the intricate blue designs that covered the insides of her ears, to the ease with which she handled her sword; the way she leapt over fallen logs or expertly cut a path through thickets and ferns; the quick reflexes whereby she seemed able to sense any falling branch or hidden ditch. It was all too clear that she was faster, stronger, and better at everything.

"You'd make better time if you abandoned that satchel," the princess said, watching Theo struggle to keep up as they climbed a hill of fern-covered boulders. "What've you got in there anyway?"

"Nothing," Theo panted, re-hoisting the pack so the strap didn't bite into his wounded shoulder.

Indigo flicked her tattooed ears. "I've never seen 'nothing' weigh so much."

As she left him to catch up to the others, Theo realized that had been their longest conversation.

~

That night Theo couldn't sleep for the ache in his shoulder wound. The Blackwings who'd patched him had as much skill with healing as he did with short arrows, and in the rush of escape he'd had little time to tend his shoulder.

Not wanting to wake his sleeping companions, he stole away from where they'd camped, taking his medicine pouch with him. Once he found a quiet hollow where he knew his noise wouldn't disturb the rest of them, he laid out his supplies and examined the puncture. He'd caught it before it became infected, but only just. He cleaned the swollen area with a mixture of water and witch hazel before putting together a compress of elm and sage powder.

As he sat back and gave the medicine time to do its work, he looked at *The Miraculous Cures of Zo*. The moon, having cleared the treetops, looked down on him with a bright, curious face.

As he examined page after page of the tightly packed words, Theo's fascination with the book grew. It told him of strange illnesses with even stranger cures—some of them involving the physical removal of a limb, the benefits of poison in special circumstances, even how a creature whose heart or lung was diseased could be saved by giving it another.

Theo looked through the descriptions and drawings with a mixture of fascination and disbelief. Could they have any truth to them? Whoever had captured these words gave the impression that these practices were commonplace. At one time healers could cure injuries and ailments Theo knew to be fatal. But then, did he know that? He thought of Commander Lyusa's words: "Knowledge is power."

What kind of power did this shaman have, if he had the knowledge to cure things even Father Oaks could never believe possible? Had he even been one of the best healers of his time? Or were there others even more skilled, who, like him, had caught the words to teach others?

How Theo wished he could show this to Father Oaks. Then perhaps Father Oaks would see the benefits of word-catching.

When Theo returned to his companions the moon was already beginning its descent, but Brune was awake and cleaning his axe head with a sheet of rough bark.

"And where have you been wandering off to all this time?"

"I couldn't sleep," Theo muttered.

The bear gave him a disbelieving eye. "I have a cure for that, starting tomorrow. It's dangerous for you to go wandering around."

"There isn't a soul for leagues, Brune."

The bear leaned his axe against a nearby tree and fixed Theo with a stern gaze. "My brother gave his life for her," he said, pointing at Indigo's sleeping form. "And I'd give mine for either of you. Do you know why? Because you're both part of Noshi's plan to bring down the whole Urzok Empire. For that I'd die several deaths and go down whistling a happy tune. You should keep that in mind when you take a fancy to strolling off by yourself. The Urzoks would be tickled as ticks to get you in their clutches."

Theo's guilt must have shown on his face, for the bear softened.

"Get some rest. Tomorrow I'll make sure you sleep like a cub in winter."

~

The next night Theo had almost forgotten Brune's promise, for he was already exhausted from a long day of travel across the Yharu plains, with its late-summer swarms of biting insects. But the bear proved to have a long memory, for as they selected a place to bed down he turned to Indigo.

"It's time Theo learned the sword."

Indigo looked from one to the other. "I'm not a teacher."

Brune grinned through his helmet. "You're the best, so I've heard. Here's a chance to prove it."

Theo felt a ripple of nerves. He dreaded the thought of looking like a fool. "I don't know, my shoulder is still—"

Brune batted away his protests with a meaty paw. "We'll be entering Urzok lands soon. You'd do well to learn how to defend yourself. And a little physical exercise should help cure your sleeplessness. Now away with you. Manneki and I will find dinner."

Theo followed Indigo towards a stand of trees where the princess began testing branches with her paw. He tried not to stare as she leaned over a fallen tree, her backside to him.

"Why have you never learned the sword? It's one of the basic skills of any warrior."

"I'm not a warrior," Theo said, wishing he was.

Her patterned ears swiveled. "But only the best are chosen to go to Mount Mahkah."

"We never had any warriors in Willago," Theo explained. "We had no enemies."

"You'll find plenty here."

She selected a branch, snapped it off at its base, and held out the improvised weapon to her new pupil.

Theo took the crude rod, hefting it in his paws.

"This will do for practice," she said. "Here, let me show you how to stand. Brace your feet apart, like so."

Theo did as she instructed, the branch feeling awkward and heavy in his paws. The wound from the Blackwing arrow still ached when he moved it.

"Shouldn't I start on something lighter?"

She shook her head. "A sword is a heavy weapon. You may as well start early and get used to the weight. Now stop arguing and watch. You grip a sword like this."

She showed him how to hold the branch, with one paw in front of the other, wrapped loose but firm around the base.

"Give me the branch." She took his "sword" and then handed it back to him. "Now, show me how you grip a sword."

"I just did."

"Do it again."

He took the branch from her.

"Your angle is wrong," she said. He thought he saw the hint of a smile.

"Are you laughing at me?" Theo asked, anger creeping on him.

She shook her head. "No. I'm remembering when I first learned swordplay, my teacher said that if we never mastered a proper grip, we would never become warriors."

"How long did it take you to learn?"

"Twenty moons," she said. Her green eyes sparked with pride. "I learned faster than any of my siblings. We'll see whether you can learn in that time. Here, let me show you."

She reached out and rearranged Theo's paws over the branch, molding his grasp. A tremor ran up his arms, making his shoulder ache again, but this time he didn't mind.

She made him repeat the exercise of grasping the branch, but every time he did it Indigo would correct him. He started to feel the hot burn of frustration, sure that she must be laughing at his clumsiness. He longed for the lesson to be over.

"You're not even trying," she accused when his grip turned increasingly sloppy.

"I'm doing it, aren't I?"

"At least try to learn."

"I am trying!"

"No you're not. Your mind is somewhere else and you're just going through the motions." She crossed her arms. "Trust me, you're not doing me any favors—I'm the best at the sword in Mankahar, and most would jump at a chance to have me teach them!"

"By Kalmac. Why can't you see that I'm not made for this? This is pointless." Theo said in exasperation, throwing down the branch.

Indigo bristled. "How is learning the sword pointless?"

"Because I'll never be a warrior!" Theo said, sitting down on a rock. "I'm nothing but a rabbit."

"Nothing but a rabbit?" Indigo shook her head and tossed her branch down next to his. "Give me your mirror."

Theo's paw reached for his jerkin pocket. "How did you know I had one?"

"I saw you staring at it last night when you thought we were all asleep. Don't worry, it's natural for males to be vain."

"I'm not—"

"Oh enough already." She motioned with her paw. He took it out and reluctantly passed it to her. She held it up to him.

"Look in there—what do you see?"

He looked. The blurry image of a pudgy and grime-smeared rabbit stared back at him.

"I see my reflection, I guess."

"Now look," she sat next to him. Two rabbits' faces gazed back at them, one grey, one white.

"We're the same, right?"

"Of course. What are you trying to prove?"

"You may never become a warrior, but it's not because you're a rabbit." She stood up and brushed off her paws. "You think like prey, that's why you act like it. Where I come from, we know rabbits make perfect warriors—keen ears, eyes that see not just what's in front, but what's behind. And above all, a brave heart."

She began walking away.

"Where are you going?" Theo called out. "Are we finished?"

Indigo didn't even look back. "You said so yourself—it's pointless."

CHAPTER THIRTY-ONE

Theo sat amidst his slumbering companions and watched Indigo's patterned ears, their tips alert and flicking even in sleep. He wondered whether she could hear the silent paws of dawn stealing across the meadow, cold and pale in its autumn garb.

At last one green eye opened, then the other.

"What?"

"How did you defeat that Blackwing in the ring?" Theo said. "It was like you could see him behind you."

She yawned. "I could."

"That's impossible."

Indigo turned so that her back faced him. "It's not important. I'm just a rabbit after all."

Theo bit his lip. "I'm sorry I said that. I meant me, not you."

When she ignored him, he tried again.

"I do want to learn. I promise to try this time."

After a pause the princess turned around. She glanced at Brune and Manneki, who still wandered in dreams. "Come on then."

~

"Throw this at me."

They were back in the small clearing where they had trained the day before. Indigo placed several pebbles in Theo's paw, then turned her back to him and settled herself on the ground.

Theo stood, hesitant, until Indigo turned around, impatient. "Well? What are you waiting for?"

Theo hefted a pebble. Hesitant, he tossed it at her. Without looking back she leaned to the left, and the pebble landed at her side.

"Is that your idea of a throw?" she scoffed. "Harder. Faster."

Theo drew his arm back and shot off another pebble, this time with more force. Without looking behind her, she moved her ears so that the pebble flew between them.

"Again."

Theo threw all the stones, one after the other, each one harder and faster than the last. Each time, Indigo managed to avoid the stone with ease.

"How do you do that?" Theo asked, impressed. "Can you hear them coming?"

Indigo turned around. "I can see them."

"See them? That's impossible!"

"It's one of the many skills rabbits have: to see front and back at the same time, so that no one can sneak up on you. How could you not know this?"

"Willago has no enemies," Theo said. "I suppose we didn't need to fear anyone from behind."

"Everyone has enemies. And enemies love blind spots."

She made him face a tree.

"Don't focus on what's in front. Try to see what's behind."

"I can't see anything beyond my shoulder."

She stamped a foot. "Stop saying you can't. Just try."

He drew a breath and did as she asked. He strained to look behind him. For several moments he could see nothing but the blurred outline of his shoulder, but gradually as he moved his eyes front and back, he could see more and more. He felt as if the corners of his eyes were expanding; first he could make out a nearby thicket, then a hanging branch, then the entire tree further back.

By the time the sun had risen above the eastern treetops, he could see Indigo standing behind him. Expanding the scope of his eyes became familiar to him, almost as natural as breathing.

"That's enough for today," Indigo said. "You don't want to do too much all at once. It might strain your eyes when you're not used to it."

As they walked back to Manneki and Brune, Theo marveled at his newfound view of the world.

"Where did you learn to fight?" he asked.

Indigo grinned. "I'm of Alvareth stock. In our clan females learn to use a sword and axe before they learn to walk. Our does are renowned warriors."

"What about the males?"

"Males mind the home," the princess answered. "They take care of the young, cook, and maintain the warrens."

"Really?"

Without looking back she asked, "Why, isn't that how it is in your clan?"

"No, in Willago it's the other way around. So if you're a princess, your father—I mean, your mother, rules Alvareth?"

Indigo's ears flicked once, tense. "She did. My mother ruled for over twenty years, until her death. Now my aunt rules as my regent until I come of age." She glanced back at Theo. "What is your lineage?"

"Me?" This was the first time she'd ever shown any interest in his background, but he sensed it was because she wanted to change the subject. "My parents were tailors, but they died when I was young."

"So what's your special skill?"

"I'm not sure I have any," Theo said.

"That can't be true." She pushed aside an overhanging branch and waited for him to pass her. "All the apprentices going to Ralgayan and Mount Mahkah have a special skill. For instance I'm best at the sword." She seemed to have no qualms in declaring herself the best, and offered it not in boast but more as a well-known fact.

"I told you, I'm not the best at anything."

"Well I hope you find out what it is," she said, resuming walking. "You're going to need it if you're going to defend the Order in the upcoming war."

Her words unsettled him. He was older, stouter, and could offer nothing in the way of the arts of war. Where everyone else had a gift, he brought an unwanted language. Brune was making a mistake taking him to Mount Mahkah, he knew it.

Indigo's initial reluctance for her task thawed each night that she taught Theo the sword. Though she treated Brune with a respect and Manneki with an affection that she never showed him, her tattooed ears no longer flicked in annoyance with his clumsy attempts at learning.

Each night before they settled down, they had a session. Manneki always hunkered nearby, watching with avid interest and cackling at Theo's mistakes.

Once he'd mastered a sword grip, they started with a basic blow, first moving just his arms. When he'd learned to perform the stroke with some semblance of ease, she taught him how to stand and lunge forward and thrust.

Each night the moves grew more difficult, and he had more trouble learning than he was willing to admit. He refused to give up until he'd learned the motions, but his muscles screamed in agony from all the exercise, especially his shoulder, and he fell into sleep at night with his entire body shuddering from exhaustion. But from the very moment that Indigo had first held his paws in hers to shape them around the branch, he had a fierce drive to prove himself a warrior.

Theo had never been one to play sports with the other rabbits in Willago, partly because Father Oaks had kept him studying, drying, and sorting herbs for most of the day, but also because Harlan always dominated the games. His brother and his friends sneered at Theo's efforts and never bothered to teach him what he was doing wrong. He'd taken it for granted that he was awkward and weak. Though he still struggled to master the sword moves, he noticed with each passing day his body growing leaner, his arms and legs lengthening with muscles that etched outlines beneath his fur. His shoulders began to bulk, and he even began to wish the sun would set quicker.

As the travelers left the plains that divided the Blackwing Forest from the rest of Mankahar, the terrain turned stony, with unruly patches of sagebrush leading to a small river of mud and silt that clove a ravine in two. The ravine's sides sprouted dense clusters of beech and maple, their ruddy leaves already shed and rotting. Moss along the river stones had frozen and grown slick, making the going difficult, and yet still Brune's strides grew more hurried. Snow could not be far off, and Theo knew that the bear wished to reach Mount Mahkah before winter. At one point the river's bend hugged a small hillock, which they mounted as the sun's rays began to flee west. They camped just over the summit.

Theo found a branch for himself from an aging maple and hacked it off to begin their nightly lesson. Brune headed to the river in search of fish, while Manneki half-heartedly cast about for kindling, his attention wandering to the rabbits and their sword practice.

"Cut a second one," Indigo said.

Theo looked at her in surprise. "What for?"

"You're ready for an opponent," she said, smiling with a wicked twinkle in her eye.

He found another straight branch from the obliging maple,

and cut it off at the base. He handed it to Indigo, who took out her sword and made a few vicious hacks to the end, sharpening it. She took his and did the same, so that their "swords" were now more like stakes.

Theo didn't object. She took a stance, gripping her "sword."

He'd barely braced himself before she pounced, silent and swift. She landed a sharp blow against his arm.

"Ow!" Theo cried, taken aback. "That hurt!"

"Then stop letting me hit you, fend me off," she retorted, and lunged in again, her arm muscles rippling as she delivered another rap, this time to his other arm.

He concentrated, watching her move as she circled him, sword ever ready.

"Never let your sword down. Keep it at chest height. Keep your arms ready but relaxed."

When she lunged again he managed to dodge the branch, but she swung her body weight around and landed a kick to his chest that sent him sprawling.

"That's not swordplay!" he protested, scrambling up from the dirt.

She shrugged, tossing her branch from paw to paw. "Sword play is not always about weapons you hold. You fight with all your body, and you need to anticipate what the enemy is going to do next. Even if you manage to dodge the first blow, it doesn't mean the second isn't right behind it."

He threw himself into the fight, watching her movements, but he could scarcely defend himself, much less change the course of action. Time and again she bested him, and the point of her stake left thin, red gashes against his grey fur.

His skin burned hot despite the chill night air, yet Indigo still appeared fresh and unruffled, maintaining a steady onslaught until Theo felt so exhausted he thought his heart would beat its last. She moved with fluid, savage grace, her endless strength and speed leaving her opponent panting for air.

"Theo beaten by girl rabbit, yes?" Manneki giggled behind his paws.

"Why don't you try it then, if you can do better?" Theo muttered, still winded.

"Truly?"

Theo glanced at the monkey. The derisive smirk was replaced with earnest hope.

"You want to try?" Indigo asked. Manneki leapt up, and Theo offered his fighting branch. He realized the monkey had hunkered nearby every night, waiting for just such an invitation.

Manneki took the branch, hefted it, and faced Indigo.

"Attack," she commanded.

The pupil needed little encouragement. He flew towards her, swinging his branch in aggressive but practiced movements. Indigo seemed surprised by his fervor but quickly recovered, parrying her opponent and studying his movements.

"Don't favor your left side so much, it upsets your balance. Better. Watch the feet. They're too close together. Too rooted."

Theo watched Manneki transformed, his furry red brow knit in concentration, his teeth bared, his legs so nimble and quick that he moved around Indigo like a dusty blur. Had he learned all this just from watching Theo practice?

"Don't lunge like that," Indigo commanded. "You open yourself to attack." When he lunged again she swept a foot out to graze the monkey's leg just above the knee, and Manneki went down like a flipped spider, Indigo straddling him with her branch point to his chest.

"See what I mean? Your teacher taught you some good offense, but neglected defense."

"Manneki have no teacher," the monkey panted, struggling to get up.

Indigo pulled him up to his feet. "You learned those moves yourself?"

Manneki nodded, slapping his arm with his weapon. "I make great Ihaktu warrior, yes?"

Indigo smiled. "Ihaktus are chosen. You'd have to prove yourself to the Order."

The monkey pouted. "Teach me then, I prove Manneki worthy!"

"It's almost dark," she said instead. "We'd best get a fire going if we want to stay warm." Manneki hurried to obey, eager to please. She gave Theo a questioning look.

"I'll go fetch the water," he mumbled.

~

The river's icy touch was a welcome shock against his flushed face and arms. But it didn't ease his wounded pride.

Even at half his height, the monkey was far better at the sword than he was. Manneki was the one who should be going to Ralgayan to become a warrior, not Theo. Why was he here at all?

"You fought well."

Without turning, he saw Brune standing behind him. At least he was learning one skill quickly. "You saw?"

Brune nodded. He took a long drink, grimacing at the silt in his mouth, while Theo sat on his haunches brooding.

"You must both think I'm hopeless," Theo said, immediately hating the self-pity in his voice.

Brune chuckled, water streaming from his furred muzzle. "Indigo tells me Manneki has the training of a day-old gnat, but shows fire. You may not have his gift for the sword, but you have something."

"How can you know that?"

"Noshi says Aktu chose you. That's all I need to know."

An owl hooted from a nearby tree, and the sound of Manneki's light chatter floated down from the camp above.

"I'll never learn to be a good sword fighter, you know. She's wasting her time."

"It was unfair to test you when you weren't ready," Brune said. "Teaching a pigeon to fly is easy. Teaching a chicken requires patience, humility, and curiosity. She would do well to learn those things from you."

Theo gazed out at the river, frowning. "You mean this isn't about teaching me the sword?"

Brune grinned. "It's been good amusement, I admit. And it's time you had a bit of the warrior's fire kindled in you. But a teacher is also always a student. Sometimes princesses need to be reminded of that."

He turned and started heading back to the camp. "As I said, you did well. You can teach each other a great deal."

Theo listened to the sound of the bear moving through the shrubbery. The owl hooted again, and, despite the comfort of Brune's words, the cry only reinforced his sudden feeling of loneliness.

CHAPTER THIRTY-TWO

The next day Walnut insisted on holding Pozzi's paw during their forced ride in the jolting wagon. His mother was dangerously weak and could no longer care for him. But today Pozzi's thoughts circled around the wolfhound's words like moths around flame. Somewhere out there was help, an army that could defeat these tormentors and let them return to Willago. That meant there was hope, didn't it?

He thought of the sheep and closed his eyes to shut out the memory of that awful sound.

"Are you crying, Uncle Pozzi?"

Pozzi looked down at Walnut's worried little face.

"Nay, Walnut," he said, "just irritated eyes, that's all." He squeezed the small paw that clung to his.

"What did the wolfhound say?" Keeva asked. Her face was as open and trusting as Walnut's.

"He told me that Theo is alive. And that somewhere an army is coming to overthrow the empire."

At this, several of their companions began pelting him with questions.

"Theo's alive?" Keeva repeated, and the wistfulness in her tone dealt Pozzi a sting.

"You lot really do have weeds growing in your heads," Harlan interrupted. "You think some army is going to come save us? We have to save ourselves."

Walnut withdrew into a crestfallen silence. Pozzi glared at Harlan and wrapped a protective arm around the small rabbit.

Walnut looked up at him. "Mama used to say that the best thing to do when you're scared or unhappy was to sing a song. Can we sing a song, Pozzi?"

Without waiting for an answer, Walnut closed his eyes, his young voice struggling against the sound of the wheels and horses all around them:

> "Over the budding rye
> And between the whistling corn
> We'll come a'nigh
> Before the dawn o' morn ..."

He stopped and opened his eyes. "Aren't you going to sing, Pozzi?"

Pozzi was about to say no, when Harlan laughed humorlessly and shook his head. Pozzi cleared his throat and fell in with Walnut.

> "Over the tall blade grass
> And through the summer rain
> We'll come to pass
> Felling the ripened grain ..."

After a few stanzas Pozzi realized that other voices had joined theirs.

> "As the spring rains fall
> Whispering seasons gone
> You I'll enthrall
> With a love that flows on

Under the sycamore
And by the river's bed
I'll wait by your door
With flowers 'round my head"

The melody soon reached the guards alongside the convoy. A short, stocky man with protruding ears turned to Commander Kotori, who rode alongside him.

"Are the animals ... singing, sir?"

"Seems that way."

"I didn't know they could sing."

Kotori grunted and examined his comrade. "And what of it? So they make noise and it sounds like song. You turning Noshi?"

The shorter man stiffened. "I'm no traitor to my own kind," he grumbled. After a suitable pause, he ventured, "Should I stop them?"

His superior shook his head. "Leave them be. It's disconcerting at first, but you get used to it. Where they're going, they won't be singing anymore."

CHAPTER THIRTY-THREE

The sudden pop of a cracking log made Theo jump. But no one stirred except for the fire, its sparks circling like lazy fireflies. Satisfied that he was still unobserved, Theo returned to his book.

He couldn't say that he enjoyed this word-catcher's work as much as the stories that he used to keep hidden back home, but his curiosity was piqued by the fantastical acts of healing. Zo gave detailed descriptions of how to seal wounds without infection, the importance of boiling one's tools before using them, the treatment of water in the lungs. By far the most farfetched of the cases, however, was one in which Zo saved a poisoned friend by pumping blood from someone else into him, in what he termed a "refreshing."

Theo shivered with distaste and wondered again whether any of it could be believed. Part of him hoped he would get a chance to try one of the cures—if only to see whether the book was truly a treasure or a collection of amusing lies.

Theo remembered with a pang how Father Oaks had first taught him to make tea from dandelion and burdock roots to cleanse the blood. As a small kit he'd hated having the burrs of the plant stick to his arms and paws. He'd been thinking more and more of Father Oaks of late, and worries about his grandfather's fate always clung to him at night, just like the seeds of the burdock.

He fed the fire another log, stoking it as quietly as possible. The moon, a scythe of silver, hung sharp edged against the night sky. He closed the book and slid it back in its place, then rolled his medicine pouch beneath his head.

That night he dreamed.

He dreamed of a palace, its corridors stretching endlessly in every direction. Shelves lined the walls, their wooden planks sagging beneath the weight of countless books.

As he walked amongst them and touched each cover, they quivered, shook, then fell from their perches. As they fell, they transformed into warrior versions of himself before hitting the ground, each one wielding a shield and sword.

With every shelf he passed, more and more rabbits leapt to the ground, until he looked behind him and saw an army of identical Theos, amassing in formation and choking the passageways.

"What is this place?" he managed to ask one of himself.

His double pointed, saying something Theo couldn't catch through the roar of falling books and swords hammering on shields. He looked up, where his double indicated, and made out the lettering carved in the arch above them: The Library of Elshon.

CHAPTER THIRTY-FOUR

When Theo woke, he found Indigo and Manneki gone, with only Brune in sight. The bear was ready for travel, his battle axe slung and his helmet on.

"I thought you'd never wake up," the bear grinned, but Theo could sense the worry in his words.

"Where are the others?" Theo asked. He felt as if he'd slept a lifetime, though his limbs were stiff and his clothes bore the sour smell of dried sweat.

"They've gone on ahead. I wanted to have a word with you." Brune began kicking dirt and stones over the telltale charcoals of their night's fire, erasing traces that Urzoks or other enemies could follow. Theo watched him for a while, unsure what to say.

"You're quite the talker in your sleep," the bear said.

Theo felt his mouth turn to sand. "I must have eaten something that gave me bad dreams." Kalmac curse it, what had he said? He remembered dreaming of the library. Had he said anything that would give him away?

The bear harrumphed, grinding out lumps of charcoal to make it disintegrate faster. "You muttered some mighty strange things. Things about Elshon."

Brune searched Theo's face, as if he could read the truth there. "You want to tell me where you heard that name?"

"Lyusa."

Brune sighed. "I want you to listen." When he made sure he had Theo's full attention, the bear's eyes bored into the rabbit's. "I meant what I said about the Forbidden Language being a bad thing. Whatever your curiosity is about it, leave it be. No good comes of asking about, or Aktu forbid, trying to learn the Forbidden Language. Do you understand? You're an outsider from beyond Mankahar, but I've sworn an oath to Noshi that I would protect you. You have a great future as a warrior of the Order, so whatever your doubts, don't let these strange dreams of Elshon or anything else distract you from it. Can you do that?"

Theo swallowed, then nodded. "Because I could end up like that badger?"

The bear's eyes narrowed. "Yes, Theo. And you've been chosen by the Order. That's a mighty privilege. Don't throw it away."

The bear finished stamping out the last of the fire's remains, and with it his bantering humor returned. "That'll do. Now let's get moving and catch up to the others before they think we're lost, eh?"

The days grew shorter and chillier as they began their northward journey into the steep, inhospitable Yharu passes, the one safe passage that linked Mankahar's east and west that didn't run through Urzok strongholds. Here the wind careened around the rock faces, bending any hardy trees that managed to grow amongst the stone crevasses, whipping the foliage from spindly branches. A brittle carpet of dead leaves covered the ground, crunching in protest beneath their paws.

As they progressed, the passes narrowed and steepened, until on the third day they found themselves on a path whittled to little more than a goat trail. Their pace slowed as the climbing grew harder, the footholds more treacherous, and the wind nipped at their backs. Several times Brune had to negotiate their next few steps before turning around and giving the others a pull up.

By late afternoon the temperature had slid to a bone-numbing low, and fatigue dragged at their limbs. Manneki's teeth chattered and he ferociously rubbed his little paws along his furry red arms, while Indigo wrapped her ears about her head in an attempt to stay warm. Theo hunched his shoulders against the cold but uttered not a word of complaint. Only Brune's thick pelt managed to resist the elements.

Towards dusk they neared a widening in the path. A tumble of boulders led to a cave that cleaved the rock face, the interior inviting despite its dark, damp mouth. Manneki immediately launched into a full campaign.

"We stop here, big bear, yes?"

Brune turned, frowning. "There's a good amount of daylight left."

Manneki's mouth bent in a surly pout. "But it's cold, and Manneki's hungry!"

"Buck up a little longer. If you want to become an Ihaktu warrior you can't hide at the slightest breeze."

Manneki's face darkened even more, and his eyes disappeared in a frown. "Go to Mount Mahkah then. Manneki's had enough of being grunt and slave and cook!"

And with that he was scuttling over the large rocks towards the cave.

"Manneki, stop!" But Brune's voice came too late, for Manneki had been swallowed by the dark of the cave mouth.

"I'll get him," Theo offered.

He'd only taken two steps when the monkey came hurtling out, his arms flailing as he landed on the path in a crumpled heap. A shaggy, horned figure emerged from the cave, snorting and bleating so ferociously that Theo stepped back and Indigo raised her pike like a spear.

The beast stepped into the light. A large, fiery-eyed mountain ram glowered at them. His disheveled beard hung in a scraggly icicle from his chin, and his horns coiled about his bony head like thick snakes. He stood with cracked, crusted hooves set far apart, swinging his head from one intruder to the other to see who would challenge him.

Manneki groaned on the ground with one arm crushed beneath him. A fracture, if not a break, Theo noted.

Indigo rushed forward to attack the goat with her pike, but Brune pulled her back.

"Leave the thing alone!"

Theo noticed the ram's eyes, the vacant, hostile stare. It chewed vigorously at something in his mouth, then spat it out at the inert Manneki as if for emphasis.

Brune dropped to all fours, his fur raised and eyes narrowed within his helmet. He roared, the primal sound drowning out the wind and making it clear to any beast, enslaved or no, that he would rip the ram from end to end if it came any further.

The ram's bravado cooled at the bear's onslaught, and giving a last bray of warning, it backed away into the bowels of the cave.

Theo darted forward to Manneki's side and took the half-conscious monkey's arm in his paws. He felt along the lower arm, then the upper, and discovered the telltale break just above the elbow.

"Is he alright?" Indigo asked.

"His arm is broken."

Brune cursed and looked from the darkening sky to the cave. Manneki fainted as Theo mercilessly probed the area.

"What do we do?"

"We need a fire, hot water, and some straight pieces of wood," Theo replied. "We need to get him to shelter as soon as possible."

Brune grit his teeth and looked at Indigo. "Bring your pike. Let's see whether Sir Goat prefers to be hospitable, or eaten."

~

Bright tongues of flame lapped at the small pile of twigs in the cooking pit, casting light on Manneki's constricted face.

Brune and Indigo had managed to drive the goat into the deepest recesses of the cave, shouting and roaring to make sure the beast knew of their presence. While Theo had propped Manneki against what clothes they could spare without freezing themselves, Brune had taken Theo's flints and raised a gusty fire near the cave entrance. Though it smoked from the damp wood that was the only fuel to be found, no one complained. It kept both the raging, bleating ram and the deepening cold at bay.

"What's that for?" Indigo asked.

Theo had flipped open his medicine pouch and plucked out two hemp bags and a bowl made of nut. "White willow bark and arnica powder." He began mixing a small amount of both together in the bowl.

"What does it do?"

"Dull his pain. Then I'll be able to set his bone."

Glancing up, he saw the genuine worry in her eyes. During their time together Manneki had managed to charm his way past her guarded exterior with his mischievous expressions and his habit of always finding some sort of delicacy for her: a mint leaf here, a pawful of rowan berries there. He was in awe of her and, Theo suspected, eager for her to help him enter the Order.

Theo rummaged around the cave for a flat stone and began to pound the willow bark shavings. The fragrance of the fresh-cut bark mingled with the wood smoke, turning the air pungent but stinging.

Theo checked Manneki's arm to make sure it hadn't shifted and noticed Indigo watching him with interest.

"You never told me you were a healer." There was a hint of accusation in her voice, as if he'd been dishonest.

Theo shrugged. "I'm not. I was going to be, but I was never more than an apprentice." He felt a pang for Father Oaks and swore to Kalmac that if he ever managed to make it back to Willago alive he'd be happy to deal in herbs and potions for the rest of his life. "Father Oaks was right, it's a good knowledge to have. The Blackwings were going to throw me to the Game, but then I told the king I could cure his ringworm."

Indigo laughed, the most carefree sound he'd ever heard her make.

"Tell me how it happened." She sidled closer to the fire and propped a chin in her paw.

Theo told her about entering the forest, being shot through with an arrow, and waking up in the cell shackled to the wall. Several years of telling stories to Walnut had made him something of a yarn-spinner, he realized with amusement.

"You tell stories like my mother," she said when he'd finished. "My mother used to tell us of Jasper the Trickster, who used his wiles to get out of trouble. She would've loved your story."

Suddenly he glimpsed the young vulnerability inside the warrior.

"What?" she asked, seeing his expression.

"Nothing." He tried to hide his embarrassment, hoping his face wouldn't betray his jumbled thoughts. She smelled of cut pine and cedar. He poured the pounded bark and powder into Brune's helmet, which the bear had reluctantly surrendered as a pot once Theo had stressed the importance of having hot water.

"Why didn't you say you were a healer? In Alvareth, healers are respected almost as much as the queen," Indigo said.

Theo shrugged, bashful under her scrutiny. For once her interest wasn't haughty or critical, but born out of genuine curiosity.

Her eyes wandered to the medicine pouch, then back to Theo. "May I?"

He nodded. She picked up the various pouches and peered inside them, sniffing and wrinkling her nose. Theo watched, nervous, as she drew closer to the pouch containing *The Miraculous Cures of Zo*.

"The healer of Alvareth has a warren full of things like these. He used to scare me with stories of how he'd poison me if I misbehaved."

Theo's paws faltered as she poked about the bundle, drawing closer to the book.

"What about this? What's in here?" She reached for the last flap.

"Nothing," Theo took the pouch from her, wrapping it back up and knotting it twice. "Just spare leathers, for gathering plants and things." He placed it on his other side, away from Indigo, then poured water into the helmet.

"There you go, telling me there's nothing in that bag again. You have secrets, don't you?"

Theo stoked the fire, his throat dry. "Secrets? What secrets would I have?"

"Like Brother Elkwood. Secrets of healing."

Theo felt relief burst through him. "They're not secrets. That's just learned."

"Can I learn then? Can you teach me what you know of healing?"

Theo turned and looked at her, surprised. In his nervousness about her finding the hidden book, he hadn't noticed. But something had unlocked between them. Indigo was proposing an exchange of equals, and not her royal due. And for the first time, he felt he had something to offer, something worthy of a princess.

"Of course I can teach you."

CHAPTER THIRTY-FIVE

With each passing day Walnut's mother weakened. The forced march had exhausted her to a point where she was little more than a furred skeleton on legs. A racking cough had set into her lungs from an infection that was running rampant through the underfed prisoners, who had little protection from the deepening cold. Without their priest to alleviate their ailments, any small illness became unbearable and sometimes fatal.

It was on a damp autumn day that Mother Walnut's head slipped, limp, from Pozzi's shoulder, where she'd been sleeping. Pozzi knew, without putting a paw to her nose, that she had gone.

That night, Walnut would let no one, not even Pozzi, touch him. They sat caged in their habitual pen, with the crackle of the captors' cooking fires some distance away. The little rabbit screamed and flailed whenever anyone came near him, though Pozzi and Keeva tried to tempt him with food, water, affection, anything to break through the stone-like barriers that he had set up around himself.

Pozzi pulled Keeva aside. "Leave him be. There's nothing to be done for now."

"There's nothing anyone can do. Except maybe me."

Pozzi and Keeva turned to look. It was Harlan, leaning against one of the prison bars, Mort and Ark hulking and somber beside him. Ark was even skinnier than he had been in Willago, and his back bore many reminders of the whip.

"We're all going to die under these brutes, aren't we?" Ark giggled, the hysteria palpable.

There were half stifled sobs from the other corners of the pen.

"Our only chance is if we have somethin' they want," Mort grumbled. There were mutterings of agreement. "The one who's got it right is Harlan. He's cooperating!"

There was a surprised murmur as the rabbits thought this over, and Pozzi could see several nodding grudging agreement.

"If we help them find Theo, they may treat us better." Mort's voice pierced the hubbub.

"And what could you tell them?" Pozzi spoke up. "What do you know about him? That he disappeared into the River Tithe? That we never saw him after that? Even if we wanted to bargain for our lives with information about Theo, we don't have any! They're just interested in making us slaves, or worse."

At this, a panic began spreading amongst the rabbits.

Harlan motioned for silence. "That's not true! Agacheta just wants Theo. If we want to improve our situation we must find ways to work with them, negotiate with them."

At this Pozzi laughed. "Negotiate with 'em? We're slaves, Harlan! Does the mouse negotiate with the cat?"

Arlo exchanged glances with Mort and Harlan, and sniggered. "What do you know of the two-legs, Pozzi? Not as much as Harlan here."

"What we need is leadership," Harlan said, raising his voice. "We need to stand together and choose a representative who'll bargain for our interests with Agacheta. They're not all hard hearted, for if they were, why'd they feed me and give me blankets?" He let his words sink in. "All of us might have those comforts. We just need to cooperate and tell them what they want to know. After all, their fight is with Theo, not with us."

There were nods and grunts of agreement. No creature could be immune to reason or fair negotiation, and surely their captors were no different. Harlan's proposal fit with Willago philosophy, and Pozzi could anticipate the next comment coming, predictable as thunder after lightning.

"I say we make Harlan our leader," Arlo said, as if the thought had just occurred to him.

"Aye," Mort seconded. "He has the general's favor, and he's our best bet in bartering for freedom."

"Aren't you forgetting something?" Pozzi interrupted. "They took Father Oaks away, killed our friends, burned our homes, dragged us all the way out here. They've got us marked for death or something worse, and the only hope is escape or finding help."

Harlan strode over and towered over Pozzi, who stood his ground, unwilling to be cowed.

"How are you going to escape, Bucktooth? You going to chew your way out of here?"

Arlo and Mort giggled hysterically.

"It's better than bowing down to 'em," Pozzi said, quiet.

"If you want to pin your hopes on some army that might or might not exist, then by Kalmac's scut you go right ahead." Harlan made a sweeping gesture at the frightened youngsters, the emaciated Elders, and the hollow-eyed youths. "But don't ask these poor souls to follow you to certain death. I say we give them what they want, even if that's Theo himself! Who's with me?"

There were cries of support and encouragement, and Pozzi saw that their need for hope made them respond to Harlan's brazen leadership like a sunflower to light.

"And so you'll do what you do so well," Pozzi said bitterly. "Save yourself. Maybe not even that. And at what price? They fear this Ihaktu army. I've heard 'em talking. Why? They think it can destroy their entire empire. D'you know what that means? It means other creatures who are sufferin' what we suffer will be freed. It means those villagers we saw won't have to live afraid. It means there's hope and that we shouldn't help these monsters."

There were hesitant, fearful glances around the enclosure.

Harlan crossed his arms. "And so we're to sacrifice ourselves, our entire village, for the sake of trying to save everyone in this accursed land? I say we look after us and ours first. If this army is so strong then they can take care of themselves, can't they?"

With a last look at his companions, Pozzi knew the battle was lost. Even Keeva avoided his gaze.

"Right then," Harlan huffed, satisfied. "Tomorrow I tell the general that we are at her service."

~

"Pozzi."

He hadn't been asleep, but he'd been so immersed in his tangle of thoughts that he thought he'd imagined his name being spoken in the silence.

"Pozzi." He turned to see the soft, small outline next to him.

"Walnut? Are you alright? We were worried, we were."

"Do you really believe it?"

Pozzi frowned, confused. "Believe what?"

"That we could be saved?"

Pozzi sighed, hauling himself to a sitting position. All the captors' fires had burnt down to embers, so that their sleeping forms were nothing more than indistinct mounds.

"I don't know, Walnut," Pozzi admitted, running a paw over his ears.

For a moment Walnut looked crestfallen, but he persisted. "But you believe it's possible, don't you?" The intensity of the question made Pozzi choose his words with care.

"I'm not sure what to believe." He paused, then let his

thoughts continue aloud. "It's fantastical, but then if they're scared of being destroyed, it would explain all this, wouldn't it?"

For a moment neither spoke, each sorting through their own thoughts.

"Why do such bad things happen to us, Pozzi?" Walnut asked. The weight of the question hung between them, as full and inaccessible as the moon outside.

Pozzi groped for an answer, but could find nothing. Instead he reached for Walnut's paw and gave it what he hoped was a reassuring squeeze.

"Do you believe that we'll be able to go home?" What Pozzi saw in Walnut's eyes made his heart contract. No one Walnut's age should possess such a look.

"Yes, Walnut. One day this'll be over and we'll all go home." And as he said it he realized he had to escape with Walnut and Keeva. He couldn't bear to see Keeva and Walnut meet the untold horror that lay in wait for them at Fort Nyatha.

Walnut's eyes shone, and he wiped away his tears with one paw. "I knew it," he whispered. "I knew you'd make sure we go home." He leaned his head against Pozzi, sidling up to him for warmth, and promptly fell asleep. Pozzi was left on his own to think. And plan.

The scales faltered, one battered base plate dipping before righting itself and drawing even to its partner.

"Two hundred forty wedges o' gold." The trader's fleshy hand tipped the plate's contents into a silk pouch which he deftly tied and presented to the general.

"That's a third less than we agreed, Ghazan," Agacheta said, ignoring the pouch.

The trader's expression curdled, his eyes disappearing into rolls of flesh. "That's before I knew forty of 'em are past breeding age, half of 'em barely have meat enough to feed a cat, and the rest have the croup." He shrugged his ample shoulders. "You can't whip the fur from their hides and then expect gold coin."

Agacheta cursed to herself. She should have been more vigilant with her troops. But what could she expect? They were soldiers, not farmers.

"Very well, but I have a condition. There's a young brown one, answers to Walnut. Find him something safe. Don't put him with the others at Nyatha."

Ghazan laughed, making his jowls tremble. "Turning Noshi, eh?" At her scathing look he raised his hands in placation. "Fine, fine, I give my word."

The tent opened, and her pageboy entered. "I'm sorry, my General, but the rabbit, Harlan. He asks to see you."

"Bring him in. Have Commander Kotori ready the prisoners for Ghazan here. And Ghazan—"

Ghazan bowed and placed the pouch of gold on the table. "Your father will not hear of your special request, General." He picked up his scales and left just as Harlan was being ushered in.

"So, have you considered what I told you?" Agacheta stored the satchel of gold wedges in her personal chest, and locked it.

Harlan nodded. "I've convinced them that we should do everything in our power to help you find Theo. You won't have any trouble from us. They'll all listen to me, including the Elders."

"Impressive."

Harlan relaxed visibly. "They've agreed to go as far as Nyatha before deciding whether to return to Willago or stay. But if they refuse, you'll set us free?"

"I already have."

Harlan's ears jerked upwards. "You mean it?"

"As we speak, Commander Kotori is organizing a group of soldiers to escort you all back home, via Nyatha. Except for you, that is."

"Me?"

"Yes. I need someone to help me find that brother of yours, remember?"

Harlan looked torn between desire to believe her and doubt at such a quick victory.

"If they're being set free, why the escort?"

She was looking forward to ridding herself of these beasts and their logic. "These are dangerous lands, Harlan. In Mankahar, our kind has the right to hunt as they please. My soldiers will guarantee your protection."

Harlan gave a grudging nod. For a moment Agacheta felt a pinprick of pity, but then it was gone.

~

Harlan's news that they would be freed had elicited cries of elation and relief from the villagers, who hugged each other and praised Kalmac.

But not Pozzi. He smelled deceit, smelled it in the sudden arrival of the fat man with the gold, at the way they were being separated into groups of males, females, and young. Why would the general suddenly let them go? It meant his escape plan would have to wait, for he hadn't counted on being separated from Walnut and Keeva.

But he hadn't the heart to voice any of his doubts. Especially to Walnut, whose face was lit by a massive grin.

By sunset preparations were complete. The army had divided into those who were accompanying General Agacheta in the hunt for Theo, and the ones who would escort the rabbit convoy. Harlan was reassuring a tearful Keeva as other rabbits urged her to board the last of the carts that would take them home.

Pozzi helped Elder Yeth up, then turned to Harlan, who was standing with arms crossed over chest. The ever posturing hero, Pozzi thought with distaste.

"Glad we didn't listen to your fears, Pozzi?" Harlan asked, grinning.

"If they're setting us free why are we gettin' back on these accursed carts?"

"It's faster, Bucktooth," Harlan snapped. "Or would you rather walk all the way back to Willago?"

"I just might," Pozzi muttered as Harlan shoved him up onto the cart next to Elder Yeth and swung the wooden gate shut.

With the cracking of whips and the loud cries of "Hah!" the soldiers urged the horses into motion. The carts, full of relieved rabbits, began making their slow way out of the camp.

Some distance away up on a knoll, Agacheta and Caldrik watched the proceedings, their cloaks snapping in the chill wind.

Caldrik glanced at his former pupil. "Guilt is most unbecoming for a general. But if you feel so badly, just tell him the truth."

"What good would that do? Besides, he needs to have faith that I honor my promises if he's going to help me capture the omatje."

Caldrik shrugged. "Look at it this way. Today they suffer from fear, starvation, despair. When they're pacified, they'll be truly free."

CHAPTER THIRTY-SIX

Setting Manneki's arm proved full of tears, curses, wailing, and bruises for everyone, and much depletion of Theo's supplies.

In the end it took all three of them to snap Manneki's bone back into position: Brune to hold the monkey's flailing good arm, Indigo to pin his kicking legs, and Theo to wrestle the two parts of the arm together and strap it to splints of wood that he'd whittled straight for the purpose. Even then, Manneki tried to bite them as they held him still, and only when Theo forced a double dose of willow bark tea past the monkey's throat did he settle down.

By the third day, Theo declared Manneki fit to travel and made a crude sling for the invalid with strips of cloth and pine branches. They continued upwards through the Yharu pass, encountering a few other wild-eyed mountain goats that they took pains to avoid. Though they spied several caves that burrowed into the wind-blown rock, Manneki never asked to bed down in one again. Instead his garrulous nature was overshadowed by a gripping depression, as he was convinced that the breaking of his fighting arm had shattered his chances of becoming an Ihaktu.

The Yharu passes evened out into a gradual descent on its other side, not nearly as inhospitable and rugged as the face it presented to the West of Mankahar. The travelers were glad to not have to fight for every foothold, and also to not be striding into the wind. They made faster time going downhill along the mountain's spruce and fir covered back, and soon reached a valley floor that separated the Yharu from the next range: the Purple Mountains.

In the valley they found remnants of a small city that had been reduced to rubble.

Indigo combed the ruins of the smithy and managed to find two short swords in workable condition, which she fastidiously cleaned and sharpened before giving one to Manneki.

"Now you're truly on your way to becoming a warrior. I used to have one just like this when I was a child," she said. This cheered the monkey and made him forget the setback of his broken arm.

Theo had a sudden memory of Walnut's face, his furry chin covered in toffee. Where was he now? Theo tried to shake his thoughts from the past. Longing for Willago would not take him there. So to distract himself, he made short excursions with his medicinal kit, mentioning to his companions a copse of lush chicory here or a growth of passion flowers there. His real reason was less to harvest roots than to steal a few precious moments with *The Miraculous Cures of Zo,* which he worked through sentence by sentence, page by page, marking his place with a piece of dried bark to easily pick up where he'd left off. He'd gradually become entranced by the tales of Zo's cures and, without realizing it, had begun to try and memorize some of them.

When they'd crossed the valley, they began the approach towards the Purple Mountains, which rose majestic and hazy in the east. The terrain to the mountains were gentle, rolling hills dotted by the odd chestnut tree or twisted birch, their branches now almost naked with the onset of winter. The mountains,

Brune explained, girded the paths that would lead to the port city of Ralgayan, where pilgrims made the trip across the Sea of Forgotten Souls to Mount Mahkah.

"From here it's another week's journey to Ralgayan, and Aktu willing we shall crush the stuffing from the empire's forces within days, and then sail on to Mount Mahkah," Brune said. His spirits had risen since they'd left the harsh Yharu passes behind, and even the bitter cold at these heights couldn't hide the warmth in his voice when he spoke of home.

"I can't believe I'll finally be meeting the Lord Noshi." Indigo paused in her braiding of dogbane into rope. She was showing Manneki how to make a crude scabbard for his new sword.

"Princess and Manneki be best warriors in Mankahar, yes?" Manneki tried raising his broken arm but winced at the effort.

Brune gave Manneki a friendly cuff on the back of the head. "With luck, some of you will be virtually invincible."

"Invincible enough to defeat an omatje?" Indigo asked.

"No good can come of talking of omatjes, Princess," the bear said.

"Why do you want to defeat one?" Theo felt something in him wilt.

"Brune, more than anyone in Mankahar, you know why I must ask."

"Breaking the beehive won't lessen your stings. Your mother and sister, may Aktu embrace them, are gone, and no omatje death will change that."

Manneki's eyes bloomed with curiosity. "How did Princess mother die?"

Indigo's dark ears stiffened. "A wandering traveler came to Alvareth, several years ago." She drew a deep breath, as if the smell of ashes and burning leaves and rotten wood from their fire had become suffocating.

"You know this, Brune. You and Kuno both knew. Why won't you tell me about what happened?"

"Some things are better left in the past," Brune growled. "Your mother chose to shelter an omatje. She was warned."

"I don't understand," Theo interrupted. "Who was this omatje? Where is he now?"

"Are you saying my mother deserved her death, because she protected an omatje? Who deserves to have their throats cut in their sleep?" Here Indigo's voice caught, and Theo thought for one awful moment that she might cry. But her eyes remained dry and hot in the dying light of the embers.

"Kuno never told you because he knew this would eat at you, Princess. You need to focus on your role as queen and warrior for Alvareth. You cannot enter the Order if the only goal you can seek is revenge."

"Have you abandoned your revenge, Brune?" Indigo asked. The fire popped, and Theo noticed the bear cringe at Indigo's words.

Brune drew a ragged breath. "I have had more time to do so. And that's all I want to hear about omatjes tonight. Understood?"

Indigo dropped her half-formed rope and stood up, ears stiff. "Fine. Keep your secrets then." With that she turned and stalked off, disappearing into the dark night beyond the fire's reach.

Theo turned back to Brune. "If there are no omatjes left, how could her family have been killed by one?"

Brune harrumphed in frustration. "It's a long time ago, best forgotten. I'll take first watch and make sure she doesn't go far. You two get some sleep." Carefully stowing away the remaining rope fibers, Manneki sidled up to the giant bear, cradling his injured arm.

Theo took one last look towards where Indigo had gone, then rolled his medicine pouch beneath his head and bedded down for the night. He tried to concentrate on sleep and not wonder about what other omatjes existed—or whether Indigo would ever speak to him again if she knew what he was.

~

He was in blackness. Comforting, embracing, inky darkness that enfolded like a warm burrow. When he emerged, it was gradual, like bubbles rising to the surface of heated molasses. He opened his eyes to a canopy of tree leaves.

Theo sat up. He was where they'd stopped for the night, but no one was in sight. The Purple Mountains loomed at his back, dark and silent sentinels against the night horizon, while all around the night air hung cool and still. Not even the usual sounds of hunting owls or the rustle of grass beneath a passing snake reached his ears. It was as if the night had been frozen in a pristine, soundless instant.

Theo began to wander, his paws moving of their own accord. Where was Indigo? And Brune and Manneki? His feet found their own way over the frost-laden grass until he reached a pool of water.

The pool's surface lay still and shallow, a perfect reflection of the curved, white moon that hovered above. A cloud of fireflies looped over the waters, their bellies glowing and fading in rhythm as they danced to some music only they could hear. He stared at the moon's reflection, hypnotized.

He wasn't alone.

A dark shape sat on the other side of the pool. At first Theo thought it was an outcrop of rock. But then he heard the sound of its breathing, deep and unhurried.

"Who are you? What do you want?" Theo was amazed at how fearless his voice sounded.

That depends on who you *are.* The creature leapt off its rock and landed next to him. It stretched, long and dark, against the cold grass. It began to unfurl: four feline legs and a beaked head, with wings that whispered in the night.

The Griffin.

The thing reached out and grabbed Theo by the ankles.

"Leave me alone!" Theo tried to pry the animal's claws from him, but the thing was so cold it felt like searing heat. He recoiled.

Am I your greatest fear, little rabbit?

At Theo's expression the Griffin hissed. *Let's make a pact. Tell me who you are, and you can fly free. Keep me shackled, and I will eat your flesh by day, gnaw your bones by night, until there is nothing....*

Theo trembled at the cold tendrils of the beast, its beak inches from him.

You have something very powerful. The question is, will you use it?

Theo sensed without being told that the Griffin meant word catching. "I'd be hated. I'd lose the few friends I've ever had."

The Griffin hissed, its eyes hungrier than death.

What are you?

Theo's limbs softened into liquid fear. His mouth hardened shut.

What are you?

With a cry that swallowed the night, the Griffin leapt, its beak and talons ripping into the rabbit's flesh. He heard words from another time and place: *Find Elshon.*

CHAPTER THIRTY-SEVEN

When he woke up, Theo thought he'd died and gone to the promised lands of Kalmac.

He was in a bed—a real bed, made of wood with four posts, on a pallet that smelled of sage. He was in some sort of cottage, made of pine slats and stone, with a window opposite the bed that allowed in a generous amount of sunlight. Next to him was a rough wooden table with a wash basin, and on the floor lay a clean rush carpet.

Where was he? And how had he gotten here? He remembered the terrifying Griffin. He couldn't help checking beneath the bed to make sure it hadn't stepped out of his nightmare.

Theo sat up and rubbed his head. Why did he keep seeing this creature in his sleep?

The rabbit tried to shake off these confusing thoughts and deal with determining where he was. But before he could go to the window and try and get his bearings, the door to the room opened.

The badger face that peeked around the corner was graying, but at seeing Theo the eyes crinkled with pleasure, and a deep chuckle rumbled from his barreled chest.

"Ach, yer up! Now now, easy does it, lad, ye don't want to be too hasty," he said, coming into the room and wiping his paws on a shirt tucked into worn but clean britches. His feet were clad in simple hemp sandals.

"Where am I?" Theo asked, watching his host waddle up to the wash basin and begin rubbing his paws vigorously in the water.

"First things first, lad. Ye need some food in ye fer starters."

Theo watched in bewilderment as he sauntered out of the room and came back with a tray of food. At the smell, Theo realized that he was famished. The meal was simple but delicious. How long had it been since he'd eaten? He had no idea, but the thick turnip soup, rough chunk of pale cheese, and a coarse black bread peppered with chives tasted divine to a rabbit who'd been surviving on foraged roots and nuts for the past few moons.

When Theo had finished, the badger placed the tray aside and sat down opposite him on the bed. He reached out a paw and felt the rabbit's right ear for fever, then motioned for his wrist. Theo obeyed, and the badger felt his patient's pulse, his brow furrowed. The frown dissolved into a carefree smile when he'd finished.

"Well, lad, good news is yer just fine."

"You're a healer?"

The badger chuckled. "Aye, lad, been the healer in this here village of Lokni for nearly thirty years now."

"Lokni?" Theo asked. "Is that where I am? Or rather, where is Lokni, exactly?"

The badger began clearing up the plates and the tray. "South o'the Purple Mountains, 'bout two days' journey."

Theo's mind raced. "I've been unconscious for two days?"

The badger nodded. "Aye, lad. No movement, not a stir—yer good at playing dead, I'll tell ya that! Yer friends'll be happy to see yer recovered. They've been quite worried."

"Where are they?"

"Oh don't worry, they'll be back soon enough."

Theo tried to question him further, but the badger only repeated that he should rest until the others came back.

When Brune, Indigo, and Manneki returned, they were elated at his recovery. Even Indigo's usually reserved attitude softened enough for her to fetch his medicine pouch, saying she'd hauled the heavy nuisance for him. Manneki had no concerns about showing emotion, throwing a scrawny arm around Theo and hugging with all his might. He proudly displayed his other arm, which was now in a much better sling than the crude one Theo had made.

"I thought we cured you of wandering off on your own?" Brune chided. "Mr. Hadar here says you must have hit your head on something while you walked in your sleep."

"We decided to make a detour and find the nearest healer," Indigo explained. "Manneki convinced us that you needed someone trained."

Manneki beamed, and Theo wondered how much the monkey had been motivated to find a healer for his arm.

"Doesn't this mean that we'll be even later in reaching Ralgayan?" Theo asked.

Brune nodded. "It does, but we've also dug up some important news while we've been here. The road through Halgath is swarming with spies on the lookout for anyone headed to Ralgayan, so we can no longer go by that route. If we'd not come here, we would've been like salmon running a gauntlet of spring-time bears."

"We must instead swing south and then north to reach Ralgayan," Indigo added. "That's our only hope of getting there, for the Blackwings have joined the Urzoks. They're interrogating anyone traveling the main roads between here and Ralgayan."

"Which means we'll need supplies and will try and skirt enemy territory," Brune growled. "You'd better recover well, Theo. With the Urzoks pressing us from the south and the

Blackwings closing the passes from the north, we'll be lucky to make Ralgayan with our skins on the outside."

~

The next day, while Brune and Manneki set out to find supplies of food, water skins, clothing and weapons for the voyage to Ralgayan, Hadar led Indigo and Theo through Lokni's winding lanes.

It felt like years since he'd been in a village, and he drank in the sights and sounds. Lokni's cobbled streets rose in steep, awkward angles, but the location had obviously been chosen for its security. Any attackers would have to scale the cliff face from the scrubby river banks below.

Lokni was small but by no means quiet, with its narrow dirt lanes crowded with stalls selling baked goods and vegetables. The cold air teemed with the smoke of cooking fires, the aroma of dried berries and nuts piled high on straw mats, and a mixture of salt, peppercorn, even exotic aniseed. The occasional vegetable seller called out to their host, but he simply waved a paw and ignored their thinly veiled curiosity.

To reach the herbal remedies section, they left the main clamor of Lokni behind and entered a back alley. Here the bitter smell of witch hazel was offset by the scents of crushed lemon seeds, ginger root, and dandelion. The badger led them to the very end, where a rotund chipmunk in spectacles sat amongst clay jars and reed baskets filled with an array of herbs.

"Rothor," the healer called out. "I've brought ye customers."

The chipmunk peered at the group over his spectacles and sniffed, sizing them in a glance.

"I'm out of licorice, or any other herbs that spice the blood and make the womb fertile."

At this even Indigo blushed.

"No, no, Rothor," Hadar chuckled in embarrassment. "They're not after that!"

"Oh?" the chipmunk replied, squinting. "Then what can I help you with?"

"I need a good supply of feverfew," Theo cut in. "As well as chrysanthemum, foxglove, witch hazel, goat weed, elm shavings. Oh, and willow bark. Plenty of willow bark." That should fully replenish his medicine pouch.

As Rothor began to measure out the order, he and Hadar busied themselves in local gossip. Indigo looked over the piles of herbs and leaves. She picked up a shiny bean-shaped seed and sniffed.

"Yellow oleander," Theo explained. "Very poisonous unless treated first. You should never touch anything unless you know what it is."

Indigo looked sheepish, but also annoyed at the reprimand. "So do you know how to make poisons that kill?"

"Yes," Theo said without thinking. "But it's forbidden."

"Teach me."

"That's not a good idea."

"Why not?" she huffed. "I've taught you the sword. You promised to teach me about healing."

Theo glanced at Hadar and Rothor, who were still busily wrapping various leaves and herbs in packets of cloth. "Healing, yes. This is different. Poison is a dark art."

Theo flinched at the anger in her eyes. He tried to change the topic.

"What will you do once you're an Ihaktu warrior?"

Indigo crossed her arms, not easily distracted. "I'll be queen of Alvareth. Once I've found the omatje who killed my mother."

"You know a lot about omatjes?"

"No one does. But my father raised me to remember that if I had the chance, I should avenge my family. Which is why being chosen for the Order has been a blessing. If I'm an Ihaktu, maybe I'll have the skills to track down my mother's slayer."

"But what about your queendom?"

"What about it?"

"Aren't you the heir to the throne?"

"When I'm twenty I'll inherit it from my aunt Kalmara."

"What if you haven't found the omatje who killed your mother by then?"

Indigo's eyes didn't waver. "I cannot go back without having found my mother's killer and set things right. My subjects deserve to know that their queen is resolute and wavers at nothing."

"Don't they deserve to have a queen who's there, rather than one who's roaming Mankahar, chasing vengeance?"

Indigo straightened, and Theo realized too late that he'd struck a hidden but dangerous nerve. "How do you know what my queendom deserves, and what makes a good ruler? You're nothing but a homeless farm runt who doesn't even know how to use a sword! What right does some hill digger have to give me lessons on leadership?"

Theo stood silent, stung by the lash in her voice.

Indigo gave him one last withering glance before marching out of the alley.

Theo was about to run after her when Rothor's voice brought him back.

"Hey lad! What about your purchase?"

He motioned for Hadar to take care of it, then ran off in pursuit of Indigo. By the time he reached the alley mouth, she'd disappeared into the market throng. Theo searched several of the main streets, but had to give up by the time he reached the town's central well.

He cursed and kicked at a nearby wall. Maybe he'd been too forward, but her backlash had laid him bare. She was right. Who was he to talk to her like that? Still, what self-righteousness! Keeva would never have said those things. Keeva would have smiled back, kept her calm. Keeva would have … *Keeva would have been boring*. Keeva couldn't have taught him the sword, or to see what was behind. Now that he thought about it, Keeva was never much good at seeing what was right in front of her, considering she married Harlan. He sat down on an overturned basket and dropped his head into his paws. What he'd felt for Keeva, he realized miserably, was a mere shadow of what he felt now. And Indigo was even more unattainable than Keeva.

"I never thought I'd see that face again, chum!"

"Pachua! What are you doing here?"

The possum stood, arms akimbo, his jaw working a piece of tobacco.

"I should be asking you the same thing! You're taking the scenic route to Mount Mahkah, chum!"

"It's a long story," Theo said.

Pachua motioned at the alley Theo had just come from. "Rothor the healer's an old friend of mine, he is. I came to warn him and the town." His jaw stopped working its tobacco. "Dear Aktu, but it all makes sense now!"

Theo frowned. "Warn him about what? What makes sense?"

"Why they're coming here!"

The rabbit was more confused than ever. "Who's coming here?"

Pachua spat out his tobacco, which landed in a sticky clump next to his foot. "See chum, I came here to give these poor folk a warning. Every mole and his blind, deaf, and mute friend in Blackwing Forest knows that the Blackwings are on the move, see, and they're headin' here!"

"The Blackwings?" Theo felt an ache in his shoulder. "Why?"

Pachua gripped the rabbit's arms. "They're with the Urzoks, who arrived in Blackwing Forest only moments after you left. I thought they were coming here for a usual raid, 'cause I figured you'd be long gone up north by now." When he still stared blankly, Pachua shook him.

"Don't you see, chum? It's not a raid at all! They know you're here, that's why they're comin' to Lokni, with the Blackwings. They're after you, not Lokni."

CHAPTER THIRTY-EIGHT

By the time Theo and Pachua returned to Hadar's dwelling, a foreboding tension had descended.

Shopkeepers who had earlier hawked wares with jovial abandon were now hastily packing up their goods. Others hurried youngsters and valuables into concealed cellars.

Manneki and Brune were just as surprised to see Pachua as Theo had been, but the possum waved their greetings aside.

"No doubt you've heard that your chums the Blackwings are on the move this way, along with a small Urzok army," Pachua said.

Hadar nodded, while Manneki, who usually greeted danger with such bravado, bit his lip.

"Any chance they're just passing by?" Brune asked with a dry smile.

Pachua shook his head. "I thought they might be, until I spied Theo here. I'd be willing to bet my last acorn they're headed for Lokni because they know you're here. I heard the king was right livid when he found ya missing, not having finished curing his fire warts and all."

"How did they know where we were?" Theo asked.

Manneki burst into tears and grabbed Brune's paw. At first

no one could make out his jabbering, until he slowed down long enough for those gathered to decipher one sentence.

"Manneki didn't mean to!"

"Didn't mean to what?" Brune asked, frowning.

"Please, Brune," he sobbed. "Manneki not mean to tell the stoat we were here! But stoat not stop making fun of Manneki, that Manneki is small!"

"Everyone knows we're here," Theo said, not understanding. "We've been walking everywhere with Brune."

"No no no!" Manneki blubbered, wiping his swelling eyes with a grimy paw. "Manneki wanted to show we not weak, Manneki tell stoat that we going to Mount Mahkah, to fight Urzoks, that we outsmart Blackwings, Manneki tell him everything!"

For a moment there was no sound but the monkey's renewed wailing.

"Spies," Pachua muttered. "They're anywhere there's a pot to piss in and a tongue to wag."

Brune nodded. "If it'd been just anyone, the news of who we were would've spread all over town by now, but no one seems to know who we are—except the Blackwings and the Urzoks."

"We should find that filthy stoat and slit him navel to chin," Pachua said gruffly. "Can't stand these beasts, working for the Urzoks to enslave us all."

He then put a comforting paw on Manneki. "What's done is done, chum. There's no use bawlin' over a cracked acorn, now is there?"

"How long until they reach Lokni?" Theo asked, his voice raised over Manneki's wailing.

Pachua whistled. "They're on the warpath, they are, so no later than sundown, I'd say. I got a head start by just a whisker, chum."

"We have to get away, before they circle Lokni and flush us out," Brune said.

"And how do you propose doing that?" Pachua snorted.

"You've got at most an hour or two before they reach the foot of the cliff, and with the Blackwings they'll tear this place apart from the air. Unless you sprouted wings and flew, it's going to be a mighty tricky feat."

Hadar, who'd been standing by listening and wringing his paws, cleared his throat. "Maybe there's something I can do to help."

At this even Manneki was curious enough to stop crying.

"My grandfather once healed someone passing through, and in gratitude gave him something that might be useful." Hadar began rummaging in an old dusty chest that stood in a corner. He pulled out old pieces of clothing, pouches of herbs and poultices, wooden measuring spoons and other odds and ends, which in his haste clattered to the floor.

"Aha!" He held up a parcel tied in faded muslin. He unwrapped it, revealing a vial full of plain, brown fluid. "I wonder whether it still works ...."

"Well chum, don't just gawk at it," Pachua said. "What does it do?"

Hadar looked up as if pulling himself from a reverie. "Ach, yes. What it does. I've never tried it, mind, but my grandfather said that it supposedly—well supposedly it's a bottle of wings."

They stared at Hadar. Brune spoke first.

"What do you mean, it's a bottle of wings?"

"Just that, lad, you drink it and puff! You've got wings," Hadar's whiskers twitched as he opened the vial and took a sniff.

"Oy, Hadar, I hope you're jestin', and ya've got a better idea up ya sleeve," Pachua said.

Hadar bristled. "You don't believe me?"

"Well ya said yourself, chum, ya never tried it."

The old healer shook his head. "My grandfather told me this traveler was so powerful, if he'd said this potion would sink the sun and moon together, then I'd be sure it could. His name was Orjo, ever heard of him?"

Brune stiffened. "Orjo? Orjo the infamous omatje gave you this?"

"Who's Orjo?" Theo asked.

Smiling, Hadar said, "A wizard, some say. A mighty odd sort."

Theo glanced out the window. Everywhere there were signs of panic, increasing as the sun began its flight for cover. Terrified mothers shushed crying infants, and villagers blocked their window shutters with anything they could find: chair legs, tables, slats from cribs. A group of stoats were hastily dumping piles of cabbage, carrots, and leeks in the village square. Theo realized they were hoping to use this as an offering to divert the marauders so that they wouldn't seek out the inhabitants.

"There's no harm in trying it," Theo said.

Pachua looked at the rabbit in surprise. "Tell me ye're jesting?"

"You said so yourself, the Blackwings will be here in a matter of hours. That's how long it would take us to climb down the cliff face alone, much less get away!"

"He's got a point," Brune said.

"All Manneki's fault!" Manneki sniveled, his lower lip trembling. "We're going to die here!"

"Shush!" Brune barked. Manneki choked down a half-released sob.

"Now another thing, lads," Hadar said, shaking the vial. "There's only enough for one of you, so it'll have to be the bear. He's the only one who can carry you all."

Taking a deep breath, Brune said, "The rabbit's right. We have no choice."

Before anyone could stop him, he plucked the open vial from Hadar's paw, tipped his head back and downed the potion. He spat out the empty vial and grimaced, one thick arm wiping at his mouth.

There was a moment's shocked silence. The five of them stood, anticipating a faint, a seizure, something. The only sounds were the hurried footsteps of villagers outside, the clatter of wood shutters drawn closed, and the stifled shouts of frightened young ones.

The bear burst out laughing, half relieved, half bitter. "Well, that didn't work!"

"Brune ..." Theo pointed.

Between Brune's shoulder blades, two light spots the size of a walnut appeared. They grew lighter and larger, to the size of a fig, then a fist. As they grew they pressed against the skin, stretching and swelling the hide on his back.

"I never dared use it," Hadar said.

"Why's that?" Pachua stood mesmerized by the swells beneath Brune's now sweat-drenched hide.

"Because Orjo said it would be very painful."

Brune frowned. "I don't feel any—"

Suddenly he cried out, then fell to the ground, his teeth gritted in agony.

The swelling had broken the skin. Small pieces of bone-like protrusions emerged, covered in slime and blood. Brune snarled as he writhed on the ground, sending chairs and pottery crashing to the floor.

Theo rushed forward to hold the giant head. The bear's forelock was drenched in sweat and his eyes rolled bone white, his skull a dead weight in the rabbit's comparatively tiny paws.

Theo silently cursed Hadar and his evil potion, which was no doubt killing Brune.

"Get water," Hadar urged, pushing Manneki. "You'll find cloths in the drawer in the other room, lad. Go on now." Hesitantly Manneki inched towards the bedroom before disappearing around the doorpost.

"Hold on, Brune," Theo said, watching the bear gasp at regular intervals. The bones coming from his back had emerged even further. They were the length of Theo's arm and curved like a sickle.

Hadar knelt and examined the growths, each touch drawing a groan from the bear. "There now lad, he'll make it through, just you see." But Theo could hear the telltale uncertainty in his voice.

"Give me a piece of wood," Theo pointed at a splintered leg that had broken off a table.

Hadar handed it to the rabbit in silence, and, prying Brune's clenched teeth apart, Theo managed to wrestle it in. "Bite this."

Brune bit almost clean through the wood, and roared in pain. Theo could have sworn that the entire village stood still, shocked into silence.

When Brune stopped, the growths from his shoulders had fully emerged. There came a soft sucking sound as they birthed from his flesh, pulling tissue and blood with them in wet, stringy clumps. They unfolded, and Theo recognized that they were not bone—or at least, not completely.

"By holy Aktu," Pachua breathed.

Hadar gently brushed away the thick film of blood and ripped skin before sponging the growths with a cloth, revealing interlocking feathers. Like Brune's coat, they were a tawny black shot through with ochre yellow, the feathers long and tapered, glistening with water and blood.

"We'll need to staunch this," the badger said, pressing his wet cloth to the swollen flesh.

Theo pulled his gaze away from the wings to look at Brune's face. The bear's shrinking pupils meant the worst was over, and his breathing evened out into regular gasps.

"Is bear gonna be all right?" Manneki whispered.

"Go get more water, and liquor. Hadar, do you have ginger root? We'll need to clean those wounds."

"They're doin' a good job of healin' themselves, chum," Pachua said, pointing to where the ruptured flesh was sealing around the protrusions.

Hadar cleaned the last of the blood off the wings. Brune twisted his head to look, then struggled to sit up.

Theo gave him what support he could with his shoulder. The

bear steadied his trunk-like legs, shook his head, then tentatively flexed his new wings.

"It hurts when I move them," Brune grimaced.

Hadar nodded. "Aye, it'll take some gettin' used to, I imagine."

Pachua peered out the window, his face grim. "Well chums, ya'll have to move fast if you're going at all, and, to be honest, I don't know what shape this bear's in."

The group hurried out of the hut, Brune following unsteadily. He folded his wings with difficulty, wincing as he negotiated his way past the narrow door.

Outside, the moon was a pale smudge in the east, while the sun's light beat a rapid retreat over the horizon.

"Look!" Pachua pointed. In the fading dusk they could just make out what looked like a cloud in the plains basin below. Hovering over the low dust cloud was an ominous winged mass.

"What that?" Manneki asked.

"The enemy, that's what," Pachua replied somberly. "The Urzoks are mounted, and the Blackwings are in flight."

"Oh no!" Theo breathed.

"Aye, there're a good number of 'em, and they'll be here faster'n you can say Blackwing bastard."

"It's not that! Where's Indigo?"

Everyone looked at him with dawning confusion.

"You lost the princess?" Pachua exclaimed.

"Where did you last see her?" Brune cut in.

"By the herb market," Theo began sprinting, with Manneki, Pachua, and Brune fast behind him.

She tossed another pebble off the ledge, still shaking with a strange storm of emotions: anger towards Theo, anger at herself, as well as another feeling that confused her. Who was Theo but some outsider who didn't know anything about royalty or leadership? He hadn't had to live through his mother and sibling being slain in their sleep. He hadn't had to try and keep his head high while others snickered that his mother deserved what she got for sheltering an omatje.

But what bothered her more than his words was the fact that she even cared. As she sat on the hidden piece of rock that jutted out beneath Lokni, she tried to understand why. He called her princess, but said it as if it were her name, not a title of deference. He was so shy, so reserved. Any rabbit in Alvareth who knew how to heal others would boast about it, impress her with his knowledge of poison. But not him.

This was not the kind of rabbit she found attractive. Nodin was attractive, with his thick fur that darkened to burnished brown, tapered ears, and broad chest. Nodin would make a good consort. Her mother would've approved of Nodin, whereas Theo ... Indigo shook her head. What was she even doing, comparing Theo to Nodin? Some queen she would be, if she couldn't focus on more important things. She hunched her shoulders and tried to shut out thoughts of Theo as anything but a fellow apprentice.

~

They searched the town streets, with not a villager in sight. Figuring that Indigo would have wanted to be alone, Theo asked Hadar where the most deserted place in Lokni was.

The barn he led them to perched on the southern fringes of the town, clinging to the cliff edge. Like the streets, it was deserted. Night had thickened around them, making it harder to search.

The party spread out and combed the surrounding areas, including an adjoining smithy, but found no one. Calling out Indigo's name brought no replies.

By this time they could hear the distant hoof beats from the approaching army echoing up the valley walls, accompanied by the shrieking war cries of the Blackwings.

Frustrated, Theo peered over the cliff face. Where could she have gone? Although she'd hurt him far more with her words than he'd hurt her with his, he now bitterly regretted having said anything about her queendom.

The moon broke through its blanket of scudding clouds, sickly-pale light spilling over the plains and rugged cliff face below. The army had already reached the base of the cliff, and the Blackwings were spreading out, ascending with great thrusts of their wide wings.

Theo's heart lurched. A dark shape, hunched near an outcropping several hundred feet below.

"Indigo!" He saw the flash of her eyes as she looked up. He was unprepared for the relief he felt.

"Is she there?" Brune asked, coming to his side.

Theo pointed. "We're not the only ones who've spotted her."

At Theo's cry a few of the inky black forms rushing up the rock face had paused and changed direction. Several of the Blackwings were now making their way towards Indigo. They shrieked the alert to their comrades as they quickly ate up the distance to the outcropping.

Theo heard the avalanche of pebbles as Indigo scrambled to her feet and reached for her sword. It came unsheathed, flashing as it caught the moonbeam.

Brune cursed and drew his axe, the curved blade like a wicked smile. "Well now they definitely know she's there. Quick, onto my back."

Theo hesitated, but the bear reached forward and grabbed the rabbit by his collar and swung him between his wings. His hide was still crusted in blood, and his back slippery. Manneki leapt up and latched onto Theo's waist, his good arm surprisingly strong.

Pachua held a bow and a quiver of arrows from the smithy. "I'll hold 'em off with this, chums, but ya better be quick about it. Even with me helpin' her, she can't fight 'em all."

Brune nodded. "Thanks again for your help, my friend. May Aktu be with all of us."

The bear's muscles bunched, and then he lunged forward, propelling them off the cliff edge.

For a moment they hung over nothingness, with only the sheer cliff face beneath them and the dark shapes of ascending Blackwings below. Theo had the odd sensation that they were reaching for the moon, cold and indifferent in its throne of clouds.

But then came the sickening pull, the give of empty space, as Brune tried to move his wings but couldn't.

They began to plummet.

"Hang on!" Brune's wings flailed like broken sails, trying to catch the wind stream.

Theo didn't need the warning. His grip on the bear's neck was so tight it could have milked stone. Manneki did the same, his one good paw digging with grim determination into Theo's chest.

As they fell the Blackwings rushed ever faster towards them, until they were more than just dark shapes and Theo could make out the scarlet gleam of their eyes.

One of them banked and made straight for the bear and his riders. Brune's balance shifted so that the wind was no longer sucking them down, but lifting them up. Theo's stomach lurched as their headlong plunge stopped, and Brune righted himself, his wings adopting an awkward rhythm.

The Blackwing was almost upon them, talons outstretched, beak open. Theo stared transfixed at the bright, menacing eye.

Just when Theo thought the beast would pluck him off Brune's back, the Blackwing reeled backwards, as if punched. An arrow protruded from its throat, and it fell towards the ravine below.

"Quick, chums, she won't last!" They heard Pachua's shout through the deafening cries of the Blackwings, and, as they drew closer Theo could just make out the outcropping where Indigo was fighting off her attackers. She'd already felled two, for he could see dark, crumpled shapes around her, but now four more were closing in.

With a great thrust of his wings Brune propelled himself towards her. Pachua let off several arrows, sending a pair of Blackwings reeling into the darkness.

Brune beat his way into the ring of attackers, swinging his axe into the nearest enemy, his teeth bared in a ferocious snarl. They scattered immediately, as much from surprise at a winged bear as anything, while Brune negotiated a foothold on the outcropping.

Theo reached down and grabbed Indigo, who was staring in confusion.

"No time for explanations, get on!" He hauled her onto Brune, sitting her in front of him.

No sooner had she gotten a grip on Brune's fur than the bear pushed out again, his wings pumping with a mighty rush of air, his back paws sending a cascade of rocks and pebbles down the cliff face as they left the ledge.

The Blackwings, recovering from their initial shock, screamed in anger and rushed forth in furious pursuit.

As the birds reached out with their claws, Brune swooped to lose them. The plains stretched away in a rugged patchwork of shadow and light. A few helmeted faces from the Urzok army pointed and gave chase, but proved no match. The winged bear, along with his passengers, were already skimming several feet above their heads, passing over them and onwards towards the Purple Mountains beyond.

"Where are we headed?" Theo shouted above the sound of rushing wind. He could feel Brune tiring, his breath coming in irregular rasps, while his fur lay slick with sweat and blood. In front of him, Indigo panted from the exertion of trying to stay astride.

"Anywhere we can hide," Brune said.

CHAPTER THIRTY-NINE

The cave was cold and eerie, but it proved dry. The tired group dared not light a fire, as they were still close enough to Lokni for smoke to be clearly visible.

Brune had flown for several leagues before they managed to find a decent hiding spot in a rocky knoll. The four had dragged themselves, bone weary and covered in grime and blood, to this cramped hiding spot. Brune had fallen into a deep sleep on the hard floor, exhaustion etched in every line of his body, his paw still clutching his axe with an iron grip. Soon after, his wings had begun to wither, the feathers molting in a brittle, blood-flecked carpet around him. Eventually even the wings themselves fell away, dead and spent.

Indigo watched Theo readjusting Manneki's splint. The wood had broken during their fight with the Blackwings, and Theo bound the two pieces back together with a strip of cloth, trying to ignore the keen sense of loss at having left behind his medicine pouch—with the book.

"How did Brune grow wings?"

Theo explained as best he could, from discovering that the Urzoks had learned their whereabouts, to trying to devise a way to escape, to the strange potion that was left by a passing patient.

At the news of the Urzoks knowing their location, Theo omitted Manneki's part in the affair, for which he thanked the rabbit silently with his eyes.

"Theo, I should say I'm sorry."

He avoided her gaze. "It's alright. What you said was true."

"What did Princess say?" Manneki asked.

"Never mind. I was unfair, and I want you to know I'm sorry. It's just that all my life I've been raised with the importance of avenging my family. That's what I've trained for, and my siblings look to me to not let them down." She fidgeted, looking away as she struggled with her pride. "And I had no right to ask you to teach me anything you don't want to."

Watching the princess covered in grime and flecks of blood, Theo wondered whether she'd ever fought anything as tough as her decision to apologize.

What was it like, to have this great expectation, this weight? For the first time Theo saw the world from her eyes: the need to always be the fastest, the smartest, the strongest, to prove to those who looked to her that she was worthy for a throne—for an entire clan. It was a weight to crush all but the hardiest.

"Forget what I said. Your queendom is lucky to have you." He finished the last knot to secure Manneki's splint. "Not everyone has your strength."

Indigo looked at him, thoughtful. "Maybe it's not strength. Maybe it's … faith. If you don't believe in yourself, why should anyone else? I can't afford to have my clan not believe in me."

As night deepened and the cold thickened around them, Manneki's snores became the only sound in the cave. He was curled near Brune, drawing comfort from the great bear's warmth. Indigo sat watching the moon, her shoulders hunched, long, smooth ears lying against her back. Theo wanted to reach out and hold her. Tell her things would be all right one day. But he didn't.

~

They stood on the edge of the knoll and watched the bright orange smudge that bloomed like a poisonous flower on the horizon. The night wind hurtling through the ravine bent the sage grass into submission and bit into Theo's back, vindictive as a cat.

"They're burning it," Theo's gut twisted at the thought of the herb seller, Hadar, Pachua, the panicked villagers, their young.

"Do you think Pachua and Hadar escaped?" Indigo asked.

"We can only hope," Brune said, grim.

"All my fault." Manneki rubbed at the tears on his cheeks.

No, all mine, Theo thought to himself. His eyes were dry but guilt squeezed him. Just as it had all those years ago, when the fire had broken out and Harlan had been sent away. Had the Urzoks found his medicine pouch and its contents? That would have sealed Lokni's death sentence, regardless of what offerings they'd piled in their squares or how much they pleaded. Perhaps they hadn't found the book. Perhaps they hadn't realized Theo's secret. But what if they had? Then Pachua and Hadar would be alive if it weren't for him, if he hadn't insisted on keeping that book, if he'd listened to Father Oaks and just not indulged his curiosity! *If only....*

"They'll be on us by sundown," Brune said, pointing with his axe. Like a snake, the enemy convoy was winding its way down the ravine that led up to the knolls they'd sheltered in the night before. Even here they could hear the distant whinnying of the pacified horses fighting their bits. Soon, they would find their prey's tracks in the half-frozen banks by the ravine, and those would lead the Urzoks up the hill.

They saw the flash of a red-crested flag.

"Ornox of Vyad," Brune growled, his hackles spiking.

"You know them?" Indigo asked.

"Aye," the bear replied. "That's the family crest of a monster who dines on poison for breakfast and blood for dinner. We'd better hurry. False trails won't throw them for long." He ran his paw along his axe blade before sheathing it and turning to head down the hill. Theo was the last to follow, his heart raw as Lokni burned in the night.

~

Agacheta could sense her targets. She recognized the quickening in her blood, the heat that came when the wait was almost over. They'd escaped her in that cliff village, where the Blackwings had proved worse than incompetent. Now they would have to catch their prey the hard way.

Harlan sat, silent and expectant, against the pommel of Agacheta's saddle as they rode. Agacheta found the anticipation so openly visible on his face repulsive. He was hoping they captured his brother soon as well, so he could claim the reward she had promised: she would put him in charge of the pacification breweries at Nyatha, with the power to choose his mates and pacify the weak in his clan.

She thought of the old rabbit when she had last seen him, before handing him to Caldrik. His eyes had burned her without mercy; they had judged and condemned without saying a word. She had wanted to kill him for that look, but knew her father wanted him alive. She gripped her reins tighter, upset with herself for being unsettled by the memory.

"Don't let your woman's weakness keep you from greatness, my Lord."

She glared at her mentor, who, as always, had the infuriating habit of seeming to know her thoughts.

"You forget yourself, Caldrik."

Caldrik smirked, but bowed his head.

"I am glad to hear it."

She slapped her mount's flank with the flat of her blade, charging forward and forcing her soldiers into a breakneck pace.

~

The clouds had completely obscured the moon, yet Brune seemed to know exactly where he was going. Manneki clung to Brune's axe holster with his good arm, tossing backward glances for signs of their pursuers, while Indigo and Theo rode on Brune's shoulders, their bodies swaying to his gait.

The ground began sloping ever upwards, and soon they had cleared the line of trees that girded the hills about the ravine. Brune stopped for a moment to gaze towards the other side, his ribs heaving from the effort of the climb.

"There." The bear's voice carried relief. "On the other side is Castle Ralgayan and safety. The Order will be expecting us."

With a grunt he secured his helmet, then fell to all fours and began running. The sudden rush of icy air whipped their faces. Theo glanced back, and though he could see no sign of the Urzoks, he could've sworn he saw the shadows between the trees move and writhe. A beaked, four-legged monster emerged from the woods.

The Griffin.

CHAPTER FORTY

It sat tall atop a rocky outcrop, its back against the rising sun, like a wolf with its head to the sky. Castle Ralgayan, last free city of Mankahar, guarded the entrance to a vast lake on its eastern flank. In the cover of night Theo had mistaken the lake for land, but now in the dim autumn morning he could see its waters, the surface sparkling like a jeweled net.

Ralgayan's fortress was hewn of limestone, its turrets rising straight and stalwart on all sides, with purple and gold banners that beckoned in the wind. Crowded fishing hamlets lined the lake, the smoky blue trails of their morning fires winding past the rooftops and floating away like prayers.

At the edges of the outlying villages, Brune slowed to a lope. Villagers came out to stare, and soon news spread of their approach. All stopped and flocked to see the helmeted bear and his riders speed past, leaving dust and yelping youngsters in their wake.

As the path to the castle grew steeper, Brune let them dismount. The fur on his muscled shoulders had darkened with sweat, and though he didn't say anything Theo could tell he was grateful to let his passengers walk on their own.

When they had climbed to the castle walls, the sun was

already in full view, a splendid golden orb that turned the ripples on the lake surface into slivers of liquid light. They found a throng of villagers already hunkering by the gangplank, waiting for the city gate to open for the day. Many were dressed in simple robes, carrying offerings of flowers, spices, candles, and wine.

The gangplank, already halfway down, settled opposite the moat. A stout badger guard, dressed in a purple vest with gold fringe, walked across to greet them.

"You're the last. The rest of the Order's disciples are already here."

They followed the guard over the gangplank, through the gate and down a main thoroughfare lined with shops and stalls preparing to open for business. This gave way to residential areas, where circular houses of thatch and greywacke stone crowded the laneways. They passed many a stall or house where residents sat, sharpening staves or whetting stones. Somewhere the clang of metal against metal rang out as a blacksmith hammered, followed by the hiss of water and steam. In one corner sat a group of hedgehogs fitting arrowheads to shafts, while the young ones clustered nearby fashioned feathers out of woven reed.

"Even the young help Ralgayan prepare for war?" Indigo asked.

"The roads through Hatuk were attacked, and so the Order's allies from the northwest haven't arrived," the guard replied. "We won't have the numbers we hoped for against the Urzoks."

Castle Ralgayan towered in the middle of the fortress. The group entered a large courtyard flanked by pillared halls leading into still more courtyards. The guard led them straight down the center to the audience hall, its walls covered in murals. Oval windows ran from floor to ceiling against the opposite wall, affording a far-reaching view of the lake.

From this height Theo could see, on the horizon, the vague

outline of a mountain, its high peak shrouded in clouds. The holy Mount Mahkah, he realized.

Manneki jabbered to himself in excitement, his neck craning to take in the high dome above. He stared in wonder at the murals, which depicted a major battle. An army of united creatures fought against two-legged, furless beasts. Theo stared at the painting in macabre fascination. He knew without being told that the two-legged beings were Urzoks.

Theo had only caught glimpses of them in the dark at Lokni. Here he could see them depicted clearly, wielding battle axes, swords and cudgels; some were mounted on horses, others drove chariots and still others attacked on foot. Without their tools and armor and contraptions, they appeared no more threatening than any other beast.

"What battle is this?" he asked.

"The Battle of Haganor, when Southern Mankahar was lost," said a voice from the other side of the room.

They turned, and Theo was shocked to see a specimen of the very beast depicted in the murals. His slate-grey beard had been tamed into two braids, while his hair hung in dignified waves past his shoulders. His rich purple robe was belted at the waist with a horsehair sash. A number of warriors and attendants flanked him, including a shaggy wolf dressed in a breast plate and leg guards made of hammered silver, and a female stoat with pale eyes and onyx earrings that marked her as someone of rank.

"The battle where the first emperor Dakus won control over Mankahar. They call it the Final Pacification, but perhaps we can reshape history," the old Urzok said.

Brune removed his helmet and bowed his head. "Lord Noshi," he said, trying to keep his face calm while his voice surged with joy at seeing his mentor.

At this name Indigo and Manneki bowed as well, but Theo stood and stared. No one had told him that the Order's leader was an Urzok.

"What's wrong with you?" Indigo hissed, tugging at his jerkin. "That's Lord Noshi, High Priest of the Order!"

Noshi motioned with his hands for them to stand up. "Enough with ceremony. We've waited a long time for you, and now that you're here we shouldn't stifle our joy beneath decorum." He held his arms open, and the bear needed little urging to wrap the priest in a tight hug.

"Lord Noshi, you always said I was slow but reliable."

Lord Noshi smiled. "Brune, reliability is worth a little time. Now introduce me to those who have come to defend Mount Mahkah and the Order."

Brune motioned to Indigo and Theo. They stepped forward, Indigo more assured while Theo held back.

"Indigo, Princess of Alvareth, welcome. We feared you lost."

"I would've been, had it not been for Brune." Indigo replied. At an indignant look from Manneki she hastily added, "And of course Theo and Manneki."

Lord Noshi chuckled, then turned to Theo. "Theo, is it? We've waited a long time for you. For all of you." Noshi scrutinized Theo for a moment longer, then shifted his attention to Manneki.

"And who's this? You've decided to bring us an extra apprentice, Brune?"

The monkey puffed himself up to his full height, and held one fist to his chest. "I Manneki the Warrior, here to become an Ihaktu!"

Lord Noshi chuckled. "Well, Aktu's cause needs more souls with your fighting spirit. We welcome you to Ralgayan, Manneki the Warrior."

Manneki's eyes blazed with satisfaction, and both Indigo and Theo had trouble suppressing laughter.

Lord Noshi indicated the grizzled wolf by his side. "May I introduce you to Commander Tarq, the Order's finest general, and Lady Drewyn, the last of the Ralgayan royal family."

"Welcome," the stoat said, her earrings chiming to her words. "Ralgayan is honored to have you."

"Now that all the apprentices are here," the commander announced, "we'll convene the war council."

Lord Noshi raised a hand. "But before that, we shall make sure you are fed, and introduce you to the other apprentices."

~

They were served a hurried but satisfying meal of chestnut and leek stew, which they all dug into with little decorum. They were joined by the seven other apprentices who crowded into the ancillary dining hall to meet the famed warrior princess and the one from beyond the known lands. Amongst them were Hazel and Lexa, two sleek and sharp-eyed foxes with an obvious rivalry; a lithe and soft-spoken lynx whose name was Oleandala (but who insisted they just call her Olea); a shaggy-haired boar with curving tusks and an eye patch by the name of Wortimer; and the triplets—three jackals with lolling tongues and laughing, tapered faces. Theo couldn't tell who was Anu, Ganu, or Danu, and they seemed to find great amusement in confusing their peers. Theo found himself surrounded, being peppered with questions and examined like a piece of fruit at market.

"We thought you'd both been killed. Were you waylaid?" Hazel and Lexa asked.

"Is it true your home is past the Petrified Waves?" Ganu eyed him with interest.

"I heard that there's nothing but tar pits and desert out there," Anu added, his ash and tan face a mask of curiosity.

"Killed seventeen Urzoks. With just my tusks. Have a scar from each one," Wortimer grunted. "You?"

Theo felt overwhelmed, although Indigo and Brune seemed in their element and Manneki basked in the glow of being amongst warriors. Theo was saved from his discomfort by the appearance of Lord Noshi and the armored wolf Tarq.

"Enough, you lot!" Tarq called above the excited din. "Let the new arrivals rest. They have much to learn about our defenses." At a firm wave of his hand, Lord Noshi sent the other apprentices into a reluctant retreat. He smiled at the remaining group.

"Now come with me. Commander Tarq and I will show you the rest of Ralgayan."

He and the commander led Brune, Theo, Indigo, and Manneki down to the central courtyard, where creatures great and small were busy at work weaving ropes, sorting blocks of stone and rubble, and sewing links of metal together with tough, woven reeds. Fires burned in pits where hulking porcupines, squirrels, and badgers sat hardening wooden spears, which they laid in growing piles.

Everywhere they looked there were signs of battle: servants scuttling from armories to storerooms, taking supplies up to the towers; soldiers shouting drill commands to their gathered brigades; the ring of hammers against metal, the rhythmic clack of bellows, and the loading of wagons bringing stones from the lakeshore.

"I didn't know that Ralgayan had so many inhabitants," Indigo remarked, looking about at the activity. Manneki stared with wide eyes at everything around him, scurrying to keep up as they strode behind Lord Noshi and Tarq.

"Over the last few years, more and more have come to find refuge at Ralgayan, for truly free lands are becoming scarcer," Tarq replied. "We knew this day would come. The emperor must control Ralgayan if he is to crush the Order and Mount Mahkah."

Theo noticed a scar that ran across the wolf's muzzle to the base of his nose, but it wasn't enough to hide a rugged grace in his voice and eyes.

"I'll show you our structures for defending the last free city," Commander Tarq said.

They had reached a tower on the eastern ramparts where a panoramic view of the surrounding lands and lake greeted them.

Rich farmland undulated in neat rows to the south and west, a patchwork of green and stubby brown where the harvests had been reaped and the fields lay in silent wait for the snows of winter. Snaking along the lakeshore were the tiny huts of fisher folk, where fish were being smoked over fires on great wooden racks.

The commander gestured to the land below with a nod of his grey head. "We have scouts who've been keeping an eye on the gathering Urzok forces, and in a day or so all these inhabitants will be within the castle walls. They've been working day and night to stock provisions for the castle, and in their spare time we've been trying to train the young and even the old basic fighting skills."

Brune looked grim. "We could've used Queen Mercusa's support. But I'm afraid all who will march for Ralgayan already have."

Commander Tarq said quietly, "Then this is truly the Order's last stand. We must all fight the Urzoks with everything we have. Even if we die trying."

"Faith, Commander Tarq." Lord Noshi smiled at Theo with kind reassurance. "Aktu will not abandon us in our last hour. She will send a sign. You shall see."

CHAPTER FORTY-ONE

He was standing on a mountain cliff as the world rushed by. Clouds roiled and tumbled over each other, and the air sang of lightning. Lokni was burning, giant tongues of flame lighting the sky. Burnt and dying villagers stumbled from the flames, and then he could make out a face: Father Oaks.

The old rabbit's ears and whiskers were singed, and his face was a mask of pain. Behind him the familiar, grotesque beast, half feline half bird, emerged from the flames. Its jaws opened as it lunged and tore into his grandfather.

Father Oaks spoke, but his voice was not his own. "Know yourself, and I will show you the Library of Elshon."

"No! No word-catching!" Theo bolted awake, his breathing shallow and his paws damp with sweat. He was in a simple but comfortable room, sunlight streaming through the shutters of a nearby window. He sat up and tried to slow the frightened beating of his heart.

The door opened with a loud creak.

Manneki's head popped around the corner, and his brows knit in an annoyed frown. "No more sleep! You must up, up, up! There is war council!"

He had overslept. Theo threw off his blankets and began

pulling on his boots.

Theo followed Manneki through several corridors and down three sets of staircases. They ended up in a large central garden with rows of towering beech trees. Leafless boughs curved over a marble amphitheatre.

Lord Noshi, Commander Tarq, and several lords sat at the high table, while the apprentices sat on stone benches flanking them. Brune and several other bears, wearing their signature helmets marking them as messengers of the Order, stood against the trees.

Theo and Manneki found vacant seats next to Indigo and tried to slide in discreetly. Several of the apprentices snickered.

"Maybe your special talent is sleeping," Indigo whispered, teasing.

Theo flushed and noticed that Lord Noshi had paused in what he was saying to take in the tardy newcomers. The leader continued once they were settled.

"What we lack in numbers, we make up for in strategy," the old man continued. "My brother's forces will feel confident in their sheer numbers, but we can use that against them. Tarq will explain."

The gathered Council thumped their paws against benches to show approval as Tarq stepped forward.

"Knowing that we are outnumbered, the Urzoks will expect us to defend, not attack," the wolf began, his deep voice rolling out amongst his gathered listeners. "We shall bring the battle to them, and give ourselves the best advantage. That of surprise."

"The walls are our best defense, Commander Tarq," a voice piped up from the benches. Theo saw a grizzled buzzard with suspicious eyes. "You want us to give that up and just march on the Urzoks?"

The wolf smiled, his teeth flashing white in his graying muzzle. "No, Lord Ibwa. I don't. There's a reason Ralgayan has withstood the empire for so long. It's the northernmost post, but it also has a secret weapon."

~

After Lady Drewyn arranged a quick breakfast for them, she and Commander Tarq led the apprentices and Lord Noshi down the castle keep, to a steep stone staircase that coiled into the bowels of the castle. They needed oil lamps to light their way, and the ceiling was low enough that Brune had to stoop.

At last they reached a thick yew door, which Drewyn opened with a large key from a ring on her belt. "This is Ralgayan's best kept secret."

The door opened onto a cold, flat stretch of pebbled beach by the lake. A brisk winter wind whipped the surface into white caps, while a lone heron fished the shallow pools. Theo looked back up the staircase in amazement. The inhabitants of Castle Ralgayan had tunneled a passageway some nine hundred feet down the cliff.

Lady Drewyn smiled at their wonder. "My great-grandfather had it built. In case of sieges. He wanted to build more, but this alone took over four hundred moles to tunnel, and several years to complete. Castle Ralgayan stands on very hard sandstone. By the end there was no one willing to desert their fields to attempt a second one."

Brune stretched his cramped back and stood looking out over the water. He turned to Commander Tarq. "This is the secret weapon?"

The commander nodded. "With this passageway, we can raid the Urzoks. They won't be expecting us to attack, at night, with a small force. My wolves and the jackals will see to the raid, draw them out early, but we'll need all the apprentices helping to defend the city." The wolf turned to each of them. "Wortimer, we'll need you positioned at the main gate to the castle for when they break through. Olea and Indigo, you'll help Brune as part of the defense in the lower bailey that leads to the rest of Ralgayan. Once the fighting reaches that, it's likely to be messy. The archers will be able to offer little support then. Hazel, Lexa, you two will join the archers on the walls and behind the arrow loops. Jackals, we're relying on you to scout the camps so we can plan a raid."

"What about me?" Theo asked.

Tarq and Lord Noshi exchanged glances. The High Priest placed a hand on Theo's shoulder. "For now, you'll help the infirmary. The healers will need to prepare supplies and equipment."

"You saying the rabbit doesn't fight?" Wortimer said.

"His place is not in battle," Noshi replied.

No one dared contradict Lord Noshi, but Theo could feel the resentment radiating from his fellow apprentices. His ears burned. He should have known. Lord Noshi, Tarq, all of them thought he would never make a warrior, and now they'd said so in front of everyone. Just like Father Oaks had. He could feel a shift in the way the other apprentices looked at him. He was no longer a fellow comrade. He was a coward who would hide in the safety of the castle while they faced the enemy.

"How many do the Urzoks number?" Indigo hurried to change the subject.

Tarq's eyes narrowed. "There has been news of several new Urzok forces moving north."

"How many? Do we know?" Brune growled.

"The guards estimate at least eight hundred amassing on the forest lines," the Commander said. "Though the herons and other birds that bring us news have reported several different battalions, each about one thousand strong, moving up from the south and east."

"Any sign of the emperor?" Lord Noshi asked.

Commander Tarq shook his head. "No. But Ornox will be here, that is certain."

Lord Noshi smiled. "Even for the killing of his own brother, he sends a henchman. I had thought him above that."

"There shall be no talk of you being killed, Lord Noshi," Brune grumbled. "Not while I can swing an axe and the commander here has teeth in his head. We shall drive them into the earth, or go to Aktu free."

~

When Lord Ornox arrived in the late afternoon, the camp was already overflowing into the forests that bordered Castle Ralgayan.

Soldiers labored alongside slaves to hammer stakes into the half frozen ground. Horses nickered, their breath bursts of white as they were brushed down after hard rides from strongholds around Mankahar. Commanders barked orders to soldiers who marked out square delineations for the various battalions. Flags were set up to demarcate the different brigades, and a group of foot soldiers cleared nearby trees for space and for battering rams. The camp was a raucous melee of shouts, hammering, and the ring of axes against wood.

Agacheta's scarlet and black tent sat in the center of it all, flanked by a set of sentries. Lord Ornox's banner snarled and cracked in the biting wind as he approached. Soldiers saluted, then melted away before his army. Somewhere a horn sounded to announce his arrival. Yod walked alongside his master's steed.

Dismounting at his daughter's tent, Lord Ornox tossed the reins to Yod. "Make sure the dwellings are erected properly and that the pacification team has everything they need. If anyone enters this tent or disturbs me while I am inside, I will have you and the intruder fed to the dogs. Is that understood?"

Yod bowed his head. "Of course, master."

Lord Ornox pushed the tent flap aside and stepped in. He allowed a moment for his eyes to adjust to the dim interior.

Agacheta stood leaning over a table, studying sketches of the surrounding landscape. In the corner a dun-colored rabbit paused in devouring a piece of pickled cabbage, his tail raised in apprehension at the sight of Lord Ornox.

Agacheta looked up, first in annoyance, and then in recognition. She stood and touched her forehead to his fingers. "Father."

Lord Ornox withdrew his hand. "You've taken to keeping pets?"

"He is the omatje's brother."

Lord Ornox's eyes darted to Harlan, who swallowed and made a hesitant bow. "How much have you told him? Words like that should not be used lightly."

"He can be trusted," Agacheta said. "He will help us capture his brother."

The rabbit prostrated himself. "Your Excellency."

Lord Ornox reached down and grabbed Harlan by the scruff, lifting him off the floor. Harlan whimpered as he was brought to within inches of Lord Ornox's appraising eyes.

"Father, you really needn't—"

"You're sure this one's not an omatje?"

"I'm sure."

Lord Ornox turned to her. "Keeping prey as pets turns you into one of them. He should be pacified at Nyatha as soon as possible."

Harlan kicked out in fear.

"If he was pacified, he wouldn't be able to deliver us Ralgayan," she said.

Lord Ornox dropped Harlan to the ground and crossed his arms. "I'm listening."

"When the great general Bromhein conquered Alamae a century ago," Agacheta explained, "it wasn't with swords and weapons, but through an eagle dressed in swan feathers."

The warlord's eyes narrowed in understanding. "The castle, once we're inside, should be an easy win, but we must ensure that the two rabbits and the messenger don't escape. You've confirmed they're inside? And that we cannot be surprised by reinforcements from Mount Mahkah?"

Agacheta shook her head. "My soldiers have burned all the boats along the shore. The scouts have been watching the castle day and night. Not even a field mouse moves in or out without my knowing it."

"Good. Make sure your soldiers know their orders. The female can be killed, as long as we have her body, but the omatje must be captured alive." He paused. "And Caldrik? He knows what to do?"

"He has already left, Father. With the cargo."

A tight smile broke Lord Ornox's stern countenance, and he reached out to touch his daughter's cheek. "Look at you, grown and leading your first siege."

She flushed, unable to remember the last time her father had ever paid her a compliment. "You know I love a battle as much as anyone, but why take Ralgayan now? If what you say about the powers of the omatje is true, we already have what we want, we don't need the other."

Lord Ornox's face hardened back to its usual mask. "And leave Noshi with an omatje? Leave Ralgayan standing? I thought you had more war sense than that. We must capture the one called Theo alive, you understand?"

"Yes, Father."

"And one more thing, Agacheta." Lord Ornox hesitated at the tent flap. "I have overheard the soldiers' gossiping about the so called prophecy, and whether these animals can really bring down the empire. Be careful what you say to your soldiers and what rumors brew in the camps." He paused. "We don't want word about the omatje getting back to the emperor."

Lord Ornox left, shouting to Yod for his horse. Agacheta turned to the rabbit.

"Are you all right?"

"Yes," Harlan swallowed, rubbing at his bruised neck. "I thought he was going to break my bones."

"I wouldn't have let him do that, Harlan." Agacheta pulled her knife from her boot and checked the blade against a finger. A drop of blood flowered on her skin. "But have you ever heard the story of how General Bromhein conquered Alamae?"

CHAPTER FORTY-TWO

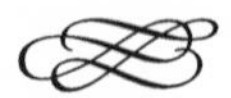

"Sir Theo! Wait!"

The scullery maid, a plump young raccoon, labored across the courtyard after him.

Theo had been so lost in his own thoughts helping the castle healer move bandages and other supplies that at first he didn't hear her. It didn't help that he also had a headache from a sleepless bout of nightmares where the Griffin had devoured him, bones and all, while Indigo and Brune watched and did nothing.

"You forgot this, Sir Theo," the maid panted when she reached him, holding out a small cloth-wrapped object in her paw. "I found it in your jerkin while doing the laundry."

Theo took it and pulled aside the cloth. Inside lay the tortoiseshell mirror that the Grey Rock had given him.

"Almost threw it out I did. Is it valuable?"

"I'm not sure," Theo answered. "But thank you."

The maid nodded and was about to go, then added, "Forgive me being forward, but may I keep the cloth?"

Theo looked at the fabric in his paw. "This?"

"Yes," the maid turned shy, her black-ringed eyes downcast. "As a good-luck charm."

"Why would this be a good-luck charm?" the rabbit asked, confused.

"Because it belonged to an Ihaktu."

Theo felt a sharp sense of discomfort. "I'm not an Ihaktu. I don't bring luck to anyone. I'm nothing but an ordinary rabbit who's only good at making bandages and dabbing cuts."

The maid held out her paw. "If it's all the same to you, Sir Theo, I'd still like to have it. You've come all this way to fight for us. That makes you a warrior in Ralgayan."

He looked at her open, sincere face and couldn't refuse her. She burst into a wide grin, thanked him, and rushed off with her trophy.

Theo stared at the tortoiseshell in his paws. What was it but a piece of old shell? Yet the tortoise had asked him to guard it with his life, and what had he done? Left it unawares in his jacket, to be tossed away by the laundress. Some worthy rabbit he was.

He sat down on a stone bench, dejected.

"You're wrong, you know."

He looked up and saw Indigo standing in a doorway, arms crossed.

"About what?"

"You're not just good at making bandages and dabbing cuts. Why'd you try and dissuade her from keeping that dirty old cloth?"

"Because she thinks I'm something I'm not. I don't want to deceive her."

"Who's deceiving her? That's not deception, Theo. It's hope. You're going to have to get used to being a symbol of hope for others. It does get easier."

"I'm not a fighter, or whatever everyone thinks I am. I'm certainly no symbol of hope," Theo said.

"You're just having battle jitters. You've been chosen to defend Ralgayan and train at Mount Mahkah for a reason, Theo. Have faith in yourself."

He didn't answer.

"In the meantime, why don't I help you with all this? What needs to be moved?"

"I can manage," Theo said, standing.

"I don't mind, you know."

"Thank you, but no."

Indigo shrugged. "I'll see you for evening meal then. Make sure you're there. It's the jackals' honorary night before their raid."

She walked away across the courtyard, accepting greetings from the Ralgayan inhabitants who recognized the princess and asked for her blessing.

From behind him, someone let out a hearty chuckle. "She fancies you."

Theo turned, and saw Lord Noshi standing near an archway, his thick white hair braided into two plaits. For once the old Urzok was alone.

"Me? Hardly," Theo muttered, embarrassed.

Lord Noshi chuckled as he walked up to Theo. The rabbit still couldn't get used to the sight of Noshi's face—the nakedness of it, with only two scraggly strips of hair above the eyes, like grass sprouting from the cracks of a fallen oak; the square shaped teeth and oval ears that seemed designed purely for holding his hair back from his face.

"And you have it even worse for her, if I'm not mistaken," Lord Noshi added.

"I'd better return to the infirmary," Theo said, trying to cover his discomfort.

"Is everything alright, Theo?"

Theo thought of brushing off his unease and letting the old Urzok go on his way, but something in the craggy face made him choose honesty instead. "I think my being here is a mistake."

"Maybe you're right," Lord Noshi folded his hands in his robes. "And if it is, what then?"

Theo hadn't expected agreement, and it took him a while to respond. "If I'm not going to fight, I have no place here. You need fighters and qualified healers, not some apprentice who can barely wield a sword. I'm not what everyone thinks I am. And if I don't join the fight, everyone will think I'm a coward."

"And you think all fights are by the sword?"

"This one is, isn't it?" Theo asked.

The old man cocked his head, weighing Theo's words. "What do you propose?"

"I just think if I'm not fighting along with the other Ihaktus, I should go."

Noshi shook his head. "I don't think you know how much we need you. Let me show you something to change your mind."

~

They climbed a set of stairs and walked through several corridors, the guards and maids bowing to Noshi and Theo as they passed. When they reached a set of wide double doors, its purple surface inlaid with patterns of silver and ebony, Noshi pushed them open and ushered Theo into a spacious chamber with a domed ceiling.

Thick woven rugs covered the floor, and a small stone brazier blazed in the center. Arranged around it were low tables, their surfaces clear except for a small wooden box. The room's lone window, framed by thick woolen curtains, looked out over the frigid lake far below. A short sword hung on one wall, while along the other a shelf held bowls that emanated pungent juniper and sage smoke.

"They calm the senses," Noshi explained, seeing him wrinkle his nose. "This is my prayer room."

Theo tried to wrestle the logic of such a place. A room dedicated to prayer was entirely strange to him.

"I come here when I need peace and space to think," Noshi moved across to the window, and drew a heavy tapestry across it, blocking their view. "I come here when I need to ask Aktu for guidance."

"Alone?" Theo asked.

"Oh yes," Noshi said, turning back to him. "I can't take those bickering council members all day, after all."

Theo found himself relaxing at the old Urzok's levity. There was something soothing in that harsh, naked face after all.

"Sit," Noshi said, motioning towards the grouped tables. "The box has something that belongs to you."

Theo gave him a puzzled look, but sat down. The box's unmarked, unfinished surface didn't look familiar. Theo pulled it towards him, and the bottom opened, sending its inner treasure clanging onto the table surface.

Theo knew Noshi was watching his reaction, but he couldn't help it. He instinctively flinched as the jeweled collar bounced on the table and then fell with a heavy thud onto the carpet next to him.

Theo looked up, his eyes full of questions.

"I know who you are, but you needn't be afraid," Noshi said. "I have sought you for quite some time."

Noshi made a low birdcall, and from the lintel over the door, an owl swept down to land on the old Urzok's shoulder. Theo would have recognized the owl anywhere, but especially now, with the collar open and winking before him.

"You know that your skill is currently unpopular amongst many," Noshi commented, moving forward and folding his legs until he sat opposite Theo. The owl hopped down onto the table, settling himself in a spot close to the brazier's warm flames.

Theo nodded. "Father Oaks and Brune have told me I could be killed for it."

Lord Noshi sighed. "That is unfortunately true. I'm afraid most on the council feel that way, but I think Aktu has greater plans for you."

His words brought up buried fears. Would Brune want him killed? He thought of Kuno, Brune's paws twisting his own brother's neck. And what of Indigo and Manneki? That night Indigo had talked of her mother's death, and how she hated all omatjes. Theo looked from the old Urzok to the owl, but the bird offered no help. He appeared to be dozing from the warmth of the fire.

"Take another look, Theo." Noshi pushed the box closer to the rabbit.

Theo picked it up, hesitant, and turned it around. "There's nothing else inside."

Lord Noshi reached forward, and tapped the box on one of the corners. "Sometimes you have to turn things inside out to truly understand them."

Theo looked closer at the edge, and realized what Noshi meant. The box had no nails—rather, it had joints that fit together like seamless teeth. A gentle tug, and one side popped open in his paws. He opened all the sides, until the box lay flat on the table, its inside surfaces revealing a complex array of neatly carved script.

"This belonged to the last head of the Order." Noshi leaned forward and refolded the box. "She said it contained a great secret, a lost secret."

"You want me to release the words?" He didn't think Noshi would trap him, but it had been so long since he'd released words in front of another that it felt awkward, almost rude.

"You're the only one who can," Noshi replied. "Aktu has told me that whoever understands this box, will have the ability to save Mankahar."

Theo looked back down at the hinged pieces of carved wood before him. "But that doesn't make sense."

"What doesn't?"

"It says 'To him who speaks the truth will be revealed the Library of Elshon.'" Theo looked up. "The Library exists?"

Noshi reached forward to tap the carvings. "Does it say where the Library is?"

Theo read further. "No. Simply that he who speaks the truth, and finds Elshon, shall bring peace."

"Then it is clear," Noshi said, leaning back and placing his hands on his knees. "You must find the Library of Elshon, and end the war."

Theo stared at him, dumbfounded. "You think it means me?"

"Who else? Admit that you are an omatje, and then the road to Elshon will be revealed," Lord Noshi said.

"Admit to whom?" Theo felt a lump of dread lodge in his chest. "You said yourself, most on the council would wish me dead. Unless you could protect me?"

"I could most certainly try," Noshi sighed. "But unfortunately, I do not have the influence that I used to."

Theo saw that the owl was awake now, his head cocked in Theo's direction. "I don't see how my admitting this and risking death will reveal the path to Elshon."

Noshi smiled. "Find your faith, Theo. Aktu would not bring you so far, to have you perish amongst friends."

"That's the thing," Theo said, quiet. "I would lose my friends if they knew what I was."

"But if it was to save Mankahar, wouldn't you do it?"

Theo kept silent, his heart thudding. He wanted nothing more than to go back to this morning, before he knew that Noshi had sent the owl, the collar, before he knew any of this.

"You have a choice, Theo," Noshi said softly. "You do not yet know how words can serve you. If you wish to leave now, I will not blame you. But I have an army of fighters who can wield a sword, while you are the only one I know who can understand the Forbidden Language, Aktu's language. You can find the Library of Elshon, and use it."

"Finding the Library won't be in time to save Ralgayan," Theo said.

"Accepting one's power to act is never easy." Noshi rose to his feet and walked over to the sword hanging on the wall. He gently removed it, and brought it back to the table. "If you do decide you prefer the sword to the Forbidden Language, then I will leave you with Q'orio. A blade my father gave me before he died, and one that will protect you in the coming battle." He laid it down next to the box. "I will leave you to think it through. But do hurry. We, and Mankahar, have little time left."

The Urzok motioned to the owl, who gave Theo another glance before spreading his wings and lifting himself onto his master's shoulder. The two left the chamber, letting the heavy purple door close behind them with what sounded to Theo like a death knell.

CHAPTER FORTY-THREE

The bugger was lucky to be alive, Brune thought, contemplating the shivering figure huddled by the fireplace. The visitor was swathed in a thick blanket, his fur plastered to his forehead and dirty tear tracks still visible down his cheeks.

Lady Drewyn sat next to him, spooning corn and carrot stew into his mouth.

"A full stomach helps all wounds," she said. "Is your arm better?"

The visitor winced as he tried to straighten it and failed. "It's in a bad way, isn't it?"

The stoat smiled. "It's a deep wound, but with care you'll be as good as new."

She took the now empty bowl and hurried to return it to the kitchens as Indigo entered. Harlan sat a little straighter.

"You're alone," Brune commented.

Indigo tried to hide the worry that dogged her. "I went back to the courtyard and asked around. Someone said that he'd come back here, and that was the last he'd seen of him."

Brune frowned. "Yet no one here's seen him?"

Indigo shrugged.

Harlan watched the exchange from beneath his blanket. "I hope Theo's all right," he said. "He never knew how to defend himself. I always worried when he was off alone."

"It must have been hard for you when you thought he'd died," Indigo commented.

"I was devastated," Harlan agreed. "As soon as we heard he was alive, we knew that we had to send someone and warn you."

"We are grateful," Brune said. "Three days is short, but we'll make do and prepare as best we can. I'm sorry that Theo himself isn't here to welcome you."

"Princess, would you escort me to my room? I'd like to hear all about how my brother has been doing since he left Willago."

Indigo looked to Brune. "Will you search for Theo, then?"

At Brune's nod Indigo helped Harlan up and together they followed a palace maid out.

Brune watched them go, then frowned as he gazed out the window. A steady flow of villagers came in the city gates. Yesterday they had started as a trickle, then turned to a flood when the Urzok tents had first appeared, like dark smudges, on the edges of the forest. There was no mistaking the signs of impending battle.

The sun was almost set. Where was Theo?

~

He wove his way against crowds flowing the other direction towards Ralgayan's safety, and passed the gates just as the guardsmen sounded the last bell to mark the city's closure. In his mind, Theo triple checked that he had everything he needed: his flints, a knife, some food he had pilfered from Noshi's prayer room.

He had decided that if he was to leave, it had to be before nightfall, before Noshi could forcibly reveal him to the council. The city gates closed at sunset, but leaving now he could join the last of the raccoon fisherfolk who still left the city at nights to stock food. A part of him had been tempted to scratch on Indigo or Brune's door, but he had thought better of it. How would he explain his leaving? Better to just disappear, slip off and be cursed as a deserter before being forgotten.

His leaving was best for everyone—Ralgayan needed fighters, not omatjes. Staying would only risk his own life. And Noshi's plan to make him confess made no sense, how could admitting his word catching to anyone win the battle?

Theo renewed his grip on his pack and forced himself to keep walking towards the lake, towards the unknown.

CHAPTER FORTY-FOUR

The jackals and their select company of wolves left the castle ramparts under the thick cover of night. Drewyn and several of her attendants helped them leave through the lakeshore passage, while Tarq and his aides gave last minute instructions. Trailing a safe distance behind was Harlan. Having heard the rumor that the jackals would become heroes that night, Harlan decided it was best to find out what he could, in case he could glean something of use to Agacheta, or himself.

Along the way to the staircase, he had pieced together from their conversation the plans to infiltrate the enemy camps, but didn't know of how they would get past the Urzok sentries. Until he saw the staircase.

While they made last minute armor checks, Harlan turned and slipped back into the shadows. When he was certain he'd put enough corridors between himself and the scouting party, he clambered up the nearest window.

He clenched his teeth at the searing pain from his arm, and for the millionth time cursed Agacheta and all her kind.

She'd insisted that the enemy would smell a ruse if he was unwounded, and had personally dealt him the deep cut to his arm. And she'd been right. The inhabitants of Ralgayan had immediately taken him in when he'd pleaded for help, then brought him up to the castle when he fed them the story that Agacheta had coached him to say: he was Theo's brother, he'd been captured by the Urzoks, but had escaped to warn Theo of their plans.

Harlan had been bracing himself for the difficult task of convincing Theo to trust him and couldn't believe his good luck when they couldn't locate the brat. Even better, the bear didn't recognize him—they had seen each other but briefly at the River Tithe, and it had been dark, but still ....

Peering up out the window, Harlan took stock of which direction he was facing. He saw the lake on his right, its surface black and impenetrable. He mentally retraced his steps and surmised that the passageway must curve a good deal if it came up to the back supply rooms, yet ended down below at the lake shore.

This was a juicy piece of knowledge, one that he'd stumbled on purely by luck. But where exactly was the door, and how well was it hidden? Would Agacheta be satisfied if he informed her that there was a secret passageway, without knowing its entrance? Harlan cursed for not having followed the jackals down to the exit.

He hurried back to his room, finding his way by retracing the markings he'd made on the walls with a piece of rough stone. When he reached his room he felt under the straw mattress for the amulet Agacheta had given him. He pocketed it and crept back out, easing the door closed behind him.

The castle inhabitants were almost all asleep, while the growl of thunder sounded from across the lake. He made his way to the round foyer in the center of the castle, where hallways led off in different directions to the front courtyard, the guest rooms, and the audience chamber.

A central hearth in the middle still held smoldering coals, which cast a faint glow in an otherwise completely dark space. Standing on the other side was Indigo, still dressed in her sleeveless jerkin, worn britches and woven boots, her short sword at her waist.

Such a pity, Harlan sighed. He would've asked Agacheta to spare her if he thought that she would agree.

Hearing his sigh, Indigo turned.

"I was worried you wouldn't come," Harlan said, looking about to make sure no one else was around.

"You said I was in danger."

"There's something I must tell you, Princess. About Theo."

Again he let his eyes dart about, to stress the importance of what he was about to divulge. He motioned for her to come close so he could whisper it to her.

As she leaned in, Harlan's paw crept into his pocket, closing around the amulet. He slipped off a protective cap that concealed the thin spike on its edge.

As he spoke, she hardly felt the prick of pain on the scruff of her neck. She was too shocked by the words Harlan poured into her ear to notice the poison seeping into her blood.

CHAPTER FORTY-FIVE

Indigo blinked. Harlan could see she was struggling to corral her thoughts, make sense of his words.

"I—I have to find Brune," she said. "And warn him."

Harlan shook his head. "I've told him. He's searching for Theo now."

"Why didn't you tell us before?" she whispered.

"There were servants, and who knows who else, listening. I didn't want to cause a panic, or let Theo on to the fact that his secret was out. He might've disappeared or done something drastic."

"Theo wouldn't run away, he's … he's not like that," Indigo murmured.

"He's an omatje, Princess, who knows what he'd do? He ran away from his own village, remember. And lied to all of you for all this time. He'll do anything to protect himself. You should get some rest. We can discuss what to do tomorrow."

Nodding, she allowed him to grasp her arm and escort her back to her chamber, where he helped her find her unsteady way into the bed.

He stood watching her succumb to her last sleep. At least it would be painless. He hoped.

When he locked the door behind her, he checked the corridor to make sure they hadn't been observed, then headed for the secret stairwell. He'd have to hurry. Daylight was but a few hours away.

~

The cobblestone alleys were quiet but filled with a palpable energy that hung heavy in the chill night air, for many knew that a secret scouting expedition on the Urzoks was planned tonight. Prayers were offered for the jackals' success. The full moon found no admirers, being greeted by windows closed and barred, with the occasional face appearing at a cracked shutter.

Brune lumbered between the houses and shops of the smithing district. Most of the dwellings were filled to capacity. The citizens of Ralgayan had unconditionally opened their homes to their neighbors, knowing that in a war like this, to deny sanctuary was to assist death.

Brune sniffed the air. It smelled like a storm, and for the first time he noticed a heavy buildup of clouds closing in from the direction of the lake. He hoped the scouts were safe. They had to be, if Ralgayan was to have a chance at victory. He had to finally admit to himself that he was worried, and not just about the Urzoks. If Theo didn't appear soon he'd be forced to alert Lord Noshi and admit that he'd lost his charge.

As if the very thought of the old priest had conjured him, Lord Noshi's figure became visible through the dark. The ancient sage, wrapped in a woolen cloak, stood in a small square with his back to Brune, gazing at the moon.

Brune approached on silent paws and stood behind his mentor.

"Aktu is great, is She not?" Lord Noshi's eyes never left the heavens. "She gives us the most exquisite beauty, even on the brink of our darkest hour."

The bear gazed up as well. "Aktu forgive me, I would trade Her beauty for a few thousand more soldiers and a crippling plague on Ornox's army. And to have Kuno back."

Lord Noshi pointed a gnarled finger. "Look, Brune!"

The moon's face grew dark, as if it was drawing a veil across itself. The clouds drifted across until it engulfed the moon and they were drowned in darkness, with not even an outline of the bright orb that just moments ago had dominated the skies. Just when Brune thought that perhaps he had witnessed a heavenly death, a sliver of light cracked open. It grew and expanded like a laughing mouth, until the darkness had been chased away and the moon gleamed forth again in rotund glory, touching their faces with cold, fresh light.

"Aktu has heard you, Brune," Lord Noshi said. "She tells us that sometimes the darkness is our light."

Brune decided there was no point in evading his mentor. "Lord Noshi, I cannot find Theo."

"He is where he needs to be, Aktu will guide him," Lord Noshi said.

The bear tried to contain his worry. "Perhaps Aktu could let us know where both of them are then."

"She will, Brune. Come, walk with me."

"My Lord, I should find Theo. He has a tendency to wander into trouble."

"Maybe trouble is what he needs," Lord Noshi began walking. "Come."

Brune sighed, but fell into step next to the old man.

They walked in silence until they had looped around the city's meandering side streets and reached the front bailey, its wide square girded by the city gates. Here Lord Noshi stopped and surveyed the area. Apart from a few sentries high above in the ramparts, the bailey was deserted.

"Do you know when I realized you no longer had need of me?" Lord Noshi asked.

The bear began to protest, but his mentor held up a restraining hand.

"I know what you would say, to coddle my pride, and there is no need. I am quickly becoming a useless old man. Deceived by my false sense of wisdom, as so many on the Council remind me." Lord Noshi's eyes were warm in the cold night. "I realized you had no need of me when you told me you wanted to join the Order, become its messenger, and I could see you weren't saying it to please me. You said it because your gut told you to, and you listened instead of doubted. I knew then you were no longer a cub."

"I remember. Commander Tarq refused to even speak to me until he had your permission." Brune smiled despite himself. They'd had long arguments about his and Kuno's future, the old mentor quietly alarmed that his two adopted protégés might commit themselves to a cruel path out of misguided obligation.

Lord Noshi placed a hand on the bear's chest, his gnarled fingers almost disappearing in the fur. "Brune, listen to that voice that told you to join the Order. Heed what it says. Theo will soon need you more than ever, I think."

Brune watched his beloved mentor walk away towards the castle's gates, his shadow behind him fading and then disappearing as the clouds returned. This time with thunder.

The skiff nudged the lake shore, its lantern casting a halo of light. Theo clambered aboard, glad to have found a fisher before the rain broke. The skiff's owner, a rough faced raccoon smelling of wind and trout, leaned on his oar.

"Crossing's usually worth two pots of beer. Or wine, if you have it."

Theo cursed silently. He hadn't thought to bring anything but what he needed to survive.

"I've flints, and some food. That's all."

The raccoon sniffed in disappointment, then brightened. "What about that there? In your pocket."

Theo looked down. He pulled out the tortoise shell, catching his murky, distorted reflection in the lantern light.

"Never seen one of those," the raccoon commented, leaning close. "But it'll do."

The raccoon plunged his oar into the water and pushed against the shore. The skiff's prow scraped the lakebed, and thunder growled from above, but all Theo could hear was Indigo's voice: *You think like prey, so you act like prey. A rabbit has a brave heart.*

He shoved the shell into an inner pocket, grabbed his pack, and jumped over the skiff's edge, landing waist deep in icy lake water.

The raccoon rushed to the prow, calling after him, but he had already splashed his way to shore, and started back towards Ralgayan.

CHAPTER FORTY-SIX

By the time Harlan had descended to the lakeshore entrance, rain had begun to fall in fat, heavy drops.

He cursed as he realized that the door was bolted shut with a massive iron lock. Why had he assumed that the door could be opened from the inside?

He struggled with it for some time, but decided that if the Urzoks wanted in, they could bloody well break down the door. He fumbled in one of his shirt pockets and pulled out a smooth piece of hollow wood.

He put one end to his lips and blew, three times, in quick succession. It made no sound, and for a long while Harlan wondered whether this was some trick of Agacheta's.

A sleet-like rain now fell in angry, steady sheets, pock-marking the lake and turning the air so cold that it sucked the warmth from his bones. Harlan rubbed his paws together and blew on them, then peered out into the darkness beyond the door's grille.

He yelped, almost knocking over the lamp, as a great scarlet eye materialized on the other side, harsh and unblinking in its purplish leathery face.

Harlan mustered his voice. "This passage leads all the way up to the castle. Tell Agacheta the troops can come in here, as long as everyone's distracted by the main fight. There's a raid planned for tonight. Warn Agacheta."

The eye blinked once, and then the giant vulture took off into the night, the force of his wings sending rainwater splashing against the castle wall.

When he was sure the bird was gone, Harlan began the long climb back to the castle keep.

~

Rain hammered against the shutters of the castle windows as Theo cautiously made his way past a kitchen door with a faulty latch. He had managed to climb up beneath the drawbridge and find a sympathetic guard who recognized him as one of the twelve, and who had let him into the city.

Theo reached the stairways that led to the main foyer. He heard the common sounds of night: rhythmic snoring from the downstairs barracks, the occasional scurry of insect legs against rock or wood, the drip of water down some outside drainpipe.

But then he heard something else. At first he thought it was the patter of heavy raindrops against the cobblestones outside, but the rhythm didn't match that of the rain.

Hurried footsteps—coming closer. Not the ambling shuffle of someone returning to bed from the latrine.

Theo stood still in the foyer, unsure what rooted him to the ground. A long-eared figure emerged from the shadows in the corridor.

An impossible, but familiar figure.

"Harlan?" His surprise turned to confusion at the sight of his brother's bandaged limb. "What happened to your arm?"

"What, no joy at seeing your own brother?" Harlan held out his arms in a mock embrace. "You don't even know what's happened, do you?"

At Theo's confusion, Harlan growled.

"You and your word-catching destroyed Willago! They came and burned our houses, slaughtered us for meat! Slaughtered us, Theo, do you understand?"

His words hit like a hammer to the stomach. Theo forgot to breathe. Images of Pozzi, Walnut, neighbors, and Elders surfaced in his mind.

"We've been living a nightmare for the last season, and what've you been doing?" Harlan's voice turned vicious as he moved closer. "Look at you! Fatter than ever and well dressed, living in a castle and traveling with princesses!"

Theo dropped his pack to the ground, then seized him by the fur and shook him. His brother's surprised gasp of pain proved to them both that he was much stronger than when they'd last met.

"Where are they, Harlan? Are they here with you?"

Harlan broke free. "What would you care? You've never cared about anyone but yourself, but I'm going to make sure that we're spared. By giving the Urzoks what they want."

"Harlan, you can't give them what they want—do you know their plans for us?" Theo protested.

"If it means making you pay for everything you've done then by my reckoning it's a fair trade."

With that Harlan leapt, using his good side to pin Theo to the ground.

Theo gasped for air. His brother clawed with his uninjured paw at Theo's throat, tearing fur and raising welts, then sank his teeth into Theo's shoulder, drawing a cry of pain.

"It's your fault! You brought them on us!"

Small sparks burned themselves into Theo's vision as he felt the heat of his brother's pent-up rage. Harlan's paw continued to claw at Theo's neck, and only when his lungs started burning did Theo manage to come out of his shock and bite into Harlan's forearm.

His brother was taken by surprise, his attack checked. Harlan examined his bleeding limb, more stunned than pained.

"So you finally learned how to fight honorably," he smirked.

Before Theo could say anything Harlan threw himself into the fight again, but this time Theo was ready for him.

He could tell Harlan hadn't anticipated resistance, nor that Theo would exploit his brother's wounded arm. He dodged several of his brother's swings, then landed a sharp gouge to the bandaged limb before backing away.

"Harlan, listen—"

Harlan barreled into him with the brunt of his skull. He pushed Theo into the hearth, where they became a tangle of flying punches and kicking legs rolling in the cold ashes.

"I'm not going to suffer any more for your mistakes! You hear?"

"Listen to me!" Theo tried, and failed, to block a punch. "I'm sorry," Theo panted through a bleeding lip. "I'm sorry. I didn't mean for Father Oaks to send you away."

This seemed to enrage Harlan more. His blows grew wild. Drawing on moves he'd learned from Indigo, Theo managed to kick Harlan in the ribs, then maneuvered himself on top of him and gripped his head in a tight vice with his arm. Harlan struggled like a trapped wasp, but couldn't get enough leverage with his legs to wriggle free.

"You weren't sorry then, were you?" Harlan spat.

Theo fought the shame stinging him. His grip tightened around Harlan's neck. "I didn't know he would ask Gaweld to take you. I didn't."

Harlan managed a bitter laugh. "No? Then why'd you lie about the fire?"

Theo closed his eyes, but he couldn't close his ears. "I didn't lie."

"You said nothing! You let Father Oaks blame me for your mistake. Yours! I became Gaweld's brewing boy while you had everything easy."

"Easy? When did you ever let me have it easy, Harlan? I thought he would just thrash you, like you always did me." He'd wanted to give his brother a taste of his own medicine. Especially when Harlan had bullied him into the chore in the first place. He hadn't meant to leave the pot boiling for so long. He hadn't expected to get lost in a volume of Kalmac's histories. Letting Father Oaks blame Harlan for the destructive blaze that brought down half the warren had felt like a sweet, unexpected form of justice. And then over the years the lie had become truth.

Harlan managed to twist around and tear at Theo's shoulder with his teeth, drawing blood and forcing Theo to let go. Harlan stood, wiping at a split lip while Theo clutched at his wounded shoulder.

"And when you realized he wouldn't just thrash me? Did you speak up then?"

"I didn't understand what would happen, Harlan! I was young."

"And do you understand now?" his brother snapped. "That everything is your fault? My life, my being here, Willago destroyed. Was your word-catching worth it? Worth Father Oaks being taken away?"

Theo rushed him, tears of anger burning his eyes. Harlan snatched up a sharp piece of wood from the fire, and hurled it with vicious precision.

Theo tried to dodge, but too late. His brother had always been best at short arrow. He felt the edge of the wood tear into the flesh above his left eye, something warm and wet rushed into his vision, and then there was nothing.

CHAPTER FORTY-SEVEN

Just as Brune reached the castle gates, chilled and soaked from the sleet, the strident blast of a bugle sliced through the pre-dawn air like a knife.

The call came from the western tower, and soon other towers had picked up the cry, sounding the alarm as lanterns were lit and guards were roused from their posts.

A ragged shout from one of the western turrets struggled its way through the rain: "The Urzoks! They're advancing!"

Brune ran up the staircases that wound up to the parapet. The stones were icing over, but Brune's wide feet found purchase like a mountain goat's.

Lightning tore through the sky, charging the landscape with a sinister glow. The advancing army was a thick venomous river as it left the cover of the trees and began flowing towards Ralgayan, and the thunder of thousands of hooves mingled with the rumbles rolling out from the clouds.

Soon the castle was awash in the sound of horns and shouts, panicked voices and the pounding of boots.

Brune leaped down into the castle's main courtyard, where bells pealed and soldiers began arming themselves with pikes, spears, and arrow-filled quivers. As he strode across the foyer, he met Drewyn, who had donned simple robes and carried a lantern.

"The jackals haven't returned," she said, her voice strained. "It seems the mission has failed. Commander Tarq asks that you help him alert all the apprentices, get them to their positions."

Brune bared his teeth in frustration. "I can't. Theo is missing."

Drewyn's eyes widened. "Have you checked his chamber this morning?"

They hurried through the corridors towards the guest quarters, passing soldiers donning helmets and castle wards herding frightened youngsters to the keeps below.

When they arrived at the guest wing, Drewyn rushed to Indigo's room.

Throwing the door open, Brune scanned Theo's empty room. "Where in Aktu's name is he?"

"Brune!"

The bear hurried to Indigo's room. He entered to find Lady Drewyn shaking a prone and stiff Indigo.

"We need a healer, and quickly," Drewyn said. "She won't make mid-morning."

~

"Theo, you hear me, yes? Theo!"

Theo tried to focus but his eyes burned in their sockets. *Concentrate!*

He couldn't tell whether the monkey's faraway voice was real or just an apparition, but he found strength enough to groan.

"Theo! Theo, up here!"

Theo's vision cleared and he saw Manneki's concerned face. He was lying in a well, its sides slick with wet moss. His head throbbed where he'd been cut, and when he reached a paw to touch it he winced at the sticky swelling above his eye.

"Theo! You all right, yes?"

Theo pushed himself to stand. Bruised and battered, but no breaks. The well had dried out not long before, and mud had cushioned his short fall. Harlan had disposed of him in the most convenient way, but clearly hadn't checked the well's depth.

"Manneki, get me a rope!"

Manneki disappeared from the ledge and reappeared shortly with a thick coil of sturdy rope, his one good arm straining under the heavy load. He deposited it on the edge.

"Theo wait! I make it safe!"

The monkey picked up one end and scampered once around the well base, fastening it in a deft knot. He then pushed the remaining coils over the edge, and the long rope slid downwards to land in a messy heap at Theo's feet.

He grasped the cord in both paws and began to haul himself up, using his hind legs to brace and push against the slippery walls. When he reached the top Manneki pulled him over the edge onto safe ground.

Manneki began asking a slew of questions. Theo cut him off.

"What's that noise?"

"I try tell you! Urzoks, Theo! They attack now!"

"Where's Harlan?" Theo stood on his aching, unsteady legs.

"Manneki not know, not see him. Everything like beehive on fire!" Manneki gesticulated. "Everyone go to gates, and Brune not find Theo, ask Manneki and Drewyn to search!"

He followed the excited monkey out into the corridor, steadying himself against the walls as they went along. Manneki dashed ahead, bursting with nervous energy while Theo tried to ignore the searing throb of his forehead.

"I save your life, don't forget!" Manneki prodded Theo with a bony finger. "Manneki great bodyguard!"

Just then Lady Drewyn appeared from around the corner.

"Theo! Thank Aktu. What happened to your head?"

Before Theo could reply she turned and hurried back the way she'd come, motioning for them to follow. "A quick binding will have to do. We haven't time for anything else. Come, we must get you and Indigo to safety before the Urzoks siege the castle."

The way she said Indigo's name made Theo hesitate. "What's happened?"

Drewyn's expression darkened, but the rabbit couldn't get another word from her as they followed her back to the guest chambers.

When Theo saw her, his first reaction was relief. She lay stretched out on the pallet, surrounded by Brune, Lord Noshi, and several moles dressed in healers' robes. If not for the slight jerk of her chest as she drew in the odd breath, he would've thought her sleeping.

Theo's relief was replaced by dread. "What happened?"

"She's been poisoned with quell root," the chief healer said. "I'm afraid it's too late."

Theo looked at the princess's face. Her pupils had expanded so far that they had swallowed nearly all the green. "But quell root is a mild poison. It can be bled out."

"No, Theo, quell root is just the medium. This is what poisoned Kuno," Lord Noshi said.

"You mean she's going to become pacified?"

No one answered him, which was worse than if everyone had shouted the truth.

"You're all priests of Aktu, is there nothing in her powers that can stop this? Indigo might be the best Ihaktu fighter you have!"

Drewyn shook her head. "The chief healer is right. This poison took hold of her hours ago. There's nothing we can do against such a strong dose."

"We shall gather the funeral shrouds and make ready to send her soul to Aktu," the chief healer said, tucking his paws in his robe and motioning for his fellows to follow.

Theo cursed to himself and put a paw to Indigo's throat, feeling the weakened pulse. He then opened her mouth to peer at her tongue.

"Bring a lamp, boiling water, a sharp knife, cloths for tying, a bottle of your strongest fermented brew, and a basket of hollow reeds from the courtyard pond." Theo began rolling up Indigo's sleeve to expose one white-furred arm.

"What are you doing?" the chief healer asked in alarm. "There's no way of saving her."

"Then you won't mind my trying." Theo felt along the princess's arm for one of her main blood paths. Lord Noshi watched his every move.

"The princess has the right to die in peace without you interfering," the mole healer protested.

"Brune, Lord Noshi, we can stand here and watch her die, or I can try something that might work."

Brune looked about to object, but Lord Noshi stopped him. "The rabbit's right. If the healers have given up, there's no harm in trying every option."

Drewyn motioned at several of the chief healer's assistants. "Come, let us fetch what the rabbit asks."

"Hurry!" Theo implored. They rushed from the room, though the chief healer remained, his face locked in a scowl. *Please let me remember Zo's instructions,* Theo prayed. *And please let Zo's cures be real.*

"What are you going to do?" Brune looked from Indigo's motionless face to Theo's.

"I don't know."

"What do you mean you don't know?"

"I've never done this before," Theo cleared the bedside table of the herb pouches and implements used by the previous healers. The chief healer rushed forward to save his wares, protesting loudly.

"You see? The rabbit knows nothing, yet you let him destroy my things and put the princess through more agony. And for what?"

Drewyn and the assistants returned bearing what Theo had asked for. He motioned for them to place everything on the cleared table. They bustled past the mole healer, his arms full of salvaged medicines and his face a purplish cloud of anger.

"Drewyn, put the knives in the water and then hold the blade in the lamp flame. You," Theo pointed at a young mole with chestnut fur and crooked teeth, "find the strongest reeds and cut them into arm's lengths. Where's the liquor?"

"I sent for it." Drewyn submerged the knife blades. "Everything in the cellars was moved to make way for artillery storage. The scullery maids will help search."

Theo plucked a long strip of cloth from one of the baskets and tied it tight around Indigo's exposed arm. Using tongs, he extracted a knife from the boiling water and, with its sharp edge, scraped away the fur from her elbow just below the tied cloth, revealing pink skin. Indigo remained inert.

"This is pointless. Bleeding won't help her!" the chief healer insisted. "The Urzoks are almost upon us. We should be preparing the infirmary!"

"Your objections have been heard, mole," Brune cut in. "Now keep quiet or by Aktu I'll string you up by the hairs of your stumpy flea bitten tail!"

At this the creature's face contorted, but his voice failed him. A plump mole burst through the door, cradling a bottle of liquid. "I found it! The strongest liquor in Ralgayan!"

Theo motioned for him to pour some into a bowl, then wadded a cloth and dabbed it in the dark fluid.

"I've cut the reeds, Mr. Theo," the crooked-toothed mole piped up, holding an armful of the plant stalks.

"Good, immerse them in the water but just for an instant, don't let them go soft, then drain them." He swabbed Indigo's exposed arm with the cloth, then motioned for one of the moles to bring the large tureen. Theo positioned it on the floor near Indigo, and turned to the mole with the reeds. "Finished? Give me one."

The mole passed him a reed, and Theo studied its two ends

before placing it on the bed. He then selected the sharpest knife from the pile and gripped it over the princess's exposed flesh.

"May Lyusa be right. May his gift be the key to healing Mankahar." He made a small slice along Indigo's arm, and immediately dark blood seeped forward like a wellspring.

Theo inserted one end of the prepared reed into the wound, feeling for the hole he'd created. He held the other end over the clay vessel, and soon a pool began to form at the bottom.

"Tie a cloth around the reed to keep it in place," he instructed Drewyn. "We have to let her bleed for some time."

"If you're trying to kill her faster you'll succeed." The chief healer's voice was icy.

Theo ignored him, and instead began winding a cloth around his own arm.

"You're not going to do the same?" Brune looked alarmed.

"Bleeding her won't help if she doesn't have new blood to replace it."

The healer snorted. "I've never heard of such a ridiculous idea! Now you'll kill yourself along with her."

"Patience, esteemed chief healer," Lord Noshi admonished. "Perhaps Aktu is about to reveal why she sent Theo to us."

Theo wished he could share Lord Noshi's confidence. What if the book was wrong? What made him even think it wasn't deliberate fantasy? And what were the odds of success when he'd never even tried this before? But then, what if the miraculous cures of Zo were true? He'd forever be haunted by Indigo's lifeless eyes if he didn't find out.

Theo grasped the knife, resolute. He held its edge in the lamp flame before feeling along his arm and making the puncture. He grabbed a reed and guided the point in, fitting it and letting Drewyn bind it with cloth.

"I hope to Aktu you know what you're doing," she murmured.

"We'll soon see," Theo tried not to look at his blood pooling at the bottom of the vessel. The dual throbbing in his forehead and in his arm made him feel faint.

"What now?" Brune asked.

"We wait until the vessel fills halfway, and then we give it to her."

Theo could feel himself growing weaker as his blood drained from him, though the vessel seemed far from half full. A tense silence fell on the room's occupants, so that the only sounds came from the scurry and shouts of battle preparations outside. Theo felt himself growing tired and cold, especially in his paws, but struggled to stay alert.

"She's nearly gone," one of the assistants said, feeling Indigo's chest for a heartbeat.

The chief healer snorted his contempt. Theo struggled against sluggishness and motioned for Drewyn to withdraw the reed. The vessel was now nearly half full, its surface black and dotted with bubbles.

"What do we do?" Brune growled. Sounds of shouting and the clash of metal armor could be heard from outside, reminding them that they had little time.

"Bring a water bag, the largest you can find, and pour this into it," Theo said. "Lady Drewyn, help me bandage my arm."

Drewyn wrapped a length of cloth around his elbow, and he pressed a paw against it to stop the flow. He stood, dizzy from loss of blood, and made his way to Indigo's bed.

When the water skin arrived, it took several moles to hold the bag open while Brune lifted the vessel with Theo's blood and poured its contents in. The water skin could not hold all of it, and Brune put down the vessel with a grunt.

Theo motioned for Manneki. "Hold the water skin just above her. Yes, like that. Hold it steady while I jab this end into the skin."

The monkey did as he was told, and Theo punctured the bottom of the bag with the free end of Indigo's reed. He undid the cloth binding Indigo's arm, then gave the water skin a squeeze to make sure its contents would flow.

"Now we wait, and hope."

Commander Tarq and the other apprentices, all in full battle garb, flooded into the room. They looked taken aback at the strange scene before them, but the wolf quickly recovered.

"The Urzoks have reached the lake. We must take positions."

"You need to find Harlan," Theo said. "He's in league with the Urzoks."

Both the commander and Brune looked at him in surprise. "Are you telling me that we let in a spy?" Tarq growled.

"He isn't your brother?" Brune asked.

"He *is* my brother, Brune, but he's the one who ran us into the River Tithe!"

Brune cursed.

"We'll have to flush him out before he can do more damage." Commander Tarq turned to the two foxes Hazel and Lexa, who had fitted themselves out with spiked leg guards and body armor. "Make sure you find this rabbit. When the battle breaks we can't have an unknown threat lurking within the walls." The two nodded and streaked from the room, their red tails following them like banners of war.

Commander Tarq turned back to Brune and Lord Noshi. "Unfortunately it's as we feared. Our raid has failed and we'll have to face the enemy outnumbered."

Brune snorted. "No time for wishing, Commander. Manneki, stay with Drewyn and help her tend to the princess."

The monkey began to protest but Brune roared, "Just obey me for once!" Manneki fell into silence.

"Theo, can you come with us? They'll be needing as many paws as they can find on the ramparts, I imagine."

Theo looked at Indigo's inert form, the limbs limp as death. Could he bear to watch her die? Could he bear not to?

"Drewyn, when the bag is empty, fill it with the remaining

blood and keep administering it. If she lives, she'll wake on her own." He turned to Brune. "Let's go."

Lord Noshi stopped them on their way out. "Take care, rabbit. Mankahar may need you beyond just this battle." Then lowering his voice so that only Theo could hear, he added, "I'm glad to see you stayed."

Theo said nothing, instead fetching Noshi's sword, Q'orio, from his chamber and following Brune and the remaining apprentices. When they'd climbed the city walls, dawn was breaking on the horizon, and the rain had hardened to an icy sleet.

The city was a hive of frenzied activity as soldiers primed catapults and took up positions. Baskets of arrows and sharpened rocks were hauled up by rope to the archers and slingers already lining the wall's parapets. The trenches were filled with archers readying their bows. Axe-wielding badgers and hedgehogs donned their armor and spiked arm bands.

Theo gazed out at the scene outside the city walls.

From the bottom of the slope to the edges of the forest undulated a black and red sea, glistening wetly in the gray dawn. Thousands of Urzok soldiers had already encircled the bottom of the hill. They were mounted, horns curving from their red war helmets, with long, hooked swords lashed to their backs in red leather harnesses. Their horses had fearsome head guards made of polished bone, with breastplates to match, so that they seemed half beast, half skeleton, their breath rising like ghosts in the frigid morning air.

Between the lines of Urzok commanders marched long battalions of stocky, broad-snouted warthogs in heavy red armor. They bristled with short spears and pikes lashed to their girths, making them living, hooved maces.

Leading the ranks were two Urzoks, mounted on frightening war steeds with shining black hides. Both wore metal helmets painted blood red, inlaid with gleaming bear's teeth and lion claws.

"Who are those two?" Theo asked Olea, who had arrived beside him.

"Lord Ornox and his daughter, General Agacheta," the lynx replied. "He's no doubt passed on his taste for blood."

Commander Tarq began barking for soldiers to take their battle positions, then turned and ordered helmet and armor for Theo.

"You're going to need it," he said.

The rabbit put on the unfamiliar contraption, its touch cold against his fur. The chainmail was woven of fine links. A metal helmet with ear holes and face guard were passed to him, which he clumsily fitted to his head, pulling the straps tight beneath his chin.

As the Urzok army came to a stop at the base of the cliff, the two sides fell into an expectant hush, as if sizing each other. The dawn birds had fled, and the steady sleet drummed against thousands of metal helmets.

The silence was ripped apart by a piercing bugle call followed by the thunderous hammering of swords against shields. The city walls trembled as thousands of boots and hooves charged up the castle hill like a dark flood rushing the base of the cliff.

"Aktu help us, there are even more of them than we thought," he heard Olea mutter. She flashed the rabbit a grim smile. "If we don't win this, then the lucky ones will be dead."

CHAPTER FORTY-EIGHT

Theo ducked as the first volley from the Urzok's archers came over the wall, their long shafts screaming through the brittle air to bury themselves in any exposed wood or flesh.

Commander Tarq shouted for the catapult ropes to be cut, and with loud cracks the giant wooden arms sprang free of their fetters, hurling boulders over the castle walls and onto the warthogs below. There was the crunch of crushed metal and pulverized bone, along with short screams as the boulders rolled down the hill, scattering the soldiers like locusts before a flame. But like locusts, it took them only a short time to regroup, filling in the gaps until they were again an angry red swarm marching over their fallen comrades.

"Archers! In position!" Tarq's battle howl echoed off the battlements. "Aim! Fly!"

The Urzoks were a frighteningly disciplined army, holding tight interlocking ranks of archers and shield bearers who protected them against the barrage of arrows raining down. Many hit their mark, but they were like water droplets against a bonfire. The troops swept on and up the hill, their war cries growing louder with each step.

As the enemy reached the city walls, the defense archers kept up an incessant wave of arrows. But their comrades simply used their bodies as shields, battering the gate with their thick pikes, while a row of climbers began amassing behind them. Soon, sharp-clawed grapple hooks were flying over the fortress walls, their metal screeching across the wet stone.

Arrows continued to hail down, and Theo could see that several of the defenders had fallen, either slumped where they stood or falling off the city wall like bags of flour.

Commander Tarq called an order for the slingers to step up to the wall so the archers could reload their quivers.

Brune bounded down the staircase to the clearing by the city gates, joining the ranks of axe-wielding badgers waiting for the enemy's first wave to break through. Brune drew his axe, hefting a handle as thick as Theo's arm, and bellowed a rallying call to those behind him.

Theo whirled around and saw that several Urzoks were already well up the city wall, climbing like monkeys despite their heavy armor. He flung the cloth covering aside and gripped Q'orio in his paw.

He raised the sword and brought it down on the rope of a grapple hook. It severed with barely a whisper, and even cleaved into the stone floor beneath it. He heard the screams of falling Urzoks as he and Olea severed the dozen or more ropes they could find. Even so, the sheer numbers meant that the defenders could not stop the onslaught forever, and soon the wall clanged with metal as Ralgayan and the attackers fell into paw-to-paw combat.

The first to make it over the wall and lunge at Theo was a stocky, hairy brute who stood a good two heads above him. With one swift movement the enemy had his curved sword free of its scabbard, roaring his challenge. As his blade flew down, Theo reacted instinctively, sidestepping and slashing at his opponent's belly. He expected to hear it slide off the man's armor, but instead the blade sliced through the hard leather as cleanly as a boat's prow cuts water, then up into flesh and through spine.

The soldier grunted in surprise before falling, his organs spilling in tangled ropes onto the damp stone.

Several enemy soldiers followed the first one, slithering over the rain-slicked wall of the castle. Theo felt faint from loss of blood and the effort of his first battle. He knew his only advantage lay in having a sword that was proving harder than any of their armor, and so relied on surprising the soldiers by aiming at protected limbs rather than the joints.

Suddenly a loud cracking reverberated from below. "The gate! The gate's about to go!"

"Stand firm!" Commander Tarq bellowed.

The line of badgers bristled as they readied themselves. The gateposts shuddered under the assault, splinters flying from where the beams were weakest.

"Archers, ready your bows!"

As the gate groaned and then cracked open, a thin line of warriors squeezed through, brandishing their swords and screaming for blood. A round of arrows from the archers in the trenches brought them all toppling over each other, while those who survived were speared through on the badgers' pikes.

Little by little, however, the gates began to give way, until the trickle of Urzoks became a stream, and the stream became a floodtide, and the bailey swarmed with them. The badgers and porcupines proved ferocious fighters, hacking at heads and limbs with great sweeps of their battle axes. The square roiled with metal, stone, and wood weapons.

Brune reared to full height and plunged headlong into the fray, his axe singing. Its curved edge cut a merciless swathe through the sea of red.

Just then a black steed burst in through the gates, its rider helmeted and holding a curved sword wet and dark with blood. It was the warlord's daughter. She stopped at the sight of the bear.

"Slay the bear! Find the rabbit!"

At her cry the soldiers lunged towards Brune with renewed vigor, and the helmeted Urzok swiveled in her saddle, her blood-flecked face looking straight up at Theo.

Was this the one who had ordered the destruction of Willago? The one who had sentenced Father Oaks, Pozzi, and everyone else to a fate he couldn't bear to imagine? Theo felt a sudden overpowering anger at all he had known and lost, the destruction of everything that had protected him from what he was.

Without thinking he launched himself off the wall. Theo saw her eyes widen in surprise before he smashed into her, pulling her from her horse. The beast neighed frantically before giving way and stumbling to the ground.

Theo could tell she hadn't anticipated his strength. They rolled for a pace in the wet mud before breaking apart, each springing to their feet with swords drawn.

"You're the omatje," she said.

Theo's surprise was enough to give her the advantage she anticipated. She lunged, her sword nicking Theo's arm as he side-stepped. A thin line of blood appeared, staining his muddy jerkin.

The two circled each other, their eyes locked. Her armor bore the dents and scars of numerous battles, and Theo realized he was hopelessly outmatched, even if he hadn't been weakened by blood loss. Was he mad, taking on a seasoned warrior? He tried to still his fear. In the din of war Theo focused on her breathing, trying to gauge her next move, her strengths, her weaknesses. He could tell she was doing the same.

When she attacked again Theo barely raised his sword in time, Q'orio shrieking as it met Agacheta's long, thick blade. The Urzok was vicious. Every blow reverberated down Q'orio's length and up Theo's arms. Her blade was made of something stronger than the armor her soldiers wore, so that Q'orio scratched its surface but couldn't break it.

She struck again and again, forcing Theo towards the rampart walls, until his back was against its cold, wet stone. As she cornered him and brought her blade down, Theo hunched and rolled towards her, avoiding the blade by a hair's breadth. He managed to hack at her ankle as he rolled to his feet.

Her armored boot slowed the sword, but couldn't stop it. Q'orio sliced through the metal until it found flesh. Blood poured from the wound, and Agacheta let slip a grunt of pain.

Her arm lashed out and grabbed Theo before he could raise Q'orio in his defense. She pulled him up by the ears, so that he thought for one horrible moment his scalp would rip at the roots. She then flung him hard against the stone wall.

The air fled from his lungs as his body hit the hard surface, cracking a rib and making his eyes water. Q'orio tumbled from his grasp, landing far from reach.

Theo lay gasping against the sodden ground, every breath searing. The sleet pelted his drenched fur like tiny blades.

She leaned over him, propping herself with her sword. "You're not of fighting stock. You cannot win this."

Theo tried to crawl away towards Q'orio, but he couldn't move fast enough. With her good foot she flipped Theo onto his back, then placed her other boot squarely on his chest. His injured rib burned.

He clawed deep into her ankle wound, trying to inflict enough pain to make her let go. Though she grimaced, she only pressed down harder.

"Well fought, rabbit, but you won't kill me with a flesh wound." She motioned around them. "What's the point in fighting? You think any of your fellows will help you, knowing you're an omatje?"

She smiled at Theo's expression. "When we find the Library of Elshon you'll have everything you could possibly want. We should be allies." She reached down and closed her hand around his throat, hauling him up to eye level. He flailed, gripping her arms to try and free himself.

"Please," Theo gasped. "Take me then. Leave Ralgayan alone."

Agacheta shook her head. "War doesn't work that way, rabbit."

Theo tried to say something, but all that came out was an unintelligible gasp.

"We're the ones who'll value your skill," she said. "Your so called friends won't."

Theo grimaced, then managed to rasp: "Maybe you're wrong."

Agacheta's eyes darted above his head and saw what Theo had been able to see all along: Indigo, eyes blazing, a bandage tied around her elbow, standing above them on the rampart wall with bow and arrow nocked. She aimed squarely at Agacheta.

"Tell Aktu Indigo sent you."

Indigo let the arrow fly. It sliced through the rain and sleet, grazed past Theo's ear, and sank into Agacheta's right eye. Bloodied liquid swelled around the wood, and her hands loosened enough for Theo to spring free, dragging raw breaths.

The point had plowed past her eye and into her head. The general sank to one knee, her hand grasping at air, before collapsing onto her side in the mud. Her hands clutched at the ground before they too fell still.

Theo studied Indigo. She was still weak from the poison, but she would live. Joy winged through him, but there was no time for even the shortest thanks. A clattering of horses' hooves and the screams of terrified villagers sounded from within the inner city.

Mounted Urzoks emerged from between the alleyways, galloping through the city towards the gates. Their swords cut a remorseless opening through anyone in their path, and their horses' bone masks gleamed like leering demons in the morning light.

How had they gotten in? Somewhere in Theo's mind he knew it had to do with Harlan. With the bulk of the army defending the city walls, the Urzoks would soon have the city encircled and trapped between two fronts. Outnumbered as they were, Ralgayan's annihilation was only a matter of time.

Theo dug out a bugle horn from where it had fallen, half buried in the trample of horses and soldiers. He put it to his lips and blew as hard as he could, waving in the direction of the oncoming Urzoks.

One of the badgers in the front lines heard him and lifted his head from battle, then turned and caught sight of the advancing army. His voice bellowed out through the rain and clamor.

"Lo! Hark the back flank, boys!"

Indigo grabbed a helmet and sword from a fallen defender, then ran to the badger's aid, but Theo knew that nothing could hold off the advancing army. He ducked into a stairwell and drew a painful breath. The fight was over unless something drastic changed the tide of battle. But what?

What are you?

He froze. In the din of war Theo couldn't tell where the familiar voice had come from. All he knew was that his nightmare had somehow crossed into daylight.

What are you, Theo?

He felt a jab in his rib and reaching in, his paw closed around something small and warm. He pulled it out. The tortoise's mirror.

What are you, Theo?

Had he lost all his senses in this fever of battle?

The mirror's surface changed. Where once it had been murky and clouded, it now cleared, like a pool of water. A smudge appeared in the middle and grew larger, until Theo could make out a creature's head, then body, then tail. Something cold and sharp prickled inside, and then it was upon him: that grip that froze his tongue and turned his mind to stone.

"I smell fear," the Griffin whispered, eyeing him from beyond the mirror.

"Please. The Grey Rock said you'd help me in my darkest hour." Each word sent slivers of pain through his ribs.

"Did he? Well that depends. Who are you to ask for *my* help? Me, your buried, blackest fear?" The Griffin punched at the glass that divided them. Theo pulled his voice back from its hiding place.

"I'm ... I'm a rabbit."

"Then go away and die a rabbit's death." The creature turned and began to fade back into the mirror.

"Wait!"

"Now what?" The creature resurfaced, its bird face impatient.

"I'm not just any rabbit. I'm a healer."

The Griffin laughed, the sound slapping Theo's face. "Healers are well respected by some. But I don't help healers. Especially those who don't value their own fear."

Something unlocked in Theo's memory—what had the Grey Rock said? *Sometimes what you fear most is what you most need.* What did he fear most?

"Griffin! Wait." *Dear Kalmac, let this be the right path. Let this be the admission he had to make.* "I'm an omatje."

The mirror flared to life, and the Griffin's face appeared again, the amber eyes fiery. "What did you say?"

Theo willed himself to stare back, unflinching, into those eyes that seemed to strip him bare. "I said, I'm an omatje. I'm a word-catcher."

The Griffin appraised him with a critical eye, as if doubtful. "And if I help you?" he asked, cocking his head. "What will you do?"

There was no going back once he made his oath. "If you'll save Ralgayan, I swear to find the Library of Elshon and use it to free Mankahar."

"So be it, Theo the Omatje. I accept the pact."

The mirror began to shudder so violently that Theo dropped it, its hot edges hissing as it hit the wet mud. It exploded with a loud crack, and the heavens seemed to open anew; lightening ripped across the horizon and torrents of icy sleet pummeled the earth.

He watched as it began to morph and contort, like a living thing, then grew and expanded. Theo had forgotten about the battle and the soldiers around him. But now he could hear the cries of surprise, then fear, as warriors paused in their fighting to watch what was growing in the city square.

It swelled and unfolded until it was the size of a house, and the flashes of lightning that snaked down from the skies laced the air with fire and unnatural light. The being began to take its giant cat shape, a ripple of feathers sprouting, row upon ice-slicked row, across its back.

Soon the lion-like legs with claws appeared, and a bony, beaked head unfolded itself from a stout neck. The Griffin opened its eyes. They were primal eyes, eyes to make the sea feel young, and a deeper yellow than the sun's heart. For the first time Theo felt no fear looking at them.

Its roar shook blades in their hilts, toppled stone from the ramparts, and ignited white-hot terror. Where previously the Urzoks had been killing anyone in their path to get into the castle, they were now butchering anyone who stood in their line of escape. The city square became a panicked sea of armor and flesh as soldiers on both sides felt their courage turn to dust in their veins.

Theo saw Brune and Indigo, blood drenched and rain soaked, staring at the beast that stood growling down at the fleeing tide below. It bunched its hind legs and then leaped onto the city ramparts, its body keeping perfect balance on the rim as its claws gripped the wall. Pieces of rock crumbled beneath its paws, and its eyes surveyed the land below as a cat surveys a den of nesting mice.

Theo ran up to the ramparts, his heart pounding. What had he unleashed? He stumbled at his next thought: *What if the beast turned on Ralgayan instead?*

CHAPTER FORTY-NINE

From the foot of the hill, Lord Ornox watched the carnage with great satisfaction. The Ralgayan forces were decoyed to the city gates, as Agacheta had predicted, leaving the second army free to infiltrate the secret passageway her pet had found.

He allowed himself a smile. His daughter had been right, the rodent had his uses. But soon Ornox would have something even more useful, something that would make him more powerful than the emperor.

His thoughts were interrupted by screams of terror from the castle gates. There had been such screams throughout the battle. But these were different. These were screams of terror from his men, not from the defenders.

From where he sat astride his horse, Lord Ornox watched the mass of soldiers at the city gates suddenly flow backwards, as if pushed by an invisible force. Some turned and ran, while others paused, unnerved.

The steeds in his battalion jerked their heads and snorted, their hooves kicking up a spray of mud as they pranced. The soldiers drew their swords as an enormous black beast leaped onto the citadel walls, its strange form hideous and unnatural in the glow of the lightning that scarred the sky.

"What in Blackhide's name ..." Yod muttered.

As thunder slapped across them, the shape reared and seemed to grow wings. Lord Ornox could make out what looked like a beak. In a jagged ribbon of lightning, the thing's eyes burned through the sleet and smoke, searching.

The shouts of terrified Urzoks floated like tattered banners on the wind.

"Retreat, retreat!"

Before Lord Ornox could curse the coward who'd uttered the forbidden word, the beast stretched its neck into the sky, loosing an eagle-like scream that froze the hearts of the Urzok army.

The beast pounced, its lion body leaping off the ramparts in a horrible yet graceful arc. Its tail snapped behind it as it landed, and its head snaked out for its first victim.

The creature snapped its prey's spine with a sharp crunch, then threw back its head and swallowed the soldier, armor and all. Before long the beast's eyes fixed on other fleeing targets, and in quick succession it pinioned several more in its beak.

Lord Ornox cursed under his breath, the anger laced with a touch of fear. The black mass bearing down on them was unlike anything he'd ever seen.

Order. An army needed order. He barked for his generals to hold their positions and regroup. The foot soldiers trampled each other in their terror. Men milled about on barely controlled horses whose eyes rolled at the beast's unfamiliar smell. Whole contingents of soldiers froze and then crumpled to the ground like stunned deer, their hearts giving out from sheer terror.

"Archers!" Lord Ornox bellowed, raising his sword as a signal to his remaining generals. "Rank one and two, formations!"

The generals set about forcing their archers into line, hacking off limbs or heads from those who hesitated or tried to flee. A group of soldiers were hounded into three lines, their clumsy hands trying to string their bows while fear raced through every nerve.

The thing was bearing down on them, its lion limbs swallowing up the distance between itself and the remaining army that had been bullied into a wall of resistance.

"On your mark! Wait for my order!" Lord Ornox shouted, trying to control his mount as it snorted and reared. The continued crack of thunder across the skies ran ragged over the soldiers' shattered nerves, making them flinch.

The nightmare was nearly upon them, its beak wide and claws outstretched, when Lord Ornox gave the order. "Loose now! Aim for its throat and eyes!"

The first hail of arrows flew towards the hellion, tentative and wobbling as they leaped from unsteady bows. The creature dodged most shafts, but some found their mark, burying themselves near the shoulder and drawing grunts of unfurled rage. The beast whipped its tail and rose on its hind legs.

The sight was enough to send several soldiers falling back in undiluted fear, their screams all but strangled in their tightened throats. Lord Ornox knew this was the one chance he had. In its instinctive movement the creature had revealed its softer underside.

"Second rank, again! At the belly!" he shouted, spurring his horse with bloodied boots.

Encouraged at having drawn blood, the archers steadied their bows and nocked a new round of arrows. They drew and loosed. As the volley of shafts sped towards the target, the giant took to the air, its wings beating back the missiles as if the arrows were but drops of rain. A couple of the arrows ripped gashes in the beast's side, but Ornox realized none of them had dealt a fatal wound. He gnashed his teeth as his only choice became clear.

"To the forest!" he screamed. "Retreat!"

What remained of his army needed little urging. Their frail

formation cracked and dissolved like ice before the sun, and soon the enemy soldiers were streaming towards the cover of the trees, all thoughts but survival having fled before them.

Lord Ornox himself was amongst them, goading his maddened stallion with hands that bled from gripping the reins. He felt a blast of hot air against his back and then a bone-rending punch. They fell, the horse screaming and flailing all hooves as it struggled to stand.

Before Ornox could grasp the stallion's reins and keep it from escaping, he was turned over like a beached fish. Eyes the color of fire held him transfixed, while a lion's paw the size of his torso pinned him to the ground. The air was crushed out of his body, while the Griffin's breath seared him with the unfamiliar flame of his own fear.

"Go back to your emperor, and tell him Mankahar will not be pacified." The Griffin leaned close, his beak still wet with retribution. "Tell your kind that Theo the Omatje is coming for them."

CHAPTER FIFTY

That night Ralgayan rejoiced as she never had before.

The city's inhabitants poured out of their hiding places in the castle's keeps, houses, and stables to hug each other, shout their joy from the rooftops, and dance in the public squares. Scullery maids, bakers, cooks, and ale makers threw open their kitchen and cellar doors to young and old, abandoning caution with their cherished winter provisions. After all, yesterday they didn't even know whether they would live to see the winter.

Time enough tomorrow for grief over the fallen. Today was for rejoicing in having escaped Pacification, in thanking Aktu for sending the Griffin to save them.

Their winged miracle had set up temporary residence in the castle's front bailey, arrows and blood still marring his hide. At first the citizens scattered and held back from the ferocious beast, but before long an unattended young raccoon whose curiosity outweighed his caution placed an inquisitive paw on the sharp beak. When all saw that the Griffin didn't react, the castle's healers were called, water was fetched, and soon a small army of nurses and healers were busy dressing the injuries.

A thorough search of the enemy's abandoned camp, led by

Commander Tarq, had uncovered the three jackal triplets and their accompanying wolves, all of them with their throats slit. The Urzoks had grabbed what they could upon fleeing, but most had abandoned their possessions in favor of their lives. Tarq could offer no words to comfort Theo, who combed the area repeatedly before facing the truth: there was no sign of Father Oaks, or anyone else from Willago.

That night, Castle Ralgayan's main hall filled to the rafters. Trestle tables and stools were gathered and moved in, casks of mead and elderberry wine flowed like water, and the common folk of Ralgayan tried to outdo each other in bringing food to those who had fought. By nightfall the tables groaned from platters of seeded yam cakes, dried fish stuffed with cranberries, and hot stews.

As the citizens of Ralgayan celebrated, the Order convened behind closed doors to deal with more practical matters. The senior Council members sat in a semi-circle around a marble table, while Drewyn, Brune, and Tarq's fellow wolves crowded the corners. The two foxes, Lexa and Hazel, had managed to flush out Harlan. They'd found him trying to disguise himself as one of the fisher folk so he could escape to the lakeshore undetected. They led their prisoner into the Council chambers, his paws bound and a thick noose fastened about his neck.

A hush descended.

A lone, harsh cry of "Death!" broke the silence. Soon others followed, raining insults and suggestions for punishment. Lord Noshi rapped his knuckles against the table.

"The law of Aktu clearly states," Lord Noshi said, "Let no one take the life of another, unless it is to preserve your own or is in accordance with the natural order."

Lord Ibwa's neck feathers stood in an indignant collar. "Enemies of Aktu choose not to live by Her law. They therefore do not deserve Her law's protection, Lord Noshi."

There were scattered murmurs of agreement, but Lord

Noshi stared them down. “As long as I am High Priest, we respect Aktu’s laws. Even if others do not.”

Lord Ibwa glowered, but remained silent.

“We cannot let him go,” Brune protested.

“Let’s give him his own medicine. Have him pacified!” suggested a fellow bear. His animosity could be traced to his most recent souvenir from the battle: a bandaged paw with a conspicuous space where his two left claws should’ve been.

“That would make us no better than he, no better than those who wish to enslave us.” Lord Noshi shook his head. “We don’t do such things to fellow creatures.”

“Let everyone know what he’s done,” Commander Tarq said, stepping forward. “In battle, those whom we trust, those who are our allies, we mark with a scent. Let this traitor be known to all by a mark on his face, so that wherever he may go he shall be known as the enemy of Mankahar.”

At this there were cries of agreement around the Council.

Lord Noshi nodded. “Let it be done, and may Aktu forgive you, rabbit.”

Drewyn ordered castle guards to take the silent Harlan. They prodded him with their staves when he resisted, and in the end had to drag him by the arms.

“Now that we’ve dealt with the traitor, let us deal with our friends,” Lord Noshi said. “Are the apprentices gathered?”

At this cue an attendant badger opened a side door, ushering in the waiting group. They filed in and stood before the Council table, joining the foxes already there. Theo felt as if he’d been sentenced instead of Harlan, for he knew that what he had to say might bring him the same fate, if not worse. In the confusion of celebrations there’d been no time to talk to Indigo, Brune, or even Manneki. He wished he could’ve at least said goodbye. Now he might not have that chance.

“Ralgayan and Mankahar owe you all a great debt,” Lord Noshi began, looking at each of the gathered apprentices in turn. “You came from all corners of Mankahar to risk your lives against a formidable enemy who outnumbered us. Some of you gave your lives. We are thankful. We are humbled. And yet we would call on you further, for though we've won the battle, the war has just begun. We would ask that you join the Order, swear an oath to help restore Aktu's balance to Mankahar."

There was a resounding cheer of support amongst the remaining apprentices, except for Theo, who kept silent. He thought no one had noticed, but one look at Lord Noshi's face told him otherwise.

"Tomorrow we shall honor you as official Ihaktus," the high priest continued. "Anyone who opposes these fine warriors from entering Aktu's highest service, speak now or hold peace."

Theo stepped forward.

"I cannot stay," he said. In the silence that followed he thought perhaps he'd only said the words in his mind. But no, the stunned expressions on the faces before him meant he'd voiced the unthinkable.

"You mean to abandon the Order's cause?" Lord Ibwa's russet feathers quivered as he gave a short laugh of disbelief.

"No, my Lord," Theo replied. "I mean to help, but in my own way. In the way that I feel I can be of best use."

"What do you intend to do then, Theo?" Lord Noshi asked. Theo thought he heard encouragement, even relief, in the question.

"I shall find the Library of Elshon and use it to defeat the Urzoks."

Lord Ibwa pointed an accusing talon at the rabbit. "An omatje! I knew it!"

There were gasps and angry mutterings at this, and Theo could feel the palpable tension in his fellow apprentices. Several of them took a step back, as if he carried a plague.

"How do you intend to find it, young Theo?" Lord Noshi asked.

"I don't know, but I'll find out."

A surprised murmur rippled through the gathering.

"There are stories of those who tried to find the Library, but paid heavily. Are you prepared to pay the price?" Lord Noshi said.

"It's the only way." Theo looked directly at Lord Noshi. "And wouldn't it be worth paying, if we can free Mankahar?"

The high priest nodded. "Winter is upon us. Stay with the Order until the thaw."

Theo shook his head. "Every day that I stay will be another day that they may find the Library before I do." He looked around the Council table. "I had hoped that perhaps the Council would consider helping me find the Library."

Commander Tarq's voice was harsh. "Wars are won with swords, with the strength of our claws and the sharpness of our teeth. Wars are not won with words, or with a forgotten language. If you walk this path, you walk it alone. We cannot spare a single fighter."

"The Forbidden Language is what gave the Urzoks their power in the first place. Maybe it can also defeat them," Theo argued.

There were scandalized mutterings around the table, and Brune looked distinctly uncomfortable, his eyes darting from Lord Noshi to Theo.

"How could the Forbidden Language defeat the Urzoks?" Lord Ibwa said, exasperated. "We have learned our lesson, no good comes from it!"

"The Forbidden Language was what saved the princess's life," Brune's voice cut through the din. Theo stared at him. How did he know? "He would sneak off nights with banned materials when he thought I didn't notice. Something in them told him the cure for pacification. Am I right, Theo?"

Theo nodded, staggered that Brune had known his secret all along.

"If he'd had that knowledge earlier," Brune continued, gazing at each of the counselors, "he might have saved my brother, Kuno."

There was an awkward silence as the Council digested this. Everyone had heard of the princess's miraculous recovery, but had credited it to Aktu's mercy.

"I don't know what powers the Library of Elshon holds," Theo said. "But I know it must be beyond our imaginations. I intend to find it and use it."

Lord Ibwa craned his neck forward, his eyes hard and severe above his downturned beak. He seemed to have forgotten any deference to Lord Noshi. "If you do this, rabbit, you do it alone. In honor of your service to the Order we will not punish you for your blasphemy, but no one here will support you in your quest."

Though Theo had known to expect this, it didn't lessen the crushing sense of solitude he felt trapping him. He didn't dare look at Indigo or Manneki behind him. He couldn't stomach what he might see in their eyes.

"I shall go," a voice behind him said. Indigo stepped forward from the other apprentices, ears high.

Theo stared at her. "What are you doing?" he hissed. "Your dream is to be an Ihaktu, remember?"

"Stop arguing with me," she whispered back. "I'm in danger of changing my mind."

Theo kept quiet, for once glad he couldn't find words.

Lord Ibwa raised his voice above the shocked whispers of his fellow councilors. "Are you forgetting your duty, Princess of Alvareth? You are a chosen Ihaktu. Your destiny is to stay and train with the others."

"I've not yet sworn my oath to the Order," Indigo replied. "I shall help Theo in his search for Elshon."

The gathering seemed in danger of crumbling into dissent. Lord Ibwa shouted testily, "This is not a blithe decision, Princess. If you refuse now, the Council may not offer it to you again."

Indigo frowned, but she gripped her sword hilt and nodded. "If that is what the Council decides."

"Very well then, Princess," Lord Ibwa snapped. "Leave by sunrise, or face the consequences. Brune, escort them out."

"I'll do more than that," Brune slapped on his war helmet. "I'll be escorting them to the Library of Elshon, Lord Ibwa."

Theo couldn't stop a smile from spreading across his face.

"You've lost your gizzards," Lord Ibwa muttered. "All of you! Lord Noshi, we cannot permit this. If one Ihaktu decides to leave, what's to prevent everyone from deserting the Order?"

Lord Noshi raised an eyebrow. "Perhaps this is Aktu's wisdom, Lord Ibwa. Sometimes we get what we ask for, but not the way we envisioned."

While the Council adjourned and chaos reigned, Theo snuck out to the front bailey to seek out the Griffin. The creature's wounds had been dressed and bandaged, and there were offerings of what meat the Ralgayan inhabitants could offer: crabs, sturgeon, and fresh-water eel from the lake. The Griffin's eyes, though still unforgiving and ferocious, had lost the unbridled savagery that had haunted Theo's nightmares.

"Thank you. For what you did."

The Griffin whipped its tail in reply.

"Why did you let Lord Ornox go?"

"You asked me to protect Ralgayan. It was you who agreed to protect Mankahar." The Griffin leaned towards him. "Besides, the nightmare that travels by word is more feared than the real thing. You are now the Urzoks' nightmare, Theo, as I was yours."

"I have no idea where to look for this library."

"Seek the one called Orjo."

Theo frowned. "The wizard?"

The Griffin shook his head. "The omatje. Perhaps the only other left in Mankahar. He knows where it is."

"Where can I find him?"

"If word spreads that you are an omatje, he will find you."

Theo thought on this for a moment, then asked, "What will you do now?"

"I shall protect Ralgayan, as I promised. Until it doesn't need my protection anymore," Griffin replied. "I expect you to keep your oath, for until you do I am bound here."

Theo nodded. "I shall do my best."

The Griffin's beak opened in a semblance of a smile. "That is all anyone can ask of you, Theo Omatje."

CHAPTER FIFTY-ONE

From the safety of the tree line, Caldrik waited to see if he'd been followed.

He'd never minded waiting. He'd taught Agacheta that waiting meant time to plan, time to observe the enemy and make sure you were undetected when the moment for action arrived.

He lay motionless, patient, while the light seeped from the trees and left the forest in darkness. He let his eyes adjust to the new world, and lay there, observant. He was several days' hard ride from Ralgayan by now, but caution made him scan the terrain behind him every night.

Satisfied that no one hunted him, he stood up on limbs numb from inaction, then crept through the underbrush. He felt his way along the trail he'd carefully tamped down in the snow. It wouldn't do to fall and injure himself. Not when the fate of the Empire lay in his hands.

At last he made it back to the glen, his gloved fingers feeling the marker of cloth he had tied to a branch at chest level.

His mare's snort of recognition guided him the rest of the way. He found everything as he left it every night: the banked coals, just enough to see by; his mare, saddled and ready for hard riding; saddlebags with as much foodstuff and water as he dared carry. And most important, the cargo.

A scratchy caw from his horse's saddlebag greeted him as he opened the satchel. He pulled out a small crow, its legs hobbled with string. He freed the bird's feet, then stroked its blue-black feathers, making sure the sky-colored band was securely fastened around its leg. Blue for cargo secured and on its way, so that the Child would know his mission was safe.

Caldrik thrust the crow up into the air and shaded his eyes from the soft snow. The bird's wings snapped in crisp farewell, and then he was gone.

The man turned to look at his prize, the prize he and Agacheta had separated from the other rabbits and kept under the strictest guard. The old rabbit named Oaks sat in silence behind the saddle, his paws bound. A fur-lined wrap protected him from the night's deepening cold, but nothing warmed the hostility in his ancient eyes.

Caldrik's pocked face stretched in a smooth smile. "Come, omatje. It's time to seek out Orjo, and the Library of Elshon."

CHAPTER FIFTY-TWO

The sky had just started to flush with dawn, hints of pale yellow and marigold pushing back the night's embrace, when Theo heard the crunch of boots on snow behind him.

He could smell that unique blend of pine and cedar that had, without him noticing, become his favorite scent. Indigo took a seat next to him on the parapet, already dressed in traveling breeches, new boots, and a thick woolen cloak.

They sat in silence for a while, staring out at the sun's progress. Behind them, Brune and Manneki were supervising the last preparations down in the lower courtyard. At Theo's suggestion they had saddled two pacified gray mares with their supplies of food, water, weapons, bedding, and a small ration of precious spices and gemstones in case they needed to pay their way out of a situation. Though there had been misgivings about using the pacified animals, Theo had argued that they provided speed and transport and that only fools would attempt a journey during the heart of winter without necessary supplies. The whinnies of the horses, along with Brune's whistling and Manneki's sniffles, drifted up to them on their perches.

"It's not too late to change your mind, you know," Theo said.

"You keep saying that. Don't you want me to come with you?"

Theo struggled. *Yes! Absolutely yes!* The thought of a world without her was colorless.

"Don't bother arguing," she said. "I've made up my mind. Alvareth law would bid me help someone who has saved my life, and as clan princess I cannot flout my own laws."

"So … this is purely obligation, then?"

She cocked one tattooed ear. "You're not suggesting I might be in love with you?"

Theo blushed so deeply that the frozen air felt on fire, and the stitched cut above his eye throbbed. "No, of course not."

"Good," she said, turning back to gaze at the ripening dawn. "Because I'm not, you know. But you'll need protection. You're pretty much the worst sword apprentice I know."

Theo nodded, grimacing from embarrassment as much as the pain his rib caused when he took too deep a breath.

"Although," she added, "that doesn't mean I shouldn't thank you."

She leaned over and kissed him, her scent enveloping them both. He could almost feel the instant his mind dissolved, all thought fracturing like a pool hit by a pebble.

"'Bout time!"

They sprang apart as if burnt and looked down at a grinning Brune and Lord Noshi.

Theo scrambled to his feet, wincing at his rib. With a shy grin at Indigo, he hurried down to the courtyard. The old man pulled the jeweled collar lock from within his sleeves and held it out.

"Take this. It may prove useful if you need to bribe Orjo."

"I have something for you as well," Theo put the collar in a safe fold of his jerkin, then untied Q'orio from its saddle belt, rewrapped in its covering. "You said that if I wasn't going to use my gift, I would need a weapon. You can have this back now."

Lord Noshi smiled, and took the sword. "I'm glad to hear it, rabbit." He patted Theo on the shoulder. "I've told Brune what I know about Orjo, that he's in the Land of the Blue Elders. But take care. I have heard it said that no one tangles with Orjo without regretting it."

Theo nodded. "Thank you."

Manneki leaped up on the horse's withers and helped Theo strap his recovered medicine pack to the saddle. The monkey rubbed at his red, swollen eyes.

"If you keep crying, Tarq may break his promise to make you an Ihaktu," Theo teased.

"Manneki not care about being Ihaktu," the monkey said, sullen.

"We'll be back before summer. By then, you'll be a mighty sword fighter."

This cheered the little imp enough to stay the tears, and he sprang off the mare to give Theo a choking hug.

Lord Noshi motioned Manneki to his side. "Now go, before Lord Ibwa convinces the Council to imprison you."

They gathered the horse's reins, said their goodbyes to Lord Noshi and a wet-eyed Manneki, and started out the castle gates.

By the time the sun had banished the last shadows of night, Castle Ralgayan was but a smudge on a whitewashed outcrop, growing ever more distant with each stride of the gray mares' legs. Theo rode on one, while Indigo sat on the other, her cloak fastened tight against the bracing cold. Brune lumbered at an easy pace next to the horses, who had gradually become accustomed to his menacing bulk.

Theo mulled over his plan and how much remained unknown. Where was the Land of the Blue Elders? Would Orjo agree to lead him to the Library of Elshon? Even if he did, what would he demand in return?

He looked at the helmeted bear ahead of him, then at the armed warrior riding alongside, and smiled. He wouldn't have to find the answers alone. And for now, that was enough.

ACKNOWLEDGMENTS

This book owes much to the support of those who read it through its various drafts. Thank you Tamara Sharp, for guiding me through two of the biggest revisions. Both David Latham and Dave Peterson showed me how to better my male protagonist voice. Gretchen Schreiber helped me brainstorm the book's market and core audience, while Tiffani Angus did an amazingly thorough edit. Tara Wilkinson and Grady Hendrix found me assistance when I needed it. Sam, thank you as always for your ever candid but insightful critiques on story and pacing.

Lastly, I'm grateful to all the wonderful pets (including rabbits) whom I had the privilege to live with and learn from as I grew up.

WHAT'S NEXT?

Continue the adventure with the second book in the series, *Theo and the Secret of Elshon,* available at your favorite bookstore. You can also join the author's reader list via www.melanieansley.com. You'll be notified about upcoming releases, and receive a free e-book copy of the prequel to the series, *The Queen and the Dagger*.

www.melanieansley.com

ALSO BY MELANIE ANSLEY

Enjoyed this book? Share your thoughts with a review on Amazon or Goodreads. You might also enjoy the prequel novella:

"A fantasy lover's delight."

- *Neven Carr, author of* Forgotten

"Outstanding. 5/5 stars."

- *Hall Ways Book Reviews*

ABOUT THE AUTHOR

Melanie was born in Canada but raised in China, and now lives in Ballarat, Australia with her husband and two children. She loves to read, write, and laugh. She also makes movies.

www.melanieansley.com
writingrooster@gmail.com

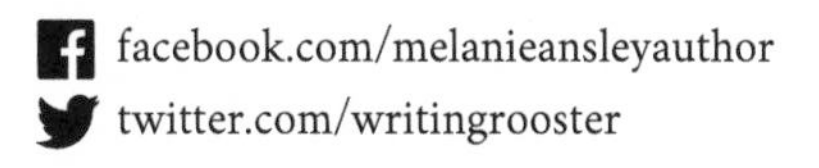

facebook.com/melanieansleyauthor
twitter.com/writingrooster

Made in the USA
Columbia, SC
26 July 2022